We Have Met the Enemy

Felicia Watson

D. X. VAROS

For Ed, who said, "Sounds good, write it" — thanks for the tremendous support, this one's for you

Table of Contents

Prologue: A Lost Kingdom of Peace   1
Chapter 1: The Past Is Never Dead   9
Chapter 2: What He Hides   29
Chapter 3: Memories of Yesterday   43
Chapter 4: The Unknown Curve   63
Chapter 5: Know the Enemy   77
Chapter 6: In Need of Justice   95
Chapter 7: Understand the Cosmos   107
Chapter 8: The Consequences of Anger   125
Chapter 9: Light Despite the Darkness   135
Chapter 10: Only Suffering in Return   145
Chapter 11: Strange Secrets   155
Chapter 12: To Survive the Day   167
Chapter 13: A Gauntlet with a Gift   179
Chapter 14: To Speak the Truth   195
Chapter 15: Into That Darkness Peering   205
Chapter 16: For Others and the World   219
Chapter 17: On the Road to the Stars   233
Chapter 18: By a Foe   243
Chapter 19: Expect the Best and the Worst   255
Epilogue: A True Friend   269
Chiricahua Glossary   272

Prologue

A Lost Kingdom of Peace

"Obsessed by a fairy tale, we spend our lives searching for a magic door and a lost kingdom of peace." Eugene O'Neill.

Year 3028

The early morning air was oppressively damp and heavy but Naiche Decker didn't mind much since it matched her mood. She looked down the double set of tracks wondering how late the train would be. The stationmaster had warned her that there had been some flooding down the line and she might be in for a long wait. Naiche wasn't sure if she cared or not. On the one hand, it would be a relief to get away from the glares of her cousin, Motsos, who had accompanied her to the station. On the other, the train would be taking her out of Luna County, away from what family she had left, away from the Chiricahua Apache people who had been her world for the entirety of her nearly eighteen years.

Naiche sighed and toyed with the strand of Dionian moonstone beads that hung around her neck, reaching nearly to her belt. The necklace was fashioned of small milky-blue crystals with a large briolette pendant of the same luminous stone. That particular gemstone had been discovered on Saturn's moon Dione, hundreds of years before and had been quite popular for a long time, but in the 31st century jewelry made from it was considered old-fashioned and somewhat passé.

She gave up the watch and sat back down on the worn wooden bench next to Motsos. He was her Great Aunt Loza's youngest son and at nineteen years her senior, he readily assumed the mien of a tribal elder with her. In spite of this, she was striving to maintain a respectful attitude towards him while they waited together. After all, he had not only brought her to the station, but he had graciously stopped at the cemetery on the way, so she could say good-bye to her late grandfather, Augustus Decker. Motsos had watched patiently as she knelt at the grave that lay between the one for the grandmother she'd never known and the fresh mound for her dog, Chato. Naiche had been grieved but not surprised that the elderly Chato hadn't survived her grandfather by more than a few months.

The cousins were alone on the platform, which evidently gave Motsos license to renew the harangue he'd been directing at Naiche for the past hour. "It's still not too late to change your mind," he said in Chiricahua, the Apache tongue they shared. She made no response, so he continued unabated. "Do you *really think* this is what your grandfather would have wanted? He was training you to be a doctor. He expected you to take his place eventually. We all expected—"

"Cousin!" She broke in at last. "Do you have anything to say that I haven't already heard from everyone else for the past two months?"

"*Have* you heard, Naiche? Or did you shut your ears? If you had listened, you wouldn't be running off to fight in the *N'daa* war that has nothing to do with us."

"How can you say that? Those alien bastards murdered my mother!"

"And? You think your presence is going to turn the tide of a war Uniterrae has been losing for ten years? No, the *N'daa* went out into the stars where we don't belong. They'd rather find new worlds instead of trying to heal the one *Bik'ehgo'iindáń* gave us. They brought this upon themselves; let them solve it. Your mother would still be alive if *she* had stayed here – where she belonged. Especially after she had you."

Naiche jumped up and faced Motsos directly. "So brave of you to criticize the dead! She's not around to answer—"

"I would say the same to her if she appeared before me now! I have every right. Your mother and I were young together. I mourn her just as deeply as you do."

"If that was true, you'd want justice for her, too."

"Is it justice you seek – or vengeance?"

"Two sides of the same coin, aren't they? If you want to call it vengeance, well, I'll own that and gladly!"

"That anger you carry is a poison that can hurt only *you*."

"We'll see who ends up hurt," Naiche muttered.

Motsos sighed heavily. "Oh, young one, you close your eyes to painful truths."

3

She threw up her hands in exasperation, asking "Like what?"

"Like your delusion that your grandfather would support you, were he here."

"How're you so sure that's not true?" Naiche snapped.

"Because if he were still alive, you wouldn't even be doing this." Motsos' voice softened. "You're trying to run away from the pain of losing him. I understand. I lost my father, too, but you can't run away from that pain. You carry it here...." He reached out his hand gently towards her heart. "You'll carry it there forever."

"I know that," she said. "I have the same pain for my mother."

"And you think vengeance will heal it?"

"It can't make it worse." When he just shook his head at her, Naiche felt the usual frustrated futility of ever trying to explain herself to people. In her experience, it never helped – why did she even try? She rubbed her right temple, feeling a migraine coming on. "Shouldn't you be getting back to the ranch? We don't know how late the train will be...no sense in both of us waiting."

"Yes, I should get back." He pulled himself up wearily from the bench and stretched his body to its full six-foot height. They shared the same tall, muscular build, deep brown eyes, and long brown hair – they even wore their hair in similar twin braids. But at that moment, Naiche felt their kinship was wholly limited to their appearance. Motsos embraced her briefly and said, "Farewell, Naiche. I wish you luck among the *N'daałigánde*, but you'll always be a stranger to them – and they to you."

"Farewell, Motsos, and good luck to you," Naiche answered, overlooking his dire warning so their parting could be an amiable one.

Her cousin moved towards the platform steps, turning back briefly to say, "You can come back to us at any time. Just don't stay away too long – or you'll be a stranger to us as well. And then where will your home be?" He didn't wait for an answer but strode away without a backward glance.

Hours later Naiche was finally on the train, headed towards the border of Chiricahua land where she would switch to the Uniterrae-run train system. She'd only left Chiricahua territory once before – at age ten to attend her mother's memorial service. From the memory of that trip she knew that the Uniterrae trains were ten times faster and somehow floated on a cushion of air but wasn't quite sure how that worked. Maybe she could kill some time looking it up. She pulled out the handheld computer the Uniterrae Defense Corps had sent her when she'd been accepted into their academy. That was her ultimate destination – the UDC Academy.

When she was a little girl, her mother had described the academy to her as an imposing fortress, set high in the Rocky Mountains, safe from the excessive heat and floods that frequently ravaged the low-lying areas. Due to both its location and appearance, the academy had become known to civilians and corps members alike as "The Rock". Naiche knew that her mother had made this exact same journey twenty-two years earlier, five years before Naiche was born. Her mother had always reminisced about her time at The Rock with great fondness; she'd been a star pupil, breezing through four-years of coursework in three years' time.

When the handheld came to life, rather than immediately looking up Uniterrae train technology, Naiche once again swiped through the UDC greeting page to the section titled, "The Hall of Honor". Her mother had several pages dedicated to her memory since Naomi Decker had been a revered diplomat of the Corps, famous for settling countless bitter disputes between the member states of Uniterrae.

Though she knew it word-for-word, Naiche read thorough it again, her heart twisting in bitterness when she reached the last section, describing her mother's tragic end. *At age thirty-two, Lieutenant Commander Naomi Decker lost her life in service to her calling and her world on a diplomatic visit to the Lead Ship of the Eternals, where she had been attempting to broker a truce. Immediately upon undocking, her ship was destroyed and all lives aboard were lost. A communiqué from the Eternals indicated that the blast was a signal that they didn't negotiate with lesser beings and that the Terrans should either surrender – or face extermination.*

As if to solidify her resolve about her new direction in life, Naiche followed the link to the description of the Eternals. The first thing that greeted her was a likeness of one of the aliens; she suppressed a shudder at the image. To her eyes, even though theirs was an undeniably humanoid race, they were hideous. Eternals had dull gray scaly skin, white eyes with no visible pupils, and durable bodies that were much stronger and taller than the average human.

You'd think with those advantages they'd do their own damn fighting, Naiche mused. *But no*, she went on contemptuously – *they leave that to the Gak. Cowards!* She followed the next link to the section about the Gak. She perused the description of the reptilian foot soldiers who'd been dubbed the Gak because of the strange repetitive sounds they made. There was some dispute among the Terrans as to whether the Gak were fully sentient, but it didn't matter since either way they were ferocious and tireless fighters.

6

Naiche debated internally whether to reread the final module on the Eternals; it was truly the stuff of nightmares. Like a flame to a moth, it drew her in and she found herself on the page entitled, "Transformation."

The original combat strategy had been to concentrate all efforts towards taking out the Eternal battalion commanders. However, UDC forces quickly discovered that these kills came at a terrible price. When slain, an Eternal crumbles to dust, releasing an energy signature, visible as a swirl of gray light, which will attack any human in the vicinity. The infected human will transform within an hour's time into an Eternal. Once the transformation is complete, the newly born Eternal inevitably defects to the enemy.

Initially, infected patients were immediately transferred to medical facilities so that doctors and scientists could attempt to isolate and study the vector, dubbed an electronic-prion or eprion for short. But no recourse to prevent the progression has ever been found. Occasionally, individual humans have proven resistant to the eprion but no scan of body, mind, or genome, has been able to discover what is unique about resistant individuals.

On the Uniterrae news stations she could sometimes pick up at home, Naiche had learned that there was a recent breakthrough regarding the eprion. It had been discovered that if a human under attack by the eprion was killed during the final throes of transformation, both human and eprion perished together. Though it should have been an effective tactic, so far it hadn't provided much advantage since it was proving difficult for most soldiers to kill someone who had so recently been a close comrade.

Naiche leaned her head against the train window and contemplated the horrors of transformation. She planned to avoid the dilemma of "kill or transform" by joining UDC Medical. Though she was indeed seeking revenge for her mother's death, she was also enlisting in the UDC to aid people, and to bolster the war effort, in short, to help her fellow soldiers – not to kill them.

Chapter 1

The Past is Never Dead

"The past is never dead. It's not even past." William
Faulkner

Year 3038

At 0232 hours, the VICI unit near the door came suddenly
to life, sending the following message into the darkened
quarters of Naiche Decker, "Lieutenant Decker, report for
duty. Priority situation."

Decker sat up as she replied, "Good – I wasn't sleeping
anyway. Ready, Kayatennae?" The dog, who'd been dozing
at her feet prior to the alert, had recognized the call to action
and sprung to life as suddenly as had the AI unit.

VICI, aka the Voice Intelligence Control Initiative,
repeated, "Lieutenant Decker, report for duty. Priority
situation."

"Yes, I know, sweetheart," Deck said. "You're waiting
for the magic words." She swung her feet over the side of her

bunk and announced, "VICI, acknowledged. On my way. Lights on."

As she slid into her uniform, Decker tried to remember the last time she had slept easy. Was it before Cat's death? *Definitely not.* Before she'd been obligated to kill four other teammates? *Nope.* Before joining the UDC? *No, not even then.* Before her mother had died? *Perhaps...perhaps, that had been the last time.*

Decker grabbed her personal gear and said to her dog, "Come on, Kay, let's go save the world." She could swear the dog gave her a skeptical look, though it was probably projection on her part. "Okay, let's go save *somebody,* at least."

Ten minutes later, Decker's entire Search and Rescue team was on a troop transport headed for Centauria's Kādivi Valley where one of the Tactical-Front squads had been waging war against a battalion of Gak soldiers. *Had,* being the operative word. Lieutenant Commander Lindy MacLaine was giving the run-down on the situation. "We've got better than half of Force-4 buried under mud in the valley. We gotta get in there quick as we can and see how many live bodies we can pull out."

A voice called out from the back of the transport, "We gonna be under fire, Commander?"

"No one left to fire on us," Lindy explained. "Most of the Gak in that area were buried at the same time."

"Great," groused Ensign Zaar. "We're gonna be digging out those goddamn iguanas, too."

"Not if you pay attention to your dogs you won't," MacLaine said.

"How'd the Eats trigger the mudslide?" Decker asked.

"Concentrated blasts near the north face." MacLaine paused slightly before asking, "How'd you know?"

"'Cause I know them."

MacLaine made no direct response but moved to the front of the transport, announcing, "Okay, we'll be dropping into the valley in five. Stay frosty."

At Decker's elbow, Corpsman First Class Wayne Spencer asked, "When you were in Tactical-Front, you ever see an Eternal, Lieutenant?"

"Sure, I saw plenty."

"Ever kill one?" Spencer asked. Before she could respond, he added curtly, "I mean a real one. Not a friend."

Deck gave him a long measuring look before answering, "They're all real, Spencer. That's the problem."

His reply was punctuated by a mean little laugh. "Yes, sir. Whatever helps you sleep at night."

"You'll never know how really funny that is. We'll just add that to the list of other things you don't know – like how to rappel more than thirty meters without getting tangled up with your dog." A rumble of snickers arose from those near-by, who couldn't help but recognize the truth of that salvo.

Spencer's face grew red and his eyes narrowed in rising anger. He faced Decker head on and sneered, "Five friends killed and yet your mother's just as dead as the day you showed up at The Rock."

Her deliberate reply iced with cold fury, Deck retorted, "One more word about my mother and that will be the last word you say clearly for a long time."

Spencer took her warning to heart and turned away, sullenly pushing his way to the front of the transport. Decker watched him go and saw the glare MacLaine aimed her way; the CO wasn't happy with that little exchange – or her. She gave a mental shrug, thinking, *What else is new?*

Hours later, on the way back to their quarters, the exhausted, mud-covered team was mainly dozing, and

11

MacLaine managed a semi-private word with Decker. "About Spencer – it would have been far better to *remain calm* and thereby dispel the perception that you're in the UDC on some misguided search for retribution."

She knew MacLaine was being somewhat conciliatory since Deck and Kay had pulled out nearly half of all of the live personnel recovered by the team, but she could find nothing better to offer than, "Sorry, Commander, but there's no sense in fighting the truth."

"All right then," MacLaine said testily. "You're still an officer. Just because a corpsman tries to start something with you, doesn't mean you have to rise to the bait. Either let him have it for insubordination - or let it go."

But Naiche wasn't hypocritical enough to dress someone else down for insubordination nor had she *ever* learned to let anything go. In a perfectly neutral tone, she answered, "I'll take that under advisement. Sir." Since its inception, UDC had employed the honorific 'sir' for all genders.

Lindy shook her head and said, "I'll give you this. That's the politest 'get bent' I've ever heard."

***

At the end of another long day with the Search and Rescue Corps, Naiche Decker keyed in the entrance code to her temporary quarters on Centauria, one of the many moons in the Alpha Centauri system that humans had colonized some forty years before. Centauria was currently the scene of the most brutal front in the war against the Eternals, taxing the designated Search and Rescue squads to their limits.

Search and Rescue was generally considered an undesirable assignment in the UDC, as it was unlikely to lead to either glory or promotion. It had become an undeniably grim duty since the war had turned against the UDC and the team attracted an odd assortment of officers, most of who either had a savior complex, a distaste for killing, or had had their fill of the front. Decker fell into the latter category. She chose S&R as a quick way to muster out of Force-1, her old Tactical-Front squad, and for the chance to work with dogs, which she loved and trusted. Genuine love she bestowed on very few humans, trust on even fewer.

Decker had originally hoped she'd also get in some time as an S&R pilot since she'd been one of the Micro-craft pilots for Force-1. The Micro-crafts were small agile one-seater planes, assigned one to a squad. They could take off and land in tight spaces, reach speeds twice those of a fighter plane and had guns fore and aft. In battle, they were mainly responsible for taking on the Eternals' bomber drones. The drones were spherical and looked like they were made of obsidian; they would spin and dart rapidly about while issuing forth a steady stream of deadly projectiles.

It was said that you didn't have to be crazy to fly Micro-crafts, but it sure helped. Probably due to that particular reputation, Micro-craft pilots were not chosen to fly for S&R teams, as Decker eventually learned.

Once inside her quarters, Naiche reflexively unzipped her navy-blue uniform jacket. It had a cinched waist and a thin silver stripe at the wrists that the matched the one down the leg of her pants. The single silver stripe identified her as a Second Lieutenant in the UDC. She shrugged out of the jacket to reveal a matching blue tee shirt underneath and her Dionian moonstone necklace.

She left her hair up in the crown of braids that kept the long mane out of the way on duty and made sure her canine partner, Kayatennae, had food and fresh water before sitting

13

down at the small desk. Placing a holo-emitter in the center, she activated the VICI. "VICI, Open secure channel. Coordinates, Whiskey-Indigo-three-nine-five-Golf-Charlie-two-one-one."

The AI answered, "Acknowledged," as it complied. No image was evident for the next ten minutes, meaning Decker's best friend, First Lieutenant Conroy Kennedy, was running late for their planned talk. Kennedy had been her CO in Force-1 and had mustered out at the same time as she had, though he chose to go to the UDC Intelligence Division, a much more desirable and coveted assignment than her own.

Decker busied herself reading messages and UDC news on her hand-held computer until she heard the crackle of a transmission from the emitter and a familiar voice say, "*Ya a teh.*" Only from Con did Decker ever hear the once familiar Chiricahua greeting that she'd taught him.

She looked up to see Con's handsome face smiling at her. His uniform was identical to hers except for there being two silver stripes at the wrists and down the pant legs. "Hey, there you are. At last."

Con's smile broadened, his teeth glowing white against his dark brown skin but he looked as tired as she felt. "Yeah, sorry I'm a little late, Deck. You know how it is."

"Sure do. How are you?"

"Whipped," he answered, while running a hand over his close cropped, tightly coiled hair. "It's been a busy week for us. You?"

"Same. Busy and rotten as hell."

"Wanta' talk about it?"

"No, not right now." Decker noticed her friend's image still hadn't completely solidified. "This connection sucks.

Where are you? Wait – should I even be *asking* that of an Intel Officer? Will you have to kill me if you tell me?"

"We're on a command ship this week, smart-ass."

"Ooh, a command ship. How special." The UDC command ships were equipped with the faster-than-light speed drives that enabled them to travel through cosmic strings. The personnel who staffed them were part of Command Operations and since the ships were solely responsible for interstellar battles, they took no part in fighting on the ground. "Are you in Operations, now?"

"No, Intel is still part of Tactical, you know that."

"*Do* I know that? I have no idea what you do anymore."

"Want to know what I do?" he asked with mock severity. Con jabbed his finger at her and announced sternly, "I do my job, that's what I do."

Deck laughed heartily, since even in the days when he was her CO, Con had never been the severe type. "Well, knowing you as I do, that's a sturdy indefensible."

"A *what*?"

"A statement that brooks no argument, so it needs no defense. Like, 'it's me.'"

"Where the heck did you learn that?"

"Remedial Linguistics."

"That was something you took at The Rock?"

"Yeah, it was for students who had Standish as a second language." Standish had been spoken by most of Earth's population for five centuries and had been adopted as the official language of Uniterrae. Even those who, like Decker, had grown up in a holdout community and spoke one of the residual languages would have studied Standish in school.

"How many cadets were in that course?"

"Like...." Deck cast her mind back to her first semester at The Rock. "...about eight. That's why I had to actually pay attention."

"If you'd paid attention in more courses, you might be in Intelligence with me."

"What a crazy idea. Can you see me doing anything that requires discretion? I'm much better suited to digging bodies out of the mud."

"*That's* what you've been doing?"

Decker sighed heavily before admitting, "Mainly, yeah, that's been my week. The Eats deliberately triggered a mudslide here on Centauria. Took out over half a battalion of ours and almost as many Gaks. But whatta' the Eats care about them? They'll just clone more."

"Man, that's rough." Con cocked his head in an obvious gesture of concern. "Are you ever sorry you went into S&R?"

"Not sorry *exactly* – I just wish we spent more time on rescue and a lot less on recovery."

"You ever miss Tactical-Front?"

"Nope. I miss you; I miss flying. I don't miss the slaughter – that's for sure." She learned forward in concern and surprise. "Why? Do you miss it?"

"No. I do miss the camaraderie our squad had, and I sure miss working with you. But yeah, the deaths...." Con shifted his gaze to the side. "The deaths had gotten to be...." The next three words were punctuated with a verbal stop in between each one, "Just...too...hard." Decker waited for more but Con fell into a gloomy silence. She realized it was as close as they'd come in the past year to discussing Cat's death but she was no readier to speak about it than he was. She was glad when Con abruptly changed the subject. "Enough of dwelling in the past. How is my nephew doing? Did he get that toy I sent him?"

16

"For the last time," answered Deck, grinning widely. "He is *not* your nephew because he's not my son, not my pet, not even just a dog. He's my partner and a UDC corpsman, third class. Right, Kay?" The mottled black and white Blue-Heeler at her feet looked up at the sound of his name and barked, as if in agreement. "But yes, thanks, he's destroying that toy as we speak."

"He get any more citations in the field?"

"No – they don't hand out citations for finding mainly corpses. I almost hate to ask, but have you guys gotten any good Intel lately? Anything that might help turn the tide?"

"Maybe." Con glanced around even though he looked to be alone in his quarters. "We're on a secure channel, right?"

"Yeah, why? You know something big? Something good?"

"Kinda'. It's gonna come out soon enough but 'til then, you can't tell anyone."

"Who am I gonna tell? Give. I could use some good news."

"A couple of months ago we captured one of the Eats' fighter planes."

Deck threw up her hand in a gesture of equal parts disappointment and disgust. "Big deal!" As far as she knew, the Eternal's AI-guided fighter planes had been captured on a regular basis since the start of the war.

"No, this time the self-destruct didn't trigger." Con leaned forward, his voice dropping to a conspiratorial whisper. "The database was recovered intact."

"Whoa. Were we able to get anything useful? ID a weakness of the Eats?"

"I heard they got *something* important, exactly what though, is above my clearance. In fact, no one but Admiral-level and above is privy to whatever it is that they were able to decode."

"What the hell are they hiding? The Brass *does* know we're all on the same side, don't they?"

"I don't know, you tell me. You've slept with most of them."

"Oh, you flatter me. Not most. My fair share," she conceded, before adding archly, "but it's not like I limit myself to the Brass."

"Ah, I know that tone. You have a new conquest. Who is it?"

"A chief gunnery officer – Stevenson. You know him?"

"I'm not sure. What's he looks like?"

"Tall, broad, blond, graying at the temples."

"Wait, that moving mountain, with shoulders out to here?" Con had spread his hands apart until they were about a foot out on either side of him.

"That's him."

"Okay. Good for you. I guess."

Deck was aware that Stevenson had a reputation as a taciturn, old-school soldier. "Oh, he can actually be *very* distracting. Just what the doctor ordered."

"If you ever saw a doctor, that is."

"If I ever saw a doctor," she agreed, unable to deny that she avoided Medical as much as possible and more than was advisable. "How about you? You seeing anyone?"

"Nah. It's hard to find someone to connect with when you're in Intel and always on the move."

"You know, you don't *have* to find love," Deck urged gently. "You could settle for lust every now and then."

"I could turn this back on you and say that just because you were burned once is no reason to give up on love forever."

"Oh no, you don't. We were talking about you. And I've become a devoted fan of recreational sex. I can recommend it without reservation. It can be very...umm, recreational."

"Yeah, I'm sure it can." Kennedy shrugged as he added, "Just not my style, though."

"Too bad."

Due to static, Deck could just barely make out Con's response of, "I am what I am." His image was quickly fading.

"Are we losing this connection?"

"Yeah, looks like--*Lovelace*--on the move---broadcast range."

"You're on the *Lovelace*?" She was suddenly glad they'd lost visual so Con hadn't seen her start at the ship's name. She had trouble making sense of his response.

"Yeah---we're---central intel---" More static. "Why---know---ship?"

Deck simply shouted, "I heard of it."

"----breaking up. What----?"

Deck shook her head, forgetting Con could no longer see her. "We might as well sign off. Talk to you next week?"

"--hope so." He shouted to be heard above the static but all Deck got was, "----IM you---" And the signal went dead.

So, Decker thought, *Con's on the* Lovelace. *He must've met the captain by now. Hope he hasn't mentioned my name to Ricci. But then...why would he?* After a moment's reflection, her ponderings grew more acerbic. *And if he has, so what? Ricci sure as hell isn't gonna say anything about knowing me.*

***

One morning a couple of months after Decker's conversation with Kennedy, Captain Matteo Ricci was at

19

UDC Planetary Outpost HQ, waiting outside the main war room. The headquarters were located on the moon Ptolemia, home of the largest Uniterraen settlement. Matt had been called to a meeting with all three UDC Fleet Admirals: Lalitha Bindroo, Juanita Romero, and Padraig Delaney. The Fleet Admirals were the highest-ranking officers in the UDC and were entirely responsible for directing the war effort.

Ricci had been given no information about the subject of the meeting, but he knew that any captain, who was called to meet with this trio, was either walking into some very good news – or very bad. Matt wasn't too worried as he was generally considered to be one of the UDC's rising stars and he hoped that long-time mentor Romero would have given him a heads-up if he was about to be reamed-out. Those facts combined with his natural optimism had his hopes high, but he had to admit to himself that his nerves were on edge.

After twenty long minutes, an admiral's aide-de-camp ushered him into the impressive room. The latest tech holo screens, displaying images from all the war fronts, could be seen on every wall and the dark wooden furnishings would have been shipped in from Uniterrae as no old growth trees were yet established in the settlements. Ricci took his seat at the large table and waited expectantly, while ensuring that he appeared unruffled and thoughtful. Bindroo, the most senior admiral, opened the conversation. "Captain Ricci, I'm sure you're wondering why we've called you here today."

"Yes, Admiral, I certainly am."

"Let's start at the beginning. I assume you've heard about the Eternal's fighter plane that was captured by the Intelligence Corps?"

"Of course."

"The data from that plane have been thoroughly analyzed and have led us to the unmistakable conclusion that the Eternal race is the result of an encounter the people of the *Intrepid* had with the eprion vector about two-hundred years ago."

Matt scrambled to make sense of the bombshell the admiral had just dropped on him. "The *Intrepid*, sir?" asked Ricci, looking for clarification from Bindroo.

"It was one of the generational ships that went out in the 27th century."

"One of the lost ships?" Matt asked, while trying to remember everything he'd ever been taught about that mission. It wasn't much.

"Yes." Bindroo pointed a remote at one of the screens and brought up a briefing presentation on the *Intrepid* and its sister ship, the *Valiant*. While holos of the ships were projected into the room, a voice intoned, "In the year 2633, prior to the formation of Uniterrae, and before the development of faster-than-light speed travel, two generational ships were launched for the purposes of deep-space exploration." More information was given on the ships' capabilities and personnel before finishing with, "Regular reports were filed for the first seventy years of the mission but eventually Earth stopped receiving any communication from either vessel and they were subsequently classified as lost, cause unknown."

As the presentation faded from view, Bindroo turned back to Ricci. "Since humans are subject to infection with the eprion and transform into Eternals, it's not terribly surprising that this contingent attacking us now arose from a group of infected humans. It explains so much – their considerable knowledge of human physiology and technology, how they can speak Standish, and so on. What we don't know is why they're so hostile, how the transformation works, and if there's any recourse to fight it. We're hoping if we return to the scene of the crime, as it were, we might learn something...useful."

"Like what, Admiral?"

Juanita Romero, who had originally been a member of the science division, answered him. "There has to be a host species for the eprion somewhere. An intelligent one, we believe. The eprions are absolutely driven to find some sort of sapient being to infect."

"Do we know that for a fact?"

"It's as close as we can come to a fact concerning a vector about which we understand so little. Eprions have never infected our dogs or any other animals in the settlements and over the course of the war, we've gathered enough data to make a strong one-to-one correlation of dead Eternal to infected human. The eprions seem able to survive outside a host for quite some time until they find a human to attack."

"Why wasn't that information ever made available to the troops?"

"To what purpose? The soldiers already understand the risk of infection well enough. If they know eprions *have* to find a human host and will wander quite far until they do, well, what's to be gained? More panic and gloom among the Corps?"

Bindroo broke into say, "That's why that particular piece of information will remain classified. Are we clear on that point, Captain?"

Matt struggled with his conscience for a moment; he felt that maybe that information should be given to the troops as a matter of basic respect for those on the front lines. But he still didn't know what the admirals wanted him for, and his keen nose for opportunity sensed a big one in the offing. "Understood, Admiral."

"Good."

"Okay, you said something about returning to the scene of the crime. How do we do that when we have no idea where the lost ships ended up?"

"Our science division has developed an algorithm which predicts the three most likely trajectories."

Delaney picked up the thread by continuing, "We're going to equip three command ships for long range exploration and send one along each of those trajectories. We would like to send more but the war effort just can't spare them. Those ships are going to be out of communication range with us pretty quickly and therefore, on their own. They'll face many challenges, we're certain of that. We're going to need our most resourceful commanders in charge of them." Matt could barely contain his excitement, as he was sure he knew what was coming next. "We want the *Lovelace* to be one of those ships."

Ricci had a devilish sense of humor, so he pretended to mull the offer over briefly before looking up at the admirals and saying, "Sirs, I'd be honored."

Admiral Bindroo spoke for the group, saying with a broad smile, "Thank you, Captain. We knew we could count on you."

"How will the *Lovelace* need to be modified?"

"Well, your crew will be increased to a hundred, so of course, the facilities will be expanded to accommodate that twenty-five percent increase and to sustain them for at least a year's time. That's the longest we expect these journeys to take. Due to the nature of the mission, we'll also be adding an extensive science lab."

"I don't have any science officers on staff, sir."

Romero interjected, "We know that. That's why we're giving you one of our best, Lieutenant Commander Aqila Lateef, to head up your new science division. She'll staff it out herself – all with final approval from you and Commander Lindstrom. If he decides to sign on, that is."

Ricci was puzzled by the implication that his first officer might not be part of the mission. "What do you mean by that?"

"Matt," Bindroo said, as she leaned forward, sliding her clasped hands across the polished cherry wood table. "We're making this mission completely voluntary for all concerned. You need to make it clear to your crew that there's no penalty for declining participation. We'll find other posts for them. We don't feel comfortable forcing anyone to take on so dangerous a mission under orders."

"I understand, sir. That's very humane of you. I'll let the crew of the *Lovelace* know. How soon can I tell them?"

"Senior officers immediately. Junior officers and enlisted corpsmen after we know what the senior staff decides. A complete mission description will be in your in-box by 1100 hours."

"Thank you, Admiral. Thank all of you for putting your faith in me and the crew of the *Lovelace*. We won't let you down."

"We know that," said Bindroo. "Before I forget, we'll also be assigning a senior linguist, Lieutenant Commander Jeffery Sasaki, to your expanded crew."

"A linguist, sir?"

"Yes, if you do find the host species of the eprion vector, you'll definitely need his help communicating with them. There's a good chance we'll finally start a dialogue with an actual alien intelligence."

"Of course," answered Matt, neatly concealing his skepticism. He knew Sasaki from The Rock as an intelligent, steady man and Ricci wasn't sorry to have him aboard even though he privately doubted they'd ever need use of his primary skill.

***

Later that day Matt was taking advantage of the sushi bar in the HQ officer's mess hall when he heard someone clear their throat behind him. "Captain Ricci?"

He turned to find a slender, pretty woman with enormous brown eyes and a white streak running down one side of her short brown hair. "Yes?"

"Pardon my informality, sir, but I wanted to introduce myself." She extended one of the hands she had been nervously twisting together. "I'm Lieutenant Commander Aqila Lateef."

Matt shook the proffered hand and answered, "Not a problem, Commander. It's a pleasure."

"That's very kind of you to say. I know Command Operations has a much more formal structure than we do in Scientific, but I have looked up the saluting protocols and I plan to—"

"Please, we're both off-duty right now and you'll find I rarely take note of formalities anyway." Ricci gestured at the stool next to him. "Won't you join me for lunch?"

"Oh! I'm sure you have better things to do than...I mean...I wasn't trying to impose myself on—"

Ricci decided the most expedient thing to do was issue a direct order. "Have a seat, Commander."

It worked; Aqila promptly slid onto the stool. "Thank you, sir." She took a deep breath and turned to Matt, saying

25

in a rush, "I'm very excited about this opportunity and I hope my lack of shipboard experience doesn't give you any doubts about my fitness for it." She seemed to relax slightly, having gotten that out, and accepted a glass of water and a menu from the waiter.

"Not at all. There aren't many in your position who do have that kind of experience, are there? The only one I can think of is Rose Franklin and I don't suppose she's interested in leaving Scientific behind for upwards of a year." Commander Franklin had headed up the UDC Science Division for the entire course of the war with the Eternals. She was considered to be a legend; no one knew more about the eprion vector than she did.

Aqila took a sip of water before replying, "Actually, sir, Commander Franklin posted into the *Tieraguinn*." The *Tieraguinn* was one of the other ships that had been awarded the deep-space mission; it was commanded by Commodore Grace Stein, a continual thorn in Matt's side. Their friendly rivalry often edged into not-too-friendly territory, all of which was complicated by their status as on-again, off-again lovers.

"Oh really? Is that confirmed?" Matt hoped he displayed nothing but surprise and was hiding his rising frustration at that unexpected bit of news.

"Yes, sir. She told me herself this morning. Have I said something I shouldn't have?"

"Oh no, not at all. Well...good for Grace. She and Rose will be quite the team." Matt brushed his irritation aside and said to Aqila, "Why don't you tell me about the work you've been doing up 'til now?"

Aqila obviously relished the opportunity to speak of her research and finally relaxed fully while doing so. She gave Ricci an extensive synopsis of it over the course of their

26

lunch. Maybe Franklin had more experience with the eprion, but Lateef didn't seem to be far behind. In the plus column, she had two advanced degrees in astrogenetics, which even Franklin couldn't boast. Matt ended up being quite impressed with Lateef and thinking that young blood just might have its advantages on this mission.

Chapter 2

What He Hides

"Man is not what he thinks he is, he is what he hides." André Malraux

A few days after Ricci's meeting at HQ, he and Commander Nils Lindstrom were sitting at the conference table in Matt's spacious office on the *Lovelace* reviewing pending tasks for the upcoming mission. Lindstrom and Ricci were an odd couple to be sure, as different in appearance as they were in personality. Ricci was just over five-foot-eleven, powerfully built, with thick, light brown hair and green eyes; his face was defined by a strong aquiline nose. He was a driven, mercurial man, laidback and easy-going until provoked, then his infamous temper would quickly flame to life. In contrast, Lindstrom had hair so blond that you couldn't make out the gray in it, pale-blue eyes, and a rail thin build; at six-foot-seven he towered over everyone else onboard the *Lovelace*. He was invariably unemotional and reserved; his sense of humor was ever present but drier than desert sand. Despite their differences, or perhaps because of them, they'd made an effective command team for the past six years and, though neither would ever admit it, they depended utterly on each other.

The most pressing concern the men were discussing was the need to find a new chief tactical officer. The long-time holder of that post, Lieutenant Commander Jon Waiguru, had declined to join the mission. It was a disappointing decision since Jon had served on the *Lovelace* twice as long as either Ricci or Lindstrom but not surprising since his husband was stationed at HQ.

"You know who I'd really like to get?" Ricci asked. Without waiting for Lindstrom to answer, he continued, "Andrea Haig. Wonder if we could get her to leave the front." Lt. Commander Haig was with Tactical-Front and well known for her ingenuity and keen combat savvy.

"*We* couldn't – but Commodore Stein did."

"What the fuck? Are you *shitting* me?"

"Yes, there's nothing I'd like to do more than extend this three-hour meeting by giving you inaccurate information," answered Lindstrom with a long-suffering sigh.

Matt ran a hand through his hair; the only response he deigned to give his first officer was a muttered, "How *does* Stein keep snatching up all the prizes? Sometimes I hate that woman."

"If that's true, then why are you having a late *dinner*," Nils paused to make finger quotes around the word before continuing, "with her later this week?"

"Now, how do you know about that?"

"Captain, I do have access to your calendar."

"I never thought you actually looked at it."

"Keeping tabs on you is one of my many *oh-so-pleasant* duties."

"VICI, how often does Commander Lindstrom access my calendar?"

The AI replied, "Commander Lindstrom accesses your calendar every day at 0600 hours."

"Well," Matt said, ignoring Nils' triumphant smile, "you're obviously only doing it to look for ammo to use against me – like you just did."

"Sir, you wound me."

"Yeah, I'd like to."

"Perhaps that could wait until after we identify a new chief tactical officer?"

Ricci stroked his lower lip as he threw a speculative glance at Lindstrom. "I do have an idea."

"I don't like that gleam in your eye, but I'll bite. Who?"

"Lieutenant Conroy Kennedy."

It took Nils a minute to place the name. "That young Intel officer who's been on board for a couple of months?"

"He's only been with Intel for the past year. He was in Force-1 for about nine years; he led it for six. He's skilled, levelheaded, and experienced. I looked up his combat record. It's impressive."

"I didn't realize you two had spent any time together. How do you know him?"

"We've been playing basketball together every now and then. Full contact basketball – just like we played at The Rock. Lotta fun." Matt loved sports and had been on every team, from racquetball to wrestling, at The Rock. Nils' only known sports were chess and sarcasm, but he was a master of both.

"Ah, I see," murmured Lindstrom. "That would explain the occasional bruises you've been sporting. Hopefully the lieutenant has more to recommend him than just beating you at basketball?"

"Hey, what makes you think—" Lindstrom gave his captain an amused look that stopped him mid-tirade. Matt sighed and ordered, "Wipe that smirk off your face and look him up."

"Yes, sir." Lindstrom quickly called up Kennedy's service record on his tablet and started reading it over. "He does seem to be a remarkable young man, Captain – with emphasis on the *young*."

"He's what, almost thirty-two?" When Lindstrom nodded, Matt asked, "Is that really *so* young?"

"I'm fifty, so yes, that seems very young to me – especially for a chief tactical officer."

"Well, I'm forty-eight and it seems plenty old enough to me. At that age I was a division lead."

"Yes, but you had been part of Command Operations for years at that time – with plenty of shipboard experience. Neither of which can be said for Kennedy."

"Kennedy's excelled at every new challenge that's been thrown at him. I believe he's up to this one."

"You seem to have made up your mind."

"I think I have. Let me talk to him tomorrow. I'd like to nail him down before...." Matt trailed off without finishing his thought.

"Before you see Commodore Stein, so she has one less thing to gloat about?" Nils suggested.

"No," Matt protested. "Before someone else gets the same idea."

"Of course, Captain."

Matt hated and admired, in equal parts, Nils' gift for saying one thing while clearly indicating another. "I think that's enough for tonight, Commander. Let's call it a night."

***

Two days later, Conroy Kennedy was opening up a high-priority, highest security channel to Centauria on his holo-emitter. Decker had agreed to the meeting, but it was his turn to wait, as she was not yet on-line. By the time he had poured himself a fresh cup of coffee he heard his best friend saying, "*Ya a teh*, big shot!"

He sat back down at the desk and answered with a laugh, "What's that supposed to mean?"

"You think *I* could arrange a high-priority, ultra-secure channel? No way."

Con just smiled and asked, "Did you read that briefing packet I sent you?"

"Yeah, that's just crazy. It's all confirmed?"

"As confirmed as anything with the Eats can be."

"We always knew humans could become them but to think we were the *source* of them...." The high-priority channel was clear enough that Con could see Deck swallowing down her grief at the thought. She abruptly changed the subject saying, "I hope you didn't break any Intel protocols by sending me that packet?"

"Not at all."

"I didn't think so – doing something like that would be more a 'Decker move' than a Kennedy one."

"No, I had permission. Plus, I can't possibly break Intel protocol because I'm not with Intel anymore."

"You're not?"

"Nope. I've taken on a Tactical command position."

Decker's reply was chilled with horror. "You're going back to the front?!"

"Of course not!" Con assured her. "Remember when you asked if I was part of Operations? Well, now I am." He couldn't keep the pride out of his voice as he explained, "I

33

accepted a post as chief tactical officer of the *Lovelace*."
Since Decker was just staring back at him wordlessly, Con
started to repeat, "I said that I accepted a post as chief—"

"I heard you. I just can't...." Decker shook her head as if
trying to clear it and started again, saying,
"Well...congratulations! That's just...wonderful."

"It doesn't sound like you think it's wonderful."

"I'm just surprised is all – I didn't know this was
something you were thinking of doing."

"I wasn't. Not until Captain Ricci offered it to me. He's
the captain of the *Lovelace*."

"I've heard," answered Decker, in an oddly clipped tone.
"When did the position open up?"

"When the *Lovelace* got assigned as one of the long-
range mission ships. The former chief tactical officer
declined to go so—"

"Oh...."

Con was surprised how much heartbreak Deck had
managed to wring from a single syllable. "What's wrong?"

"Well, you'll be going on this long-range mission, right?
For as long as a year. Do you know how far out holo-
messaging works without relay stations? Not very far. I can't
even imagine going *a year* without talking to you."

Con grinned at her. "That's why you need to come with
me."

Decker gave a short, bitter laugh. "Right!"

"I'm serious, Deck. I want you to be my second in
command at Tactical. Tactical gets *two* spots on the bridge.
We'll be on the bridge of a command ship together – can you
imagine?"

"I wish."

"What does that mean?"

"It means no one is going to give *me* a plum assignment like that."

"Why not? Look at your qualifications – you're a pilot, you know your way around a weapons console, shit, you could teach hand-to-hand at The Rock if you wanted to! I can't even *think* of anyone who'd be better. Tell me you'll put in your application."

"I'd like to—"

"Then do it! Promise me now."

"But, Con—"

"What, you don't want me as your superior officer again?"

Decker snorted in amusement. "We both know that no matter what your rank, you'll *always* be my superior officer."

"Then *as* your superior officer, I'm not going to take no for an answer."

"Oh...all right, all right. I'll do it. I'll *apply*, anyway."

"Tomorrow?"

"First thing."

Con rubbed his hands together, jubilantly. "This is gonna be great, us working together again."

"So...." Deck was toying with her necklace and not meeting his eye. "Is this appointment completely up to you?"

"Well, the captain and first officer have to approve my appointments but that shouldn't be a prob—"

She looked up at him at last, asserting, "Yeah, that's the thing. It might."

"Why?"

Deck shrugged and admitted, "Ricci and me...there's some bad blood there."

"What happened?"

"You don't wanta' know."

With a reproving look, Con insisted, "I *do* want to know, that's why I'm asking."

"We had a...run-in. Back when I was at The Rock."

"Maybe he's forgotten all about it."

"I haven't," she snapped.

"That's a long time to hold a grudge."

"I'm sorry, I guess we haven't been introduced," she said in falsely chipper tone, while extending the insubstantial image of her hand to him. "I'm Naiche Decker, and you are?"

"Give him a chance, Deck. He's a good captain and a good man."

Con didn't quite know what to make of it when Decker mumbled, "You're half right."

***

Later that same week, Ricci rolled over in bed and looked at Grace Stein lying next to him; her short auburn hair, lightly frosted with gray, was slightly damp with sweat, her hazel eyes were closed and her breathing even. They were in Grace's bedroom in her rather luxurious quarters high above the Ptolemian capital city of Rigelkent. If Ricci was a rising star in the UDC, Stein was the undisputed rock star. She'd been the youngest captain ever at age thirty-seven and missed being the youngest commodore by mere months. Everyone in the UDC knew the only thing holding her back from making admiral was the lack of an open spot. As soon as one of the more senior geezers died or retired, Grace was in.

The room was dim so Matt couldn't quite tell if she'd fallen into a doze after their extended lovemaking session. "VICI, what time is it?"

"The time is 2137 hours."

Without opening her eyes, Grace asked, "Looking to make your get-away so soon?"

"No, just wondering if we have time for another round before I have to leave."

"I hope that's not bravado, Captain."

"Just give me a few minutes, Commodore."

She rolled over to face him. "Glad to. We can catch up in the meantime." As Lindstrom had correctly guessed, Matt and Grace hadn't actually had dinner or even exchanged many words when they met at her place. Since they were more fuck-buddies than lovers, and hadn't seen each other in over a month, they'd headed almost directly for the bedroom. Stein now took the opportunity to ask, "How're your preparations coming for the deep-space mission?"

Matt knew she was looking to needle him and decided to play along. He propped himself up on one elbow and said, "Just great. How 'bout yours?"

She rose into a similar position, responding slyly, "Much better than you and Chen." Captain Kei Chen was the commander of the third long-range ship, the *Ramanujan*. "I'm not having to settle for the B-team."

"If you happen to be talking about my chief science officer or my chief tactical officer—"

"Or lack thereof."

"I believe you've been misinformed. I *have* a chief tactical officer."

"Waiguru changed his mind?"

"No, I signed Lieutenant Conroy Kennedy."

37

"For your sake, I hope you meant to say lieutenant *commander*...."

"No, he's a first lieutenant."

"Okay," she laughed. "No wonder I've never heard of him."

"Don't worry, he'll make a name for himself soon enough. Especially when we return triumphant from our successful mission."

"While you're concocting wild fantasies, why don't you award yourself an admiralty and the Founder's Medal of Honor?"

Matt shook his head while saying, "As always, your pillow talk leaves a lot to be desired."

"After all these years, I'd've thought you'd recognize foreplay when you hear it."

"When I hear it."

Stein stroked the side of his face, purring, "Oh, admit it – you're going to miss me. Or at least this."

"No argument there."

"What are you planning to do for sex, by the way?"

"Was something lacking about what we just did?"

"On the mission I meant! You'll be away for about a year; your first and second officers are both coupled, so they're off the table. And fraternizing with the crew is frowned upon...so?"

Matt raised his right hand and said, "This old friend will be taking care of me, I suppose. You?"

"My first is asexual and my second is taken; that puts me in the same boat, so to speak. I do have a power-cell operated toy though, that is just—"

"Thanks, I don't need any more details about *that*."

Grace laughed and said, "They always told us it was lonely at the top. I thought they meant giving up love – not sex."

"Have you ever been in love?"

"Oh God, no." Stein gave him a speculative look, asking, "Why? Have you?"

"Yes." Matt almost left it there but felt compelled to add, "Once."

"Ah, Ricci, you can still surprise me after all these years. What happened?"

"It ended."

"Badly?" She seemed genuinely curious.

Matt shifted his gaze away from her before finally answering, "Is there any other way for love to end?"

To stop any further inquiries into the subject, Matt pulled Grace to him and kissed her.

***

The next morning, the brand new chief tactical officer of the *Lovelace* was busy arranging his few personal possessions in what was now his office. The office was small and narrow but still possessed a desk, two basic guest chairs, and some shelving on the walls. Kennedy put the two holo-frames he owned on the shelving and switched on the emitters.

The first image had been captured at his UDC graduation; his parents and sisters were gathered around a beaming young Conroy, who was waving his diploma triumphantly. The remaining frame displayed a likeness of his teammates from Force-1; they were all crammed into a large booth in a bar on Rieyuu. They had been celebrating Decker's promotion to second lieutenant; an honor she'd mainly won by being one of the few Micro-craft pilots to take on two drones and live to tell the tale. In the holo, you could see Con and Decker on the outside positions of the booth while arranged in between them, in order, were Cat, Mac, Sasha, Fil, and Ato. *All dead*, he thought; he and Deck were the sole survivors from that night just a few years before.

His reverie was interrupted by a chime at the door. Con looked up to see the former chief tactical officer, Jon Waiguru, standing in the doorway. "Sir, please, you don't have to chime at your own office."

Jon crossed the small space in two strides, saying, "No, son, it's your office now. Don't you forget it." Con felt a pang at Jon's use of the term son, since Waiguru reminded Kennedy strongly of his own father, dead eight years now, from a sudden heart attack. Not only did the two men resemble each other in appearance, but they also shared a warm, genial manner. "I just came to say good-bye and wish you luck. Not that you need it, you'll do fine. I was pleased as hell that Ricci suggested you for this post. He's a sharp man; he'll do right by you. Always did by me." Jon paused as if wondering whether to add more – he apparently decided in the affirmative. "There were times over the years I thought he cared just a mite too much 'bout what the Brass thought, but then again," he said with a rueful chuckle, "I guess that's why he made captain at forty and I'm gonna muster out at lieutenant commander."

"You're not retiring, are you, sir?"

"I'm thinking of it. Van and I, Van – he's my husband, are gonna take a month's liberty Earth-side and decide. We've both got more than thirty years in the UDC so...we'll see. This war sure has taken its toll."

"I was just thinking the same thing." Con pointed to the one holo-frame and said, "That's the command team from my old Tactical-Front squad. All gone except for me and Decker."

Waiguru walked over to examine the holo. "Decker? Is that Naomi Decker's little girl?"

"Yes, that's her."

"I'll be damned." The commander scrubbed a hand over his lower face and turned back to Con. "I was one of the honor guards at her memorial service. Never saw so many hard-bitten soldiers crying like that. After the service, I handed the flag to Decker's old man. Looked like he wanted to slap me with it. I wouldn't've blamed him a bit. Probably that little girl clinging to his hand was the only thing that stopped him."

"He gave it to Deck; she keeps it with her always." Con didn't feel it necessary to add that the flag was never on display, but always hidden away from prying eyes; he was probably the only one in the UDC who had ever actually seen it. Kennedy also knew that he was the only one to whom Decker ever talked about the searing pain of missing her mother. And even that was infrequent and usually only when she was very drunk.

"Sounds like you know her really well."

"She's my best friend." Con smiled fondly and added, "And soon I hope she'll be second in command of Tactical here. She just submitted her application."

"Good idea. On a mission like this you'll need someone you can trust at your side."

"That would be Deck."

"Excellent. Well, I gotta get going. Godspeed, Kennedy."

As he turned to leave, Con, stayed him. "Commander?"

"Yes?"

"If this mission is a success...well, sir, what I mean is, don't rush into retirement too soon. We just might find a way to end this war and UDC will be all about space exploration again."

Waiguru gave a weary chuckle. "You read much history, Kennedy?"

"Just enough to get by at The Rock."

"Well, I'm a big fan myself. Particularly of one of the ancients, George Santayana. He wrote something once and when I read it, I knew it for truth."

"What's that?"

"Only the dead have seen the end of war." Waiguru tossed off a casual salute and left.

Chapter 3

Memories of Yesterday

"Anyone who limits her vision to memories of yesterday is already dead." Lillie Langtry

Lindstrom was taking a very late dinner in the officer's mess hall aboard the *Lovelace*. They had less than two months to go before the planned launch date for the deep-space mission and every officer on board had been working twelve-hour days. Other than the captain that was. Based on the frequent, round-the-clock directives from him, Nils couldn't confirm that Matt had been sleeping *at all*. Needless to say, the first officer wasn't in the best of moods; his mood wasn't improved when the, in his estimation, annoyingly chipper Conroy Kennedy sat down beside him.

"Good evening, Commander. May I join you?"

"It seems as if you already have."

"If you'd like me to leave, sir, I can—"

"Oh, sit down. Pay me no mind. It's the exhaustion talking. Something you don't seem to suffer from."

"I'm used to it. More than once at the front we would go a week with less than ten hours sleep, total."

"And yet you signed up for this."

"Well, I expect things will get better when the additional staff comes aboard. Speaking of which, when will you and the captain be approving our requests?"

"It's on our list, Kennedy, our very long list," he said wearily. "Why?"

"You see, my friend has applied for second in command of Tactical and I'd like to get that approved before her S&R team moves to Antiliac. That far out, it could hold up—"

"Ok, I understand. I'll see what I can do about expediting our review of those appointments. It's mainly a formality, anyway. What's her name by the way?"

"Lieutenant Naiche Decker."

"Decker? Are we talking about Naomi Decker's daughter? She wants to serve on the *Lovelace*?"

"Yes, sir. I talked her into it."

"May I ask *why*?"

To Lindstrom's surprise, he thought he actually saw a flash of anger spark in Kennedy's usually calm eyes. "Commander, I know you've probably heard that she's a bit...unconventional."

"If that's a euphemism for occasionally insubordinate, then yes, that's some of what I've heard. To say the least."

"You may know her reputation, but I know *her*. We served together in Tactical-Front for five years and she saved my life more times than I can count. She's tough, resourceful, and dedicated. On top of all of that, she's the finest combat pilot in the Corps. Bar none."

"Are you thinking we'll be involved in many dog fights out there, Lieutenant?"

"Frankly, sir, we have *no idea* what we'll find out there. Which brings me to my last point about Decker. She's just done a year with Search and Rescue. That's another skill no one else onboard has; Deck and her dog could really come in handy."

"I appreciate your enthusiasm and loyalty, Lieutenant, but I'm not sure she's right for the *Lovelace*."

"Well, then, sir, with all due respect, I'm not sure that *I'm* right for the *Lovelace*."

"Meaning what?"

"Meaning, I don't know that I want to do this without her." They stared at each other in silence for a second while the weight of the statement hung heavy between them. Con rose from the table, tray in hand. "If you don't mind, Commander, I'll finish my dinner in my office."

"Of course, Lieutenant."

***

Because of that particular conversation, Lindstrom cornered the captain the next day and forced him to review the Section-head appointments.

They were flying through them until they got to Kennedy's list. "So, the next candidate is Lieutenant Naiche Decker."

"What? You're kidding, right? Let me see that."

Nils made a swift swiping motion across his tablet in the direction of Ricci's, neatly transferring the data from one tablet to the other. "Unfortunately, no, I'm not kidding. She applied for second in command of Tactical. You know her?"

"Yes," Ricci answered without looking up. "Yes, I do." He met Nils' eyes. "You?"

"I know of her."

45

"Yeah, who doesn't?" Matt seemed to actually be considering the appointment, but he eventually laid his tablet down and said, "I don't think signing her on would be advisable."

"I agree."

"Well, that was easy. How many more of these are there?"

"Maybe not so easy. There is a complication – Kennedy *absolutely* wants her on his staff. They served together in Force-1 and he apparently thinks a lot of her."

"Too bad. I guess Kennedy's gonna learn that we can't always get what we want."

"Yes, but he may not stay onboard the *Lovelace* without her."

"He actually said *that*?"

"He most certainly did."

"Think he means it?"

"I most certainly do."

"You *really* think he'd resign his post over this?"

"He was most insistent about needing her onboard." Lindstrom leaned back and sighed at the inexplicable nature of Kennedy's obsession with that particular second lieutenant. "Perhaps they're lovers," he suggested.

"You think?"

"Well, he's only four years older than her but I don't know the precise nature of her requirements there."

"*Meaning*?"

"Please. Before her fame as the revenge-fueled 'comrade killer' she was known far and wide as 'daddy-issues Decker'."

"I'd never heard *that*, and I definitely didn't need to hear it now."

"Sorry, Captain. I'll redouble my efforts to keep you in the dark about commonly known corps gossip."

"How would you like some commonly known corps gossip about the captain of the *Lovelace* decking his first officer?"

Recognizing the captain's genuine ire, Lindstrom offered a rare sincere apology but also took note of the fact that he had struck an unexpected nerve. "That still leaves us with the matter of Lieutenant Decker's application."

"Yep, it does. So, what's your recommendation?"

"I recommend that the captain make this call."

"Thanks a lot."

"You're the one who wanted the pretty gold braid on your wrists. Sir."

Gold braid at the wrists and down the pant leg was the UDC captain's insignia, and "getting the gold braid" was many officer's driving ambition upon graduation from The Rock. Lindstrom's uniform was decorated with silver braid, which only a first officer was entitled to wear. Due to his temperament and distaste for corps politics, he was well content to muster out having never seen the flash of gold on his uniform.

"Right," Matt said, with a shake of his head at his first officer's jibe about his rank. He picked up the tablet again, perusing the application with a weary sigh. Finally, he shrugged his shoulders and rolled his head, saying, "Let me sleep on this one."

Based on Ricci's reaction to the subject of Decker, Lindstrom was fairly convinced that he already had.

***

Two days before its scheduled launch, Lt. Decker was walking up the entrance ramp of the *Lovelace*. She gave it a thorough once over, admitting to herself that the command ship was extremely impressive. Previously she'd only seen them flying overhead – huge striking silver tubes, the bridge visible as a semi-circular disk on the front. They were no less imposing up close, even in land-dock. Especially since the *Lovelace* was now half again as large as it had been before. The new sciences labs bulged out on the port side and the new hydroponic gardens expanded the starboard side.

The faithful Blue-Heeler Kayatennae was close at Decker's heels, his nose twitching at the unfamiliar scents, his ears perking at the cacophony of sounds that signaled a ship being prepared for a long voyage. As Deck crested the top of the ramp, she was overjoyed to spot Con in the entrance bay. He was in conversation with one of the thinnest, palest men she'd ever seen. He was taller than Con, but definitely couldn't come close to matching him in weight. From the silver braid adorning his uniform, Deck knew he had to be the first officer, Lindstrom.

She gave the greeting whistle of their old Tactical-Front squad and Con immediately turned towards the sound. Con jogged over to meet her and pulled Deck into a bear hug. "Hey, you made it at last!"

"Yeah, our transport from Antiliac was delayed." She shifted the strap of the navy-blue regulation issue duffel bag off her shoulder, letting it fall onto the floor and saying emphatically, "It's *so good* to see you in person again." She and Con had briefly re-united, seven months previously, for a visit to his family Earth-side.

"It sure is." Con bent down on one knee and greeted Kay, saying, "And this fellow, too. Think he remembers me?"

48

"I don't know, he was little more than a puppy when you saw him last." As if to prove her wrong, Kay offered his paw up to Con in a friendly greeting. "Ah, there you go. Looks like he does."

While this exchange was taking place, Lindstrom had approached the group. Deck turned to him and saluted. "Lieutenant Decker at your service, Commander."

He nodded in return, and said, "Welcome to the *Lovelace*, Decker," but his tone was unimpressed. "Since you're not only the very last recruit to board, but have a dog with you, I'd gathered it was you." He looked down at Kay and asked, "So, the dog *does* go everywhere with you, is that right?"

Kay threw a questioning glance at Con as she responded, "Yes, sir. That's protocol. I would have thought you'd been briefed—"

"Yes, I was but we're just not used to having *pets* onboard the *Lovelace*."

"Kayatennae is not a pet, Commander. He's a corpsman, third class and a member of your crew now."

"I'm honored," Lindstrom responded dryly, clearly indicating he was anything but.

Con picked her bag up and offered, "Come on, Deck. I'll show you around."

"Not quite yet, Lieutenant. Decker needs to get her physical but first—"

"Oh, I don't need that, sir." She pulled her hand-held out of her pocket, continuing, "I have a waiver from S&R Medical. They just saw me a week ago and—"

"I don't really care what S&R Medical did or said or waived. *Lovelace* protocol requires a physical for every new recruit and it will be followed. Understood?"

49

"I was merely trying to save Medical some unnecessary work—"

"Are you arguing with me, Lieutenant?"

Deck took a deep breath and answered evenly, "It seems that I am, sir, though that was certainly not my intent."

"Good. Report to Med-Bay, immediately after you meet with Captain Ricci."

Con broke into the exchange, asking with surprise, "The captain wants to see her? Now?"

"Yes, he was *very clear* on the subject. I was about to explain that when Lieutenant Decker attempted to establish her own on-boarding procedures." He turned back to Decker. "Captain Ricci requested to speak with you in his office immediately upon your arrival."

Deck gave a little shake of her head to let a visibly worried Con know that this was no big deal while she muttered, "*Of course* he did."

"I'll escort the lieutenant to the captain's office. You may take her bag and her dog, err, the corpsman to her quarters, Kennedy."

"Commander, canine corps protocol states—"

"All right, Decker, bring him along. I don't think the captain will be happy about this."

"I'm very sorry to hear that, sir," answered Decker, letting him know that she was just as gifted as he was at indicating the opposite meaning of what had just been said.

A couple of minutes later they were on the command level of the ship, which encompassed the offices and quarters of both the captain and first officer, as well as those of third in command, Chief Engineer Carla Ramsey. As they approached the captain's office, Lindstrom looked at the necklace Decker wore and said, "*Lovelace* rules don't permit visible jewelry while on duty." Decker knew that once she was in the captain's presence, she would be considered to be on duty but failed to see why her necklace would present a problem. She was about to tell Lindstrom that, when he added, "Unless, I suppose...it's a tribal thing?"

"A tribal thing?" Decker asked with amused surprise.

"Yes, your mother wore one, didn't she?"

"She wore *this one*. This is hers."

"Oh, I didn't know anything was recovered from the wreck—" He caught himself, suddenly seeming to understand the insensitive nature of his statement.

"Very little was recovered, but this was."

"That's something, I suppose," Lindstrom offered awkwardly. He straightened up to his full height and said, in a much more confident tone, "I didn't know your mother well, but we were in the same class at The Rock and I followed her career with great interest. Extraordinary woman."

"Thank you, sir. Yes, she was."

"Her death was an immense loss to Uniterrae in general and the UDC in particular."

"Yes, a loss to Uniterrae and the UDC," Decker echoed sardonically. "*Exactly*." She sighed and changed the subject back to the forbidden necklace. "I always wear it under my jacket when I'm on duty." She swiftly zipped up her jacket so the offending item was out of sight. "See? All better."

They stopped in front of a smoked-quartz door and Lindstrom waved his hand in front of the lighted panel in the jamb. A chime sounded, and a deep voice said, "Enter."

Decker followed Lindstrom into the large airy office to find Ricci sitting behind a massive wooden desk. It took some effort, but she managed to refrain from looking around at the personal effects displayed on the walls and kept her eyes trained on Ricci. He hadn't changed

51

substantially in the six years since she'd last seen him in person. He rose from the desk, she saluted, and when the captain nodded in response, assumed parade rest; Kay stood at attention beside her.

"Captain, here's Lieutenant Decker, as you requested."

"Yes, thanks, Lindstrom."

"I'm sorry about the dog, Captain, but it seems that it's standard protocol. He accompanies her everywh—"

"Yes, I understand. Not a problem." He gave the first officer an impatient nod, but Lindstrom didn't budge. Since he seemed immune to the hint, Ricci added, "You're dismissed, Commander."

While Lindstrom exited the office, Decker tucked away for later contemplation the information that he was a nosy son-of-a-bitch and had apparently been given no explanation as to why Ricci had wanted to see her.

She and the captain stared silently at each other for a few long seconds before Ricci said, "At ease, Lieutenant." Decker relaxed her stance but was hardly at ease. She gave Kay the signal to sit at her feet as the captain explained, "I thought it best that we get some things cleared up right from the start. Starting with your intentions."

He looked at her expectantly, obviously awaiting a response, but Decker was slightly bewildered. "My intentions, Captain?"

Her answered seemed to irk him. "Yes," he enunciated clearly. "Your intentions. I was quite surprised that you requested this post."

The light was beginning to dawn for her, but Decker couldn't refrain from giving the smallest snort of amusement. "I was *equally* surprised when you approved it."

"Well, that's a very snappy comeback but it doesn't answer my question."

She raised an eyebrow and protested, "I didn't *hear* a question, sir."

Deck wasn't absolutely sure whether she'd meant to provoke him, but she clearly had. The captain took one step forward and retorted, "See, that? Right there?" He shook his head, emphasizing his next statement. "Not gonna fly on *my ship*. If you think I'm going to put up with even the *slightest* bit of insolence from you, think again."

She felt that was an unwarranted over-reaction and really wanted to tell him so. "Request permission to speak freely, sir?"

"De—" Ricci's eyes narrowed as he finished, "—nied." He let out a puff of exasperation and said in a much more even tone, "Now, since you're obtuse – or pretending to be – I will ask plainly, *why* did you request assignment to the *Lovelace*?"

Decker's hackles had risen to meet Ricci's, but she realized he had the upper hand and she had no one to blame but herself. She was glad Kay had witnessed many a confrontation between her and superior officers and could observe the rising tensions between these two humans calmly. She took a deep breath before answering, "Because Conroy Kennedy asked me to, and I'd do just about *anything* for him." She really hoped he'd gotten the message that she considered serving under him to be the ultimate sacrifice.

"I see." He turned on his heel and paced the room, turning back to ask, "Are you and Kennedy romantically involved?"

Of all the many times Naiche had been tempted to tell a superior officer to go fuck himself, she felt this one would have been the most deserved. But once again, she managed to avoid uttering the career-ending phrase and instead answered, "Frankly, Captain, that's none of your business."

"Want to try that again, Lieutenant?" Ricci demanded sharply.

Belatedly Decker remembered that one of the rules of a command ship was the two top officers' right to inquire into such matters. "My mistake, sir, I stand corrected. It *is* your business. For the record, no, Con and I are just friends. Good friends." She would never understand why she felt it necessary to add, "And I don't have many friends in the Corps."

"That's not how I hear it."

Decker's immediate thought was that Ricci had now topped his previous efforts in the "Deserves a Fuck You" sweepstakes. She took a second to push her anger below the surface before pointedly asking, "Was *that* a question, Captain?"

"No, I actually have no interest in discussing your *colorful* reputation. What I am interested in, is your assurance that you can serve on this ship, like any other corps officer, without regard to our...." Ricci paused as if measuring his words carefully. "...past..." he hesitated again before concluding with a jerk of his head, "...that is to say, our relationship."

Biting off every word, Decker answered, "Captain Ricci, I can serve on this ship, under your command, just like *any other* corps officer, because the only *relationship* I want with you is one of captain and lieutenant."

"Good. Just what I wanted to hear," he answered in an unexpectedly satisfied tone. Decker was still weighing a response when he cut off that option by saying firmly, "Dismissed."

She gave Kay the signal to follow her and gladly exited the office. She waited until she was well out of earshot before turning back and hissing at the closed door, "Jackass!" Feeling immense relief, Decker looked down at Kay and said, "Let's go find Med-Bay before we have that other jackass up my butt about violating his precious on-boarding procedures!"

When Decker and Kay entered Med-Bay, they found Commander Lindstrom lounging against the reception desk talking to a short, plump woman with a mass of curly dark hair pulled back into a ponytail. She was wearing the unmistakable white uniform of UDC Medical. The contrast between the two officers couldn't have been greater and Deck took a moment to drink it in before approaching the pair. After Decker greeted them respectfully, the doctor introduced herself as Dr. Rita Clemente, chief medical officer, and said she would be conducting Decker's physical.

Lindstrom pulled himself up to his impressive height and said, "Lieutenant, I am most gratified to see that you and your canine shadow did manage to find the way here."

"I certainly hope you didn't actually feel the need to check up on me, sir."

"Let's just say that your attitude didn't fill me with confidence."

"Commander, I assure you, I would never disobey a direct order on my first day." When Lindstrom continued to frown down at her, Deck added, "I usually wait at least two weeks before I start *that*."

"What a coincidence, two weeks is at least how long you'll spend in the brig if you ever disobey an order of *mine*."

"Now, Nils," Clemente admonished, "I think the lieutenant was making a small joke."

"Do you have some sort of instrumentation that allows you to see something that small, Doctor?" While Decker was briefly pondering if it was too late to go back to S&R, Lindstrom turned to her and asked, "How did things go with the captain?"

She saw a chance to get her own back by blocking the first officer's attempt to satisfy his curiosity. "I'm sure Captain Ricci will fill you in, sir."

"I asked you a question, Lieutenant Decker."

"Well then, it went just great," she replied with mock enthusiasm.

"Really?"

"Yep, I'm still a crew member!"

"For now," Lindstrom drawled as he turned to leave.

Naiche looked towards the door the commander had just exited. "Wow, he's just a singular ray of sunshine, isn't he?"

"Give him a chance," the doctor said. "He'll grow on you."

"I don't know. Back home we had a saying about guys like him."

"What's that?"

"He seems like a half a shot of strong whiskey and a piece of ass would kill him."

"I can personally vouch that neither thing is true," Clemente answered dryly. She paused briefly before explaining, "He's my boyfriend."

"Ah, sorry, Doc. No offense."

"Why would anyone take offense at that?" she asked, while shooting Decker a quelling look. Then Clemente held out a patient gown and pointed at an exam room. "Strip. Everything off but your underwear; then put this on. I'll be right in." Deck told Kay to wait for her by the door and went to undress.

***

Clemente entered the room to find Decker sitting on the exam table, swinging her legs and looking around with an expression Rita couldn't quite name. She told VICI to open up a new patient file and arranged her instruments in neat order while musing about Decker. It was certainly evident why Nils and the brash lieutenant hadn't hit it off, but Rita wondered how she'd already run up against Ricci. The captain could be notoriously hot-tempered and emotional, but he was generally an easy-going man, who often disregarded any procedures or regulations he considered cumbersome.

Clemente had just begun the physical when she stopped to examine an odd scar on Decker's left thigh. "What happened here?"

"Oh, I was pulling some survivors out of a crash when some jagged metal caught me there. By the time we got everyone back to base, Medical was swamped so I just stitched it up myself."

"Stitched it up? What does that mean?"

Decker made a sewing motion with her hand and said, "You know...closed the wound with stitches."

"What?! With a needle and thread? Like they did a thousand years ago?"

Deck nodded, and said, "Actually a sterile needle and filament; I always have them in my pack. Don't worry, S&R Medical looked it over last week. There's no infection or anything. They wanted to heal the scar, but I told them not to bother, it'll eventually fade."

Clemente couldn't get past the use of so archaic a technique, asking, "Where *in the world* did you learn to do that?"

"My grandfather. He was a doctor. Not like you, though. He practiced traditional medicine and that's what he taught me. Our band of Chiricahua is quite spread out and he traveled far to see patients. I always went along with him and became like his assistant or nurse, I guess you would say."

"What else do you know how to do?"

"Oh...lots of things you guys don't do anymore: help set bones, insert IVs, take vital signs manually...."

"Huh. I'll be damned. Didn't you think about joining Medical when you came to the UDC?"

"I did, actually. It just didn't take." Decker swallowed hard and added, "Turns out I'm just not cut out for *N'daa* medicine."

"*N'daa* medicine? What's that mean?"

"White man's medicine."

Clemente, whose family still resided on the South American continent, paused her exam and glared at Decker. "Lieutenant, did you just call me *white*?"

Decker seemed unfazed by her faux pas, explaining airily, "Oh not white per se. More like...not-Apache."

"There's a specific word meaning 'not-Apache'?"

"Well, the direct translation is stranger, or enemy." Decker shrugged. "All the same thing."

"Do you ever think about what comes out of your mouth? Before you blurt it out, that is."

Decker admitted without a shred of shame, "Rarely."

Rita took a step back and put her hands on her hips. "Then it's high time you start, Lieutenant Decker. There's a hundred of us on a relatively small ship, setting off on a long, dangerous journey. You're a UDC officer – start acting like one."

At last, Decker seemed suitably admonished. She answered with surprising sincerity, "Yes, sir." She swallowed and offered the phrase they'd all been taught at The Rock, "I will do better."

Other than Clemente's verbal notes for the patient record, and her observations about her patient's robust health, the next ten minutes of the exam were conducted in a silence that started to get on Rita's nerves. Finally, she said, "Hmm, seems like I may have over-estimated you."

"Doctor?"

"I thought you were the type that bounces back from a dressing down pretty quickly."

Decker gave a slight chuckle as she assured her, "Oh, I do. It becomes second nature after the first hundred or so."

"Then why the silent treatment?"

She shrugged her shoulders, explaining, "It's not that. I know it probably comes off like I talk a lot, but when I have nothing to say, I say nothing."

"Is that a fact?"

"Yes, small talk is such an *N'd*—" Decker stopped herself mid-word, evidently not wanting to repeat her recent mistake.

"*N'daa* thing?" Clemente finished. "Do the Apache really divide the entire world so neatly into Apache and not-Apache?"

"Yeah, we kinda' do. More so since the Big Split I think."

"The what?"

"You know, when most of the world went one way and we went another – and reclaimed our ancient ways. Though to be fair, it's not so much an Apache thing as it is a Chiricahua thing."

"I'm not sure I understand the difference."

"Okay, let me see if I can explain it. It's like if I said to you, 'Wow, *Lovelace* senior officers actually care how junior officers feel about them', and you answered, 'To be fair, that's not so much a *Lovelace* thing as a Medical thing.'"

Clemente was well aware that Decker's amusing analogy neatly contained both a compliment for her and a slam at Lindstrom and probably Ricci too, yet she couldn't help but laugh. It was certainly true what they said, Naiche was nothing like her gentle, tactful mother, so Rita wondered why the young woman still seemed so familiar. She supposed that it was because, other than having a much taller, more muscular build, she was the very image of Naomi.

That notion was fresh in her mind when a few minutes later she met Decker coming out of the exam room, now back in uniform; Rita's eyes were drawn to the necklace she wore, visible over her half-zipped jacket. The doctor nodded at it, asking, "That's your mother's locket isn't it?"

"Yes." Deck's surprise was evident. "How did you even know it was a locket?"

"I knew your mother. Well, I met her," Rita amended. "I was stationed at UDC HQ for a while when she was there. She rarely came into Med-Bay, but the couple of times she did, she'd invariably start talking about you and show everyone holos of you on her locket."

"Oh," was all Deck could manage at first. "I never knew she did that."

"It was apparent that she loved talking about you. I'm sorry you didn't get more time together; it must have been terribly hard for you when she died."

"It was. It still is." Decker squinted at her before continuing, "Thank you for acknowledging that."

"What?"

"The personal nature of the loss. So many in the UDC go on and on about what a blow it was for the corps and even for Uniterrae but forget...." Decker stopped, shaking her head, and biting her lip, unable or unwilling to finish the thought.

"That's awful. I can't believe people do that."

"Oh, believe it."

The pointed nature of Decker's response gave Rita the sinking feeling that she might need to have another discussion with her boyfriend about his people skills. "Anyone I know?"

"You'd be surprised." She called to Kay who'd been napping near the door during the exam and left Med-Bay with a jaunty wave. "See you around, Doc."

Chapter 4

The Unknown Curve

"Faith and doubt both are needed, not as antagonists, but working side by side to take us around the unknown curve."
Lillian Smith

After nearly two weeks aboard *Lovelace*, Deck was having to work at keeping Kay happy. The energetic dog just didn't have enough to do. He'd gone from ten to twelve-hour days, working in the field, to watching Naiche train on bridge protocols and run drills for the tactical corpsmen. Even running the halls with Deck and Con every morning wasn't enough for Kay, so Decker had taken to playing fetch with him in the long corridor outside of the science labs. She waited until after dinner when the labs, which only ran an alpha shift, were usually empty. Con always joined her sooner or later and they took the opportunity to discuss the happenings of the day since Kennedy was quite often still tied up in department head meetings.

She'd just pitched the small rubberite ball down the hall and watched Kay race after it, when Decker heard someone coming up behind her. She turned to find the chief science officer headed that way. Deck gave Lateef a short salute. "Evening, sir."

When she got the usual nod and "Lieutenant," in return, Decker considered the exchange finished so she was surprised when Lateef said, "I did that right, didn't I?"

"Yes, sir." Decker couldn't help smiling at the science officer's apparent relief.

"I'm still getting used to all of this 'saluting' and people calling me 'sir', and on so on. We don't do that back at Scientific HQ."

Decker didn't quite know what to make of an unfamiliar senior officer confiding in her like that, so she simply answered, "I see." Just then, Kay came running up to her triumphantly with the ball in his mouth.

"Oh my God! You're the officer who has that dog."

"Yes, this is Kayatennae." Decker then realized she'd introduced her dog before she'd introduced herself. "And I'm Lieutenant Naiche Decker."

"Aqila Lateef." Lateef looked back down at Kay and said, "I hadn't realized you could have pets on a command ship."

"Oh, Kay is not a pet. He's a member of the canine corps and carries the rank of UDC corpsman, third class."

"Wow, that's—" Lateef stopped and said, "Wait, you're having fun with me, aren't you?"

Decker surreptitiously re-checked the silver stripes on Lateef's uniform. Yes, there were indeed three. "Why would you think that, sir?"

"Oh, everybody did it back at HQ. I'm known to be very gullible."

"*Everybody*? Even junior officers?" When Lateef nodded, Deck said, "What kind of egalitarian paradise is

64

Scientific HQ that you can get away with mocking a senior officer?"

Aqila shook her head and gave a dismissive laugh. "It's hardly a paradise, the politics are brutal, it's just rank we don't pay much mind to. So, you would never mock a senior officer?"

"I didn't say *that*." Deck grinned at her. "I just said I wouldn't get away with it."

Lateef smiled in return and then said, "I should get back to the lab."

"Are we in the way? I didn't realize anyone was working."

"No, not at all. It's just me and Bly; we took some detailed scans of that star system we passed through this morning and we're still crunching the numbers. Have you seen our labs?"

"No, I haven't been in a lab since I was at The Rock."

"Oh, I must give you a tour, they're fabulous." Deck wanted to explain that it would be wasted on her, but Lateef seemed so eager that she and Kay went along. Lateef pointed out the many wonders of the labs, which Deck pretended to appreciate, and at the very end of the space they found a young woman working at one of the consoles. The holographic screen in front of her displayed a dizzying array of multi-colored mathematical formulae, while the white stripes on her uniform wrists and down her pant legs identified her as an ensign. Her most striking feature was her long curly hair, which had been genetically engineered to be a vivid purple color and almost overpowered her dark blue eyes and short, curvy figure.

"Bly, we have company," said Aqila.

"Hello," said the ensign. "I'm Blythe Brodie, known to one and all as Bly."

"Bly, I think you should have saluted," Lateef admonished.

Decker waved her hands to negate that idea. "No, no, not among junior officers. It's fine." She turned to Brodie and introduced herself. "Naiche Decker, you can call me Deck." She pointed to Kay saying, "And this is Kayatennae."

"He's not a pet," Aqila explained, very deliberately. "He's a corpsman, third class."

"Puppy!" Bly exclaimed and rushed over to pet and coo over Kay. "What's his name again?"

"Kayatennae, it means 'fights without arrows, or weapons' in Chiricahua, my native language."

"Ah," Aqila said. "Because he's a soldier but he doesn't use a weapon."

"Exactly." Deck pulled out her hand-held and checked the time. "Thanks for the tour but we should get going. Con might be looking for me."

"Who's Con?" Bly asked. "Not Conroy Kennedy, that *dreamy* lieutenant?"

"The very same." Deck grinned at that descriptor. "Is that what people are calling him?"

"Well, *some* people are," answered Bly, with a significant look at her boss.

Aqila's blush seemed to confirm Deck's rising suspicion. "I'll IM him, and he can meet me here," she suggested. Before Aqila could object, Deck sent the message. She looked up to find Bly starting at her regulation tee shirt, embroidered with the UDC crest. "Is there...do you have something *glowing* under your shirt?"

"Oh, yeah, my locket." Deck pulled it out to show her. "It's Dionian moonstone, so it has its own luminosity."

"Oh, it's beautiful. Why do you call it a locket?"

"Because it is. It was engineered to project holos." Deck activated a tiny device on the pointed end of the pendent and held it in her open palm; the first holo appeared above her hand. "See, that's me and my mother when I was little. And that's my mother's official UDC portrait—"

"Oh, you're that Decker," Lateef said softly. "Your mother was the diplomat who died when the Eternals...."

"Yes."

"I'm so sorry. That's a terrible loss. How old were you?"

Deck swallowed and said, "Ten." To change the subject quickly she went back to flipping through the holos. "Here's me with my grandfather...and two more of my grandfather..."

"You must be close."

"We were. He's gone, too. But yes, he raised me."

"What about your other parent?" Bly asked.

"I never had one. It was just me and my mom – and a sperm donor."

In that age of genetic manipulation and triggered parthenogenesis, the concept of "sperm donor" was so archaic that it was invariably greeted by an awkward silence. Deck was convinced that people were usually trying to figure out whether she was joking – and if not, how to respond appropriately.

Fortunately, the scientists were spared the necessity of a response by the entrance of the aforementioned dreamy lieutenant. Con called out, "Hey, are you deserting Tactical for Scientific?"

"Yes, I found out they can freely mock their superior officers."

"And that's different from what you usually do – *how*?" Without waiting for a response from Naiche, he asked Aqila, "Settling into life on a ship?"

67

"Yes. It's strange how you can't tell we're moving at all, isn't it?"

"Thank God," Bly interjected. "I think that would be too weird if we felt constant motion."

"I can't agree." Decker said, "I actually wish you could feel it."

"Why?"

"There's nothing like the feeling of soaring."

"Do you have wings I can't see?"

"Heh, first time I ever got asked that. No, I was one of the Micro-craft pilots for our squad."

"You flew one of those scary little planes?"

Con said, "She loved those scary little planes!"

"Oh, they're *not* scary. The bigger planes took on the fighters, we just took out the drones, did recon."

Con said to the scientists, "Yep, that's all, she just took on those flying balls, throwing explosive rocks at us. No big deal."

Kay started whining, restless from the extended inactivity, showing he definitely needed more exercise. "Up for an evening run, Con?"

"You bet. Good to shake the cobwebs out from sitting in meetings all day."

The two tactical officers walked towards the laboratory exit, escorted by Lateef. Naiche stopped at the door to ask, "Aqila, would you like to join us for a run?" When Lateef looked doubtful at the suggestion, Deck said, "Or some other time? We run every morning."

"I'm not much of a runner, I'm afraid."

"Well, then join us for breakfast, maybe?" Decker was ignoring the quizzical look Con was shooting her. "0630?"

"You eat that early?!" Aqila was shaking her head as if the thought was impossible.

Brodie came up behind them saying brightly, "Why don't we *all* meet up for dinner?"

The two junior officers settled the matter between them while their bosses looked on helplessly, though Deck strongly suspected that they both rather approved of the idea.

***

The dinner Decker and Brodie had arranged that first time was a huge success. The incongruous quartet quickly became fast friends and dinner together a regular event. So much so, that a few weeks later the absence of one of the four dining partners drew the notice of two observers. Lindstrom and Clemente were eating within sight and earshot of the younger officers' table, but they were partially obscured behind a thin bamboo partition and therefore the eavesdroppers went unnoticed.

"Smart of them to ditch Lieutenant Lippy, isn't it?" Lindstrom said. Clemente didn't answer but simply rolled her eyes at her companion. Just then, Decker appeared at the table with her tray of food. "I guess I was giving them too much credit."

"Now, now," Rita admonished.

At the other table, Con was asking why Deck was late. "What happened to you?"

"I had to break up another fight between some corpsmen." She sat down wearily.

Con said, "Geez, that's the third one this week, isn't it?" Decker nodded in reply.

"I wonder why?" asked Aqila.

"Maybe because we're flying through endless darkness trapped in a small vanadinlum can?" Decker answered. The

69

Lovelace had entered a particularly empty stretch of space and the monotony was wearing on the crew.

"On the front when it got like this, downtime waiting for the next battle, we used to throw the biggest, wildest party we could manage," Con said. "Remember those, Deck?"

"Not *all* of them. Especially not the ones where Ato made his infamous garbage-can punch."

"Could we do that?" Bly enthused.

"Make garbage-can punch?" asked Decker. "Believe me; you do not want to do *that*."

"No, throw a party."

Deck shrugged. "Maybe. Talk to the morale officer. Who *is* the morale officer?"

"We don't have one," answered Kennedy.

"Ah, that's the problem. No morale officer, no morale."

Aqila said to Decker, "You should ask Lindstrom to appoint one."

"Me?" Decker retorted, pointing to herself. "You want *me* to ask him? There's an idea. We could sell tickets to that conversation."

Lindstrom was unamused by that observation, more so when Rita nearly spit her coffee onto the table. "And you wonder why I don't like her."

"Well, she's not wrong."

When Nils turned his attention back to the other table, Decker had moved onto complaining about the food. "Just because I eat a lot of it doesn't mean I like it. On the front, we learned to eat anything. And I do mean anything."

"What's wrong with it?" asked Aqila.

"It's all so...*healthy*. Didn't they equip this boat with a deep fryer?"

"Good nutrition enables you to perform at your peak," she explained primly.

70

"My performance is pretty peak on cheese fries and bison burgers."

"But," Bly broke in, "you'll live longer if you eat better."

"I have no intention of doing that," Decker said as she leaned across the table conspiratorially. To Nils' great amusement, he noticed the captain, tray in hand, had stopped behind the table and was listening in, also unobserved by Decker. The oblivious lieutenant continued, "I'm gonna live fast, die young, and leave an in-CRED-ibly good-looking corpse."

"Now, that's *just* what I want to hear from one of my tactical officers." To Decker's credit, she didn't jump at the captain's observation, but she definitely went rigid with displeasure, while her companions all broke out into smiles and entreated Ricci to join them. Lindstrom wasn't surprised when the captain agreed since he liked eating with the junior officers and did so frequently. He slid into the chair next to Decker, asking smoothly, "Okay by you, Lieutenant?"

Decker inclined her head ever so slightly and answered quietly, "It's *your ship*, sir."

"Yes," Ricci agreed with a smile. "Yes, it is."

Lindstrom's glee at seeing the irrepressible Decker put in her place was soon to turn to dismay as he heard the captain discussing and then endorsing the proposed party. Kennedy and Brodie supplied most of the ideas while Lateef approved but seemed to have little experience with parties. Decker was uncharacteristically silent.

"Great," Nils said to Rita. "Did you hear that? 'Talk to Lindstrom'. I suppose I'm adding 'party planner' to my list of duties?"

The dinner at the other table broke up and everyone rose. Bly looked at Decker's tray and said, "Wow, you really *are* sick of the food. You didn't eat a thing!"

"Yeah, guess I wasn't that hungry."

The group passed right by Lindstrom and Clemente's table, so they were able to hear the captain say sotto voce to Decker, "You might find it a bit easier to eat, Lieutenant, if you'd *unclench your jaw.*"

She answered in an equal undertone, "I'll take that under advisement, *Captain.*"

When they'd all left the mess hall, Lindstrom leaned forward and said, "Mark my words. Those two are gonna be hate-fucking in an equipment locker inside of a week."

"Nils!"

***

Lindstrom's fears about becoming an unwilling party planner proved to be overblown as the main thing he had to do for the party was approve the use of the spaces. It had been decided the prudent thing to do was have the enlisted personnel in the gym and the officers in the mess hall; that way more people could celebrate without undue scrutiny. The remaining item on Lindstrom's list was sanctioning the deployment of a skeleton crew for that night; considering they were still traveling through a vast emptiness, that decision was no hardship. Indeed, the only real hardship he was facing was Rita's insistence that he attend.

Decker was finishing dressing in her quarters a few minutes after the party had started in the mess hall. She said to Kay, "You have the night off, buddy. Don't wait up." When door chimed, she assumed it was Kennedy, who was her most frequent visitor. She called out, "Just a second, Con!"

"It's not Con, it's Bly. I need your help."

Decker said, "Enter," and Brodie stepped into the room; she was dressed in a long, flowered, spaghetti-strap gown, which displayed her arms, heavily decorated with colorful Celtic tattoos. "My, don't you look nice," Deck declared.

Bly stared back at her open-mouthed, and said, "Wow, you look...*amazing.*"

"That's what I was going for." Decker was wearing a leaf-green sleeveless blouse tucked into slim black Capri pants. The very deep-v neck of her thin top showed off her moonstone necklace; her hair flowed to the waist.

"How do you get your hair that straight?" asked Bly.

"Genetics. You said you needed my help?"

"Oh yeah, Aqila is still working. She said she might miss the party."

"Like hell, she will!" Decker grabbed Bly by the hand. "Come on." Together the two marched towards the science labs. A few minutes later, the junior officers were coaxing Lateef out the laboratory door. "You're coming with us – now," said Deck. "No excuses."

Aqila looked at the others, then down at her uniform and said, "I'm inappropriately dressed."

"*No*, that would be *me*," Decker insisted. "Come on. No one cares what you're wearing."

Inside the dimmed mess hall, pulsing with music, Aqila seemed lost so Decker suggested, "Let's find Con." She looked around, finally spotting him at the bar. "Ahh, there he is." He looked great, she thought, in black jeans and a brightly patterned, long-sleeved shirt. She elbowed Aqila gently, asking archly, "He sure can fill out a pair of jeans, can't he?" Lateef finally smiled. "Let's join him and see if he'll buy us a drink."

"I thought they were free."

"They are. It was a...never mind, let's just go." Con gallantly welcomed both of them to the bar and quickly procured a beer for Aqila and a rum cooler for Deck. The three of them talked together for a short while, but once she saw Con and Aqila engrossed together, Deck headed over to Bly, who was surveying the dance floor. "So, what're the likely prospects?"

"What do you know about the linguist – Sasaki?" Jeffery Sasaki's slim, elegant height, topped with a mop of thick, jet-black hair always commanded attention.

"I know he's not into women."

"How do you know that?"

Decker gave Brodie an affectionately exasperated look. "How do you *think* I know?"

"Oh."

"Yeah, he asked me to teach him Chiricahua." Deck gave a bemused shrug. "Turns out, he actually wants to learn Chiricahua."

Bly laughed and turned her attention to one of the tactical specialists lingering at the bar. "What about Bayer?"

"I think you have a definite shot. Ask her to dance."

Twenty minutes later Decker was chatting up Engineering Specialist Howe Phillips, when Lindstrom approached her. "I'm sorry to interrupt your search for a bed for the night, Lieutenant, but a word?"

"That was not fair, sir." On seeing the first officer draw back looking slightly abashed, Deck continued, "I never spend the night." She winked at Phillips.

Lindstrom pointed at a quiet corner saying, "*Now*, Lieutenant." Decker followed Lindstrom over to the indicated spot. Without ceremony, he said, "Your immediate presence is required on the bridge."

Decker looked around and belatedly realized that Con, Aqila, and Sasaki were all missing. The captain had never appeared, and this was the first time all night she'd seen Lindstrom. "What's up?"

"On the bridge," was the only answer she got.

***

When they got to the bridge, they found the rest of alpha shift crew on duty, the captain in his command chair, and Chief Engineer Carla Ramsey, standing beside him. Carla was a tall, serious woman in her late forties whose mahogany skin showed no wrinkles and her wiry brown hair no trace of gray. Her fit, muscular figure spoke of years spent climbing around engines and prying at recalcitrant fittings.

Arrayed behind Ricci and Ramsey were Kennedy, Lateef, and Sasaki. Everyone was wearing a deadly serious expression.

Lindstrom said, "Captain, all required personnel accounted for." He saw Ricci's eyes flick towards them and linger on Decker unnecessarily long. He almost didn't blame the man; the change in her appearance was rather startling.

Without ceremony, Ricci said, "Sensors have detected what we believe to be an alien vessel in the path of our approach. This information is staying on the bridge for now. We have no reason to believe they're hostile, but I want to be ready. Kennedy, what's the status of Tactical?"

"Sir, we have four designated crew units ready for deployment at any time. We've performed active hostile boarding drills six times since launch. Every tactical corpsman and officer is up to date on weapons and combat

75

training." He turned to Naiche. "Decker, report on systems' status."

"All sensors and main weapons checked out daily. Torpedoes checked, ready to load on your signal. Particle weapons have been checked out on a weekly basis."

"Good." Ricci turned towards Ramsey and said, "Engineering?"

Carla answered, "Engines performing at peak efficiency. Nav-sat calibrations performed last week. Ready to drop out of light-speed on your signal, sir. We can ramp back up to L-speed in eighteen-seconds."

Ricci took a deep breath and spoke to the pilot, Lieutenant Tanja Petrović, "Petrović, drop our speed and give me a visual on the source of that signal you detected."

Every person on that bridge thought that they were prepared for anything. They were wrong. When the visual came up, they were looking at a command ship-sized version of the Eternals' deadly bomber drones. It hung in space, a huge, threatening round black rock.

Ricci reached over and wordlessly hit a button on his armrest. Klaxons sounded in every corner of the ship. DEFCON-alpha.

Chapter 5

Know the Enemy

"If you know the enemy and know yourself, you need not fear the results of a hundred battles." Sun Tzu

Ten minutes after the alien ship had appeared, the entire crew was at battle stations, and the command staff was tensely alert on the bridge.

Kennedy and Decker had taken their places at the tactical consoles, still in their party clothes; Deck had her hair looped around itself into a makeshift ponytail. Ricci strolled over and silently handed her his uniform jacket, leaving him in his regulation tee shirt. Decker very reluctantly shrugged into the jacket. She glanced at him briefly and murmured, "Thanks."

The captain nodded, then demanded tersely of her, "Any progress on those scans, Lieutenant?"

"Nothing can penetrate that hull, sir. Everything we've tried ends up bouncing back."

"Lateef, any way to tweak those scanners further?"

"Not at the moment, Captain. We'll keep working on it."

Lieutenant Leticia Evans, at the communications console, suddenly said, "I'm receiving a transmission, Captain. Shall I put it through?"

Ricci considered it briefly. "Put it through." He waited expectantly for a few minutes and then barked, "Well?"

"Sorry, sir, it's still downloading. The file is extensive."

The captain and first officer exchanged a look of apprehension; Ricci jerked his head at Lindstrom to let him know to meet back at the command chair. In an undertone he asked, "Wonder what the hell it is?"

"Declaration of war? Demand for surrender? Latest holonovel? I don't know."

"Very helpful, Commander."

Evans cut into to say, "I've got the file, Captain."

"Put it though to Sasaki. See what you can make of that, Commander." All eyes on the bridge turned to the linguist's workstation. They waited a very long ten minutes. "ETA, Sasaki?"

"Uh, working, Captain. The translation algorithms are coming up empty so far."

Ricci passed the time listening to Kennedy and Decker's murmured conversation at Tactical.

"It's got to be Eternals."

"We don't know that, Deck."

"Then it's the biggest coincidence in recorded history." She drummed her fingers on her console for a few seconds before asking, "If a scan can't penetrate that hull, what are the chances our weapons can? I think our best bet is to go right for the torpedoes. Full barrage."

Lindstrom proved he had also been listening in by saying, "We're *not* attacking just yet, Lieutenant."

Decker turned and said, "Just the ever-present tactical mindset, sir."

"Is *that* what you're calling it?"

Matt made a mental note to do something about those two. Considering his own tense situation with Decker, his only idea so far was to lock them in a room and tell Lindstrom to sort it out. He hadn't proceeded with that plan because he didn't relish the idea of explaining a dead first officer to the Brass.

He was startled out of his reverie by Sasaki exclaiming, "I've got it." He projected a holographic screen from his console and pointed at the image. "This is a depiction of what could be...the golden ratio...yes, almost certainly. And...that's definitely pi and what appears to be...a solar system map...I think it's a...." He turned towards the command chair. "It appears to be a hand-shake package, Captain."

"A what?" Ricci asked.

"An introduction one species would make to another. Similar to the Golden Record humankind sent out a thousand years ago."

"Transfer what you have of this...package to the main screen, Commander."

"Yes, sir."

The bridge crew stared at the view screen while Sasaki narrated. "Their language is very dense, I haven't been able to make much of it, but I did decode anything numerical as well as some data into holo-vids...right there."

"Why did they send us pictures of rocks?" asked Lindstrom. "Wait, are those rocks...moving?"

"That's them!" exclaimed Aqila. When everyone looked at her, she explained, "That must be their species."

"They're rock people...in a rock ship? Is that what you're suggesting, Lateef?" asked Ricci.

"Yes, sir, that pretty much sums it up."

"Okay. Anything else, Sasaki?"

"It will take a while. In the meantime, should I send a similar communiqué to them, Captain?"

"You have one ready?"

"Yes, sir. We've had one ready for a hundred years."

"By all means, then." He turned to Lindstrom with a raised eyebrow, saying, "We wouldn't want to appear rude."

The package was sent, and the crew was discussing next steps when the alien ship suddenly spun around, dropped ten of the deadly, all-too-familiar drones, and disappeared.

Decker's hands were already on the weapons when Ricci yelled, "Fire!" and she was able to blast the first one immediately. The next few drones were destroyed within ten minutes, but the ship was taking heavy fire. By the time the ninth one was shattered, she was firing blind.

Kennedy was at his console yelling out systems damage reports. "Weapons-sensors off-line, main-sensors off-line, Nav-sat off-line, external-scanners off-line. Hull integrity at 68%."

A few minutes later, the last drone could be spotted circling the ship, but then it suddenly stopped firing. "What's it doing?!" Evans asked

"Looking for targets," Kennedy explained. "They've gotten everything on the surface which moves, blinks, or protrudes. It's scanning for the next target."

"Decker, can't you get it?"

"Negative, Captain. Without sensors I can't target it and if I start firing blindly—"

"It will fire back," he finished.

"Yes, sir."

"Lindstrom, Ramsey, Kennedy, Decker – war room, now!"

When they were assembled around the table in the war room, Ricci demanded, "Let me hear some options."

Ramsey asked, "Can we just wait it out?"

Kennedy responded, "If those drones don't find a definite target after a while, they just dump their entire payload on the closest thing to targets they can find. Which will be us."

Ricci rubbed his hand across his forehead, asking, "How long does that usually take?"

Kennedy turned to Naiche. "Deck, you have the most experience with the drones. How long?"

"It depends on how many projectiles they've already fired. The fewer they've fired, the shorter the wait since they have more to spare and don't have to be so choosey." She shook her head before estimating, "Shortest time I ever saw was about ten minutes...longest...maybe forty. The longer it waits, the better off we are, though."

Ricci responded, "Could it be almost empty at this point? We took a lot of fire."

"It could. I lost track. There were ten of them and they all look alike."

"Can't we risk jumping to L-speed? It can't follow," suggested Lindstrom.

Ramsey answered, "Jumping to L-speed without Nav-sat...well, in this area it might not be *too* risky, but we could still—"

"End up pulled apart," said the captain.

"Right. It's a small risk but maybe only as a last resort. I could send an engineer out to replace the weapons sensors so we could target it—"

Decker said, "It would kill your engineer in ten seconds flat."

"Couldn't you send some Tactical out with hand cannons to cover him?"

"Okay, then, thirty seconds flat."

"Well, how the hell did you fight those things at the front?"

"We had air-cover from the Micro-craft," Kennedy answered. "They not only take out the projectiles, they distract the drones and provide cover for the soldiers on the ground."

"And we don't have air-cover," said Lindstrom.

"Yes, we do!" Decker exclaimed. "Me."

"And what were you planning to fly, Lieutenant?" Ricci asked. "We don't have Micro-craft."

"We have shuttle crafts."

"Our shuttles are just transport vehicles; they don't have weapons."

"We could put a gunner in the back – with the hatch open," Kennedy suggested. "If we wear low-O suits we'll be okay. And we'll send out two Tactical with guns on the surface to cover the engineer."

Ricci said, "Your plan would arm the shuttle, but it still won't be *anywhere* near as fast and agile as a Micro-craft."

Decker said, "I'll *make* it as fast and agile. Or die trying," she added honestly.

"There's a plan," Lindstrom snapped.

"Gotta better one?"

Ramsey said, "We could still wait it out. If that thing is just about empty, the ship could take the barrage."

"Empty is a relative term," Decker told her. "Even if it fires after twenty minutes, it will still have about fifty of those projectiles left. Can the ship take that?"

After a moment of consideration, Ramsey said, "Not without heavy losses – most of them in personnel."

"Then, we have no choice and we're wasting time."

Lindstrom objected, "You're describing a suicide mission out there."

Con insisted, "It is not—"

"Maybe it is," Decker interjected. "But that's five out there versus ninety-five in here. It's worth the risk."

"That's pretty brutal math."

"That the kind of calculation you make, Commander, when you're on the front." She waved a hand between herself and Con and enunciated clearly, "Like we were."

Lindstrom observed, "Yes, you're very good at cold calculation."

Matt warned, "This is hardly helpful, you two," as Decker exploded out of her chair – but Kennedy was faster.

He grabbed her, spun her around, and ordered, "Sit down, Lieutenant, or you'll be relieved of duty!" She was breathing hard and staring up at Kennedy who, at six-foot-one, had four inches on her. He added softly, "And I won't have a pilot then." Deck let out a long shuddering breath and sat down, staring at the table surface.

Lindstrom didn't take his eyes off Decker but said, "It's your call, Captain."

"We're not going to sit and wait. Ramsey, get your engineer ready to go up. Kennedy, who's going to be the gunner on the shuttle?"

"Me," answered Con.

"Okay. Everybody, move! We don't know how much time we have."

***

Without sensors, the bridge crew didn't have a good visual on the battle going on all around the *Lovelace*. They could distinguish the effect of near-by explosions and could hear the communications between the five outside over comms. Kennedy was yelling, "Son-of-a-bitch! Five incoming! Can you dodge—" The *Lovelace* was rocked by a blast and then his relieved voiced blurted out, "That was too close!"

They'd heard nothing from Decker, but murmurs of, "Oh, no you don't!" and what they all assumed to be expletives in a language none of them spoke.

Kennedy shouted to the engineer, "How much longer, Avery?"

"Five more minutes, maybe?"

"Can you make that a firm five?"

"If you guys keep taking all of the fire, then yes."

"Keep it on us, Deck!"

Lindstrom glanced over at the captain; outwardly, he looked calm and alert but if he grasped those armrests any harder either the chair parts or his fingers were likely to snap off.

They felt another huge blast near the bridge and held their collective breaths until Decker yelled, "Mighty fancy shooting, Boss!"

"Shut-up and keep flying!" Con bellowed back, laughing.

Aqila asked, "How can they be so...." She just shook her head.

"They're soldiers," Ricci explained simply. "This is what they do." He turned towards the weapons console, which was now manned by Tactical Specialist Evelyn Bayer. "The minute those sensors come on-line, lock on and blast that damn thing to hell, Ensign."

"Yes, sir."

Everyone jumped back as the shuttle suddenly flew past the main view screen, spinning and swooping so wildly with the drone lagging behind, that for a minute Lindstrom thought Decker had lost control. Then she suddenly pulled up and zipped out of sight.

Avery shouted, "Almost done!"

Seconds later Bayer said, "Weapons sensors on-line, Captain!"

Ricci hit the comm button and ordered, "Decker, get clear so Bayer can blast that drone!"

"Don't wait for me! Blast it!"

"Like hell! Get clear!"

"I intend to!" announced Decker. "Bayer, I'm gonna lead it right in front of the main gun."

"Got it!" Bayer said, as she fired. The drone exploded.

"Where's the shuttle?" Ricci demanded.

Bayer was frantically scanning the weapon sensor display. "It's not on my screen, sir."

"Decker, where the hell are you? Decker?!"

There was a long tense silence, then Kennedy's voice came on-line. "Give us a minute, Captain. We're a little winded, here."

"Where?"

"In shuttle bay-2."

**

Ramsey had just wanted to check on the status of the L2 shuttle. It was the fastest of the three and Carla would be sorry to find it irreparably damaged this early in their journey – though it would have been for a worthy cause. She'd waited forty minutes on the bridge, until most of the damage reports were in, before heading down to the shuttle bay. She certainly hadn't intended to eavesdrop on the two tactical officers since it was reasonable to assume they'd have gone to shower and change by then. She had forgotten to factor in the time they needed to get out of the Low-O suits, so she'd been wrong.

Ramsey had started to examine the rear damage when she heard the quiet voices from inside the shuttle. "Do you think he's expecting an apology?" That was Decker.

Kennedy said, "I think he owes you one, actually."

"Yeah, let's tentatively schedule that for the day after hell freezes over. I'm free then."

"I'm going to talk to him."

"No, don't do that. It won't help. He's another one who doesn't see me; he only sees 'the comrade killer.'" Decker had to be talking about Lindstrom.

"I *know*, that's why I want to—"

"Look, you can't fix that. He likes you; they both do. Let's keep it that way."

Carla knew immediately who "both" were – Ricci and Lindstrom. The ship gossip was that the tactical second officer didn't get along well with either man in command of *Lovelace*. The reasons for the animosity were a favorite source of idle speculation. Ramsey's conscience told her it was high time she made her presence known but her curiosity got the better of her.

"If Ricci doesn't like you, then why're you wearing his jacket?"

"Oh, God, I forgot. Here, do me a favor and take it back to him." There was the sound of Decker roughly stripping off the jacket. "And he only gave it to me so I wouldn't disgrace *his bridge*."

"He said that?"

"Believe me, I know."

86

"Am I ever gonna get the whole story there?" That was interesting, even Kennedy didn't know what was up between Ricci and Decker.

"I'll tell you what...I'll put it in my will. You're the executor so you get to read it first."

"Why're you so sure I'm gonna outlive you?"

The affection was tangible in Decker's voice as she answered, "Because *Bik'ehgo'iindán* loves a good man."

Carla was immediately concerned that things were about to get romantic between the pair, since that was another source of ship gossip. Spying on passion was too sordid for her scruples so Ramsey finally made some noise, ensuring that it appeared as if she had just walked in.

Kennedy and Decker emerged from the shuttle interior. They were both sweat-soaked and looked utterly exhausted. Ramsey smiled at the pair, saying, "Well, I see you brought L2 back in one piece."

Con said, "And it brought us back in one piece, sir."

"I think that had more to do with your pilot than my shuttle," Ramsey said, nodding in Decker's direction.

Kennedy smiled at the warm praise of his friend. "Yes, I think you're right, Commander." He turned to Decker, "Well, hero, ready to go get some more kudos?"

"Those kudos should be shared at the very least; you did the shooting. It's a lot easier to just fly than to shoot and fly." Decker stretched and yawned but said, "You go 'head, Con. I want to ask Commander Ramsey something about the shuttle."

"Okay, I got a report to write. Catch up with you later." He wagged a finger at her. "Get some sleep tonight. That's an order."

Decker saluted with a laugh. "Yes, sir."

Once Kennedy had left the shuttle bay, Carla turned to Decker and said, "What did you want to ask me?"

Obviously not one for niceties, Decker immediately launched into her subject. "What would it take to weaponize this shuttle?"

"Do you think that's going to be necessary?"

"Based on today, I sure do. I want to have at least one shuttle with guns."

"Today was probably a one off, don't you think?"

"Enemies are like ants – there's never just one. And while it's good to be prepared for the next attack, it's better to be over-prepared."

"It looks like you see enemies everywhere, Decker."

"I guess I do, sir." She nodded at the damaged shuttle. "Hazard of the job. And having twenty-twenty vision."

Ramsey guessed she wasn't supposed to have gotten the significance of that last statement, but she had. "Okay, you're the expert here. I'll put one of my engineers on the project. They'll talk to you and then get you a couple of proposals in about a week. You pick the best one and we'll make it happen." Decker was already studying the shuttle as if planning where the guns would go, so Carla made sure to add, very deliberately, "All of that's *after* you get the captain's sign-off, of course."

"Of course." Almost to herself, Decker added, "Con can get that." She smiled at Carla and said, "Thanks, Commander. I appreciate your support."

"Glad to give it." Ramsey hesitated for a moment but then said, "Can I also offer you a piece of advice, Lieutenant?"

"You don't need my permission, sir."

"Well, I'm asking for it anyway."

Decker gave her a slightly skeptical look but immediately said, "Fire away."

"Lindstrom – he can be a difficult man to know; he can often be a difficult man to like. He's not a difficult man to serve under. He's a bit prickly but beneath all that, he cares deeply about his crew. Give him a chance."

"Thank you, sir. I appreciate the advice."

Carla almost laughed aloud – no wonder Decker couldn't get along with Lindstrom, they must be in constant competition for the best stealth "fuck off." "Which you have no intention of taking."

"Commander, you're the second person who's told me to give Commander Lindstrom a chance. With all due respect, sir, why should I give him, what he won't give me?"

Ramsey shrugged, surprised at this hidden well of naiveté. "Because you need to be the one to start – and before you ask why again, because he's in charge. Same's true of Ricci, you know. They both earned it. And the respect that comes with it." Carla waited for a response, but the young lieutenant remained expressionless and silent. Ramsey tried elaborating, "And that's what you signed up for, Decker, when you joined the *Lovelace*. I sure don't remember us going out and drafting anybody."

There was finally a weary sigh and an admission of, "Yes, sir. You're right," from Decker. She glanced around the ship, as if appreciating what she had gotten herself into for the first time. "This *is* what I signed up for." Carla wished her goodnight and was walking away but still heard Decker say quietly, "And that's why I see an enemy even in the mirror." Ramsey just added it to the pile of things she hadn't been meant to hear.

***

Very late that night Lindstrom was in his office compiling all of the damage reports so the captain would have them on his desk first thing in the morning, when he heard a chime. Matt usually walked right in, so Nils said testily, "Whoever you are, I'm sure this could wait until tomorrow."

"No, it can't, Commander."

Nils had never heard Kennedy use that tone of voice so his head jerked up in surprise. "By all means, come in." They stared at each other for a second and then Lindstrom waved his hand at a nearby chair and said, "Have a seat, Lieutenant."

Con sat down and without preamble said, "About Decker—"

"She's a loose cannon."

His attitude respectful but determined, Kennedy said, "Sir, you provoked her."

"She's easily provoked. Do you really expect me to believe that the *daughter of Naomi Decker* can't comport herself better than that? In a tense situation, you've got to be able to keep your head."

"She *did*."

"Only thanks to you. How long do you think you can keep saving her from herself?"

Kennedy sat back and said with a smile, "As long as there's breath in my body."

"That's your choice, Lieutenant, but a word of advice? You are one of the most promising young officers I've seen in a long time. The captain spotted your potential and he was right. But if you're not careful, that girl will drag you down."

"I think you're wrong about Deck, Commander, but even if you're right, I'll go down with her willingly."

90

"Because you think she saved your life a few times? I'm sure you saved hers, too. Soldiers save—"

"No! Because she saved...." He stopped mid-sentence, took a deep breath, and then started again. "Did you know that after I took over Force-1, it was the only Tactical-Front squad that never had a soldier go over the hill?"

Lindstrom recognized the phrase soldiers at the front used for a transformed human defecting to the enemy. "No, I didn't."

"Do you know why that is?"

"I would imagine it's because Decker kil—"

"It's because we had *a pact*. We swore an oath to each other that we'd never let that happen. We all swore that oath, so we all should have taken the responsibility when the worst happened. But...." Kennedy's voice was cracking. "But we let Decker do it, time and again. Not because she wanted to but because she *could*. Even the last one...the one that should have been mine."

Lindstrom waited but based on how wet Kennedy's eyes were, he wasn't sure the lieutenant intended to go on. "Who was the last one?"

"Cat. Caterina Xavier. She was the chief corpsman in our squad. She'd worked her way up through the enlisted ranks, so she was a little older. She mothered Deck a fair bit...." Kennedy was smiling faintly. "It was good, she needed that." He swallowed and continued, frowning now, "That battle, the one where we lost Cat, was brutal. I lost contact with Cat; I was worried she was KIA but I didn't think about infection – there'd been no Eats' life signs in the vicinity, so why would I?" It was obviously a rhetorical question, so Nils let him talk. "By the time we found her...it was almost too late." Con took a deep breath and asked, "Have you ever seen a transformation?"

91

Lindstrom cleared his throat and admitted, "Only on holo-vids."

Kennedy gave a small bitter laugh and said, "You can't even imagine *the horror* until you've seen it in person. They writhe and scream and foam at the mouth. Their skin changes almost immediately but their eyes stay the same, right up until the end. They look at you with those eyes you know so well – like they're trying to tell you something...." Kennedy swallowed hard but didn't elaborate further. Lindstrom understood for the first time just how much the UDC asked of soldiers at the front.

"Anyway," Con said in a shaky voice, "Deck and I found her. And Deck...she asked me to take this one. She said she couldn't. And I should have; it was way past time for me...." Nils could see him swallow several times, before he continued, "But you see, Cat and I had recently started...that is, we were...together." Kennedy had tear tracks down his cheeks. "So, I couldn't...and Deck had to. I let her do my dirty work *again*." He smacked his hand against Lindstrom's desk while stating, "She doesn't even have the sense to resent me for it!" Kennedy looked up briefly at Lindstrom before saying, much more calmly, "And it almost broke her...and me. We both mustered out of Force-1 first chance we got. So, you see, sir, that's what I owe her – and it's a lot more than just my life." He closed his eyes briefly, clearly spent. "If you'll excuse me, it's late." The young officer rose from his chair to head for the door. When he reached it, Con turned back to say, "Commander, if I *did* have to sacrifice my career for Decker – well, I'd toss it on the pyre and never even look back."

***

92

A week later Decker and Kennedy were eating lunch together in the mess hall when Lindstrom suddenly appeared at their table. "I don't wish to interrupt your lunches, but I wanted to let you know I've put the highest possible commendations in both of your files for your actions during the drone attacks."

The tactical officers stared open-mouthed at each other for a second before Con said, "Why, thank you, Commander. That was very good of you."

"Not at all. Well deserved." He looked pointedly at Decker. "Both of you."

"Thank you, sir."

Lindstrom nodded, and then asked, "Enjoying your lunch, Lieutenant Decker?"

"Yes, actually I am. The chef added burgers and fries to the menu."

"I know. I asked her to tweak it a bit. Enjoy." He then walked briskly away.

Decker stared after him with narrowed eyes, saying, "Who *was* that man?"

Con laughed and said, "Just finish your lunch. We have to look over those proposals for modifying the shuttle."

Chapter 6

In Need of Justice

"Nobody is poor unless he stands in need of justice."
Lactantius

At the end of alpha shift Con was swiping through Decker's weekly status reports as she sat on the edge of his desk watching his progress. Reports had never been a part of her work at the front or with S&R and it was clear that she hadn't quite resigned herself yet to this part of the job. "Yes," she drawled, "I remember my first day at The Rock, thinking, 'Now it begins. Soon I'll be filing *the hell* out of a bunch of reports. Then those Eternals will rue the day they attacked us!'"

"They also serve who only sit on their boss's desk and file reports." Con glanced up at her. "Beats fighting at the front, doesn't it?"

"I don't know," answered Deck with a sigh. "I'm like Kay, I get antsy. I need to shoot something, or carry wounded, or hit something...maybe I'll run some more hand-to-hand combat drills."

"No way. We've had *enough* of those." Con thought of the half-dozen crewmembers who'd needed pain relievers and chill-wraps from Med-Bay after the last drill. "The corpsmen are gonna report you for war crimes if you beat them up any more."

"*Tsiłkizhéne ndé!*"

"Call them cowards—"

"Fools."

"Whatever – but enough. If you need some hand-to-hand combat, go see your engineering friend." Con knew Decker was engaged in an extended fling with Howe Phillips.

Deck smirked in response. "Ooh, you opened yourself up there!"

"Meaning?"

"You start in on my love life; I'll start in on yours."

"Go ahead." By now, Con was grinning widely as he stared at the last report on his tablet. "I spent a year in Intel, remember? I know how to keep my mouth shut."

Decker pushed off the desk, saying, "You just told me *all* I wanted to know."

Con was puzzled by that assertion and looked up at her in surprise. "What? I didn't tell you *anything*."

"For once, you didn't deny *having* a love life...." She paused at the door and winked. "Say hello to Aqila for me."

"Get out of here before I write you up for insubordination," Con laughed.

"Wait...are you up-to-date on your birth control shots? I can ask Clemente to—"

"Out!"

***

The next day Decker was looking over the modified shuttle with the two engineers who had done the work when the VICI unit near the door buzzed and the AI's voice announced, "Lieutenant Decker, report to the bridge."

"VICI, acknowledged. On my way."

When she and Kay got to the bridge, she saw Ricci and Lindstrom huddled over the science console with Aqila.

Con, motioned her over to his station. "You've been wanting some action?" He nodded towards the group at the science station. "We might be seeing some. Today."

"What's up?"

"Long-range sensors have detected a near-by planet with definite Gak life signs. And where there's Gak—"

"There are Eternals."

"Ostensibly, yes. Except we can't detect any Eternal life signs."

"Not good if those bastards have learned to mask their life signs. Can you imagine? The soldiers at the front would be so screwed."

Decker saw Con looking over her shoulder and turned to see Ricci listening in with a deep frown. She quickly re-ran the conversation over in her mind but couldn't understand what they'd said that might have upset the captain.

"Captain? Do you need us?"

Ricci said, "Soon, probably," and returned to his command chair. Deck gave Con a quizzical look and he simply shrugged.

As soon as he had settled into the chair, Ricci spoke to the pilot. "Petrović, drop out of L-speed and maintain a distant orbit around the planet." He turned to the science station, "Lateef, run every known scan once we're there. I want to know *exactly* what we're up against."

There was a chorus of, "Yes, sir" in response.

Deck took up her station and waited. Soon Aqila was reporting on the planet, "Countless life signs, including the Gak. No Eternals, no eprion signatures, no technology to speak of, Captain."

"No technology?"

"None, sir. No energy signatures at all, not even electricity. I am detecting large amounts of carbon dioxide and monoxide, as well as formic and acetic acids, so there does seem to be a vast amount of wood combustion going on."

"What's the terrain like?"

"Varied. Most species seem to be concentrated in some marshy areas around the equator."

"I want to proceed with caution here. Kennedy, you and Decker take a shuttle down. Mission is recon only. Do not engage local populace unless forced to. Is that weaponized shuttle ready yet?"

Decker answered. "Was just giving it the once over, Captain. I can green-light it."

"Good. Kennedy, take that one. And as many of your corpsmen as you see fit; break out the particle rifles."

"Yes, sir."

"Captain?" Lateef spoke up. "I think Scientific should have a presence on this mission."

"I appreciate your enthusiasm, Lateef, but let's ensure it's safe first before we send down civil—" Ricci apparently caught himself before calling his chief science officer a civilian. "Before we send down scientists."

Aqila pointed to Kay who, as usual, was lounging under Decker's station. "You mean the dog gets to go down before I do?"

Ricci shrugged. "Looks that way. Sorry, Commander."

"He's a *corpsman, third class*," Deck insisted, as she, Kay, and Kennedy passed by Aqila's station.

"It's science that's third class around here!" Lateef called out good-naturedly.

As soon as they had exited the bridge, Decker said to Con, "Whoops. I hope I didn't get you in the dog house." She really didn't blame him at all for the light shove he gave her.

***

Kennedy, Decker and two corpsmen, Nike Modi and Amy Perham, had landed and were situated on a small hill overlooking a huddle of mud huts. The hand scanner showed around forty Gak life-signs. Modi and Perham were on lookout while Kennedy was recording holo-vid on the scanner and Decker was observing with the oculiscope.

"I don't see anything – wait, there's something moving...." She homed in on the image, refocusing the scope to get a better view. "Wow, it *looks* like a Gak, but not like one I've ever seen." The creature had the same reptilian form but rather than the muddy-brown skin she knew from the front, Decker saw iridescent skin that shimmered with a rainbow of color. "There's another one...and another." She sat back on her heels, saying, "Maybe they're distant relatives."

"Could be. I'm sure they're no less dangerous," answered Con. He turned his scanner towards the spot Decker had indicated. "Are they...are they cooking?"

Decker zoomed in. "Yep, fish I'd say." She saw a group of six Gak come out of a larger hut. "Wow, never saw Gak that small. They must have huge variat—"

"What?"

Deck didn't answer immediately as she was trying to understand what she was seeing. The movements that the small Gak were making, the way they were interacting was so familiar. "Oh. They're playing." She turned to Con. "They're children."

"You sure?"

"Positive." She handed him the oculiscope. "Take a look."

Kennedy studied the group for a minute. "Yep, I think you're right. I guess we should have realized these Gak couldn't be sterile clones." He handed the scope back to Decker. "Like you said, they're probably distant relatives." They watched and recorded the settlement for thirty minutes more before Kennedy said, "I think we have enough. Let's get back to the shuttle."

They had hidden the shuttle in some high grass. They had almost reached it when Decker, who was slightly ahead of the others, spotted five Gak, including a child, heading their way.

"Drop!" she ordered, in a low voice. Immediately the entire tactical group, including Kay, who had been thirty feet ahead of Deck, dropped to the ground.

With mounting fear, Decker watched as the Gak approached. They were going to spot Kay; he was right in their path. She readied her weapon. "What're you doing?" hissed Kennedy

"I'm not going to let them rip into him." Even without weapons, the Gak had been able and eager to attack Terran soldiers with their powerful jaws. The results could be fatal and were rarely pretty. "Not on my watch." She put the riflescope to her eye and waited. They all waited in hushed silence.

The youngster spotted Kay first; he gave a Gak fear yell, which was almost risible coming from a child. He ran back to the others and pointed at Kay, who was still under orders and remained motionless. The five Gak surrounded Kay. Decker still had the riflescope to her eye and now, she had her finger on the trigger. However, no attack came – the group studied Kay with great curiosity, but no movement was made until the child slowly approached. He gently put one small hand on Kay and then the young Gak did the most extraordinary thing. He giggled.

Deck put her weapon down and stared. She heard Con say, "Was that a laugh? They can laugh?"

Decker almost felt like she was hallucinating as she watched the entire group reaching down to pet Kay; they were chattering in a variety of noises she had never heard them make. The patient dog finally broke protocol and sat up. More excited chattering and petting. Then Kay started wagging his tail and the entire group broke out into laughter.

Con said, "Well, I guess they're not hostile." He looked at Decker and said, "Might as well say hello; our cover's blown." He gave the signal and the four Terrans rose. "Hello!" shouted Kennedy. The Gak turned towards him. "Umm...we come in peace."

Five Gak fear yells immediately sounded and the group ran in abject terror, only looking back to ensure they weren't being followed.

Decker came up to Con, clapped him on the arm and said, "Wonder what 'peace' means in their language?"

***

That first unsuccessful encounter with the Gak of this planet was repeated the next day, when Lateef insisted on trying an unarmed landing party with a Gak group hundreds of miles away. It made no difference; the scientific contingent was also met with abject terror. A third try in another location yielded identical results. Aqila finally gave up and made do with analyzing Gak skin samples that she had retrieved from Kay's coat prior to decontamination.

Most of the command staff was assembled in the war room awaiting Lateef, who planned to present her findings. The only ones missing were Tanja Petrović, who was at the helm, the captain, and Lateef herself. Brodie was an invited guest since she had helped to analyze the data.

Ramsey asked, "What was there to analyze? I thought we never got close to them?"

"We took swabs of Kayatennae's coat," explained Bly. "He was the only one who did get close."

"When you think about it, Kay is the *real hero* of this mission," said Decker. "I think he should get a commendation. Put him up for one, won't you, Con?"

"Absolutely!" Con knew Decker wasn't serious, so he played along. "I was thinking the Founder's Medal of Honor, actually."

At the mention of that coveted prize, Lindstrom snapped, "What are you planning to give him a commendation for? Being adorable?"

"Why, Commander," Decker cooed. "I never knew you thought Kay was *adorable*."

"I don't. You're the one who brought up the ridiculous idea of a commendation."

"Yeah, but you're the one who said 'adorable'. Admit it, sir – you think he's adorable."

"You know, I'm still in charge of the duty roster, Lieutenant. I could put you on gamma shift for the next month."

"Ooh, a month of sleeping in!"

"That only works if you actually sleep, Deck." Con often worried about his friend's chronic insomnia but he could have easily predicted her next statement because it was her standard comeback.

"I'll sleep when I'm dead."

"My, that's strange," said Lindstrom archly. "That's what the captain always says."

Con immediately saw that Deck was irked by that observation. He braced himself for a sarcastic reply and breathed a sigh of relief when she merely said with a shrug, "Oh, everybody says that."

"Everybody says what?" asked Lateef, entering the room with Ricci.

Lindstrom ended what he'd begun by answering, "That we should get started now."

"Of course." Lateef launched into presenting her data, beginning with an in-depth genetic analysis of the skin samples. This was mainly appreciated by Clemente and Brodie; however, interest rose in the room when she turned the data screen to a side-by-side comparison of these samples to those on file for cloned Gak. "It's incontrovertible. These are the same species. There's been absolutely no genetic drift."

Sasaki said, "My analysis of their vocalization patterns concurs. They make more varied sounds, but the basic structure is the same. The two groups could communicate with no problem."

"But they don't look – or act – anything alike," Con protested.

"That's an artifact of the cloning, I believe," Aqila explained. "Much of their...personality, for lack of a better word, is suppressed by the process. "

"Not an artifact," Ricci said. "The entire purpose."

"What do you mean?" asked Brodie.

Deck immediately snapped, "He means that the Eternals took a peaceful, happy species and turned them into cannon fodder." She slammed her fist on the table. "Those bastards have to be made to pay!"

Aqila sat down, demurring, "But if it's true that they arose from a group of infected humans—"

"I don't care what they once were. I care what kind of evil bastards they are now!"

Con instinctively knew that Decker wasn't just thinking of her mother; like him she was thinking of the thousands of Gak that they had killed at the front. Beings who had been snatched from an idyllic existence to fight in a war they had never wanted. He put his hand on her arm and said, "Deck, we all care." He promised firmly, "And they *will* pay – one way or another. It's the whole point of our mission."

***

That night Aqila and Con were sitting in the officer's lounge on one of the small sofas enjoying an after-dinner drink. She appreciated the down time and even more so her companion, but her mind kept straying back to the meeting.

Con noticed. "You're very quiet. What's on your mind?"

Though she hated to break the spell, Aqila felt compelled to ask, "What you told Deck in the meeting today – about the Eternals. Do you really believe that?"

He pondered for a moment and then said, "What? That we're gonna make sure the Eternals pay for their crimes?"

She nodded in reply. Con snuggled his head into her shoulder saying, "God, Aqila, I *have* to believe that. All they've taken from us, all we've lost – Deck's mom, our...friends, our...."

"What?"

"Maybe even our souls...I don't know. Ten years I've been fighting this war. Don't tell me there's no payoff coming."

Aqila let it go. The feel of Con next her was too good to do otherwise. But she wondered about Con and Deck, and the thousands of others of supposedly hardened soldiers, who maintained a child-like belief in the inevitability of justice. How would they would cope if it turned out that there was no dragon slain at the end of the story?

Chapter 7

Understand the Cosmos

"One may understand the cosmos, but never the ego; the self is more distant than any star." G. K. Chesterton

Weeks later, they were orbiting yet another planet of interest, but the ship was at DEFCON-gamma because Eternal life signs, albeit very faint ones, had been detected. There were other life signs and definite signs of advanced technology on the planet, but all of that information took a backseat to the presence of their dreaded enemy.

Ricci was pacing the bridge while Lateef tried to get more detail. "How's it coming, Commander?"

"Sorry, sir. The signals are so faint that when I try to zero in on them, they get lost in the noise."

"Can you at least approximate the location?"

"Within a margin of error of twenty to thirty kilometers, yes."

"How close is the source of these signals to the civilization you noted?"

"Another hundred or so kilometers away."

Ricci and Lindstrom met at his command chair. "Ideas, Commander?"

"No signs of war, so maybe the local population has made a deal with the Eternals?"

"That doesn't sound like the Eternals to me. Could be they don't know they're here yet. This might be a small Eat scouting party. Especially with no Gak life signs anywhere." Matt took his chair and said, "Still, that's a distinct possibility, so let's avoid the locals until we know what's up with this Eternal presence."

"How do we do that?"

"We get in and get out – quickly. A small focused team."

Ricci looked over at the main tactical console. "Kennedy, I want a scouting party for that thirty-kilometer area. No more than you need but enough to cover it in an hour. Ensure everyone has their scanner on at all times. Hopefully you can observe the Eternals from a safe distance. If those Eat life signs jump up, abort immediately. Am I clear?"

"Crystal, sir." He turned to the other tactical station saying, "Deck, let's go."

"Just one second. I want the scanners tuned to detect eprion signatures as well."

"Can we do that? We never bothered at the front. It's easier to detect an Eat life—"

"We're going to bother now," he decreed. Ricci spoke to the chief science officer. "Lateef, get your people on that."

"Yes, sir."

"How long?"

"Give us an hour, Captain."

"Good. Kennedy, in the meantime, assemble your team."

***

The landing party scoured the surface with little luck, until a tactical specialist noted a faint jump in her readings at the bottom of a rock face. She called to her CO on the comm line. "Lieutenant Kennedy, I've got something."

Minutes later Kennedy and Decker had joined her and corroborated her findings. "The source is definitely that cave up there, I think."

Decker objected, "Doesn't make sense. If there was *even one* Eat that close, the readings should be—"

"I know. Maybe this is a wild goose chase," Kennedy said.

"You think?"

"Yeah, I think the scanners have confused something entirely alien with Eat life signs."

"Makes sense. The eprion scans are at absolute zero."

"Still, we should check it out and confirm." He raised an eyebrow at her.

Deck acknowledged his silent message. "I know; I'm the best climber in the group."

"I'll send the shuttle back for some gear."

"Don't bother. That's not even that steep and there are plenty of footholds. There's a hook in my pack. Piece of cake." She looked down at Kay saying, "Stay here with Con. He might need you to make friends if the locals show up again.

"Ha ha. Get going."

Decker was good to her word and had no trouble reaching the cave in less than ten minutes. With his oculiscope, Con could make her progress out clearly. He had reported back to *Lovelace*, and Ricci concurred that the signals had probably not been Eternals at all. They were all just waiting for Deck to confirm and then the mission would be aborted.

"Talk to me, Deck, whatta' ya' see?"

"Hard to say...I'm gonna turn on my wrist-light." There was a moment of silence and then Con heard Decker exclaim, "*Naaghéé!*"

"What is it?"

"I can't...I don't...."

"What's going on? Are you okay? Decker?!"

"I think I've entered the mouth of hell."

"What? Turn on your scanner feed. Send me the visual."

Con looked down at his scanner, which was now receiving the signal from Decker's. It took him a minute to make sense of what he was seeing. Everywhere in the cave, there were stacks and stacks of Eternals, frozen, unmoving, eyes open and staring. "What the fuck?!"

"Are you *seeing* this, Con?"

"I sure am. Get the hell out of there. Now!"

"You bet!" The scanner feed ended as Decker said, "Preparing to descend. And I'm sleeping with the lights on tonight."

Just then, someone yelled, "Lieutenant, local species approaching."

Kennedy trained his scope on the spot indicated. "It's just some big blue birds." He watched in dismay as the birds headed straight for the cave. "Shit." He tapped his comm link, saying, "Deck, there's company on its way to you. Just a couple of birds, but don't engage if possible."

"Got it." A few seconds later Kennedy heard, "Wow, that's what I call a big bird. Hey now, I don't want any trouble...nice birdie...hey, what the fuck!"

"What happened?"

"One of the things attacked me. Sunk its goddamn beak right into my...."

"What?" No response; he pounded at the comm link in his ear. "Deck, are you okay?" Feeling more frantic with every second, Kennedy yelled, "Talk to me, Decker. Please!" When there was no answer, he immediately switched his comm to *Lovelace*. "Mayday! Mayday! Need emergency evac NOW. Have Medical standing by. Decker's been injured. Apparently unresponsive."

***

Conroy Kennedy had seen many horrors in ten years of war. He'd seen friends killed, and the woman he loved transformed; but nothing would ever match the sight of his best friend in Med-Bay, stretched out, rigid, completely unresponsive, eyes staring up at him but unseeing.

A pale and livid Captain Ricci was standing beside him, gripping the bed rail with white knuckles; he'd been snapping at everyone, his temper apparently frayed to the limit. It barely registered with Con, lost as he was in his own grief.

Clemente was reporting on the results of her examination. "It's a completely vegetative state; there's no apparent cognitive function or motor control."

The captain barked out, "What the hell caused this?"

"There are traces of an unidentified toxin in her bloodstream; it's undoubtedly the culprit."

"Find something to counteract it!" Ricci demanded.

"We're trying every—"

Clemente was interrupted by VICI. "Captain Ricci, your presence is required on the bridge. Priority situation."

111

"VICI, acknowledged. Ask Bridge what's so fucking important."

The AI apparently relayed that message, hopefully less profanely and then responded, "Captain Ricci, Bridge reports communication from planet's indigenous civilization."

"VICI, acknowledged. On my way." He sighed and said to Clemente, "Let me know immediately, if there's any change." Ricci strode from the room; as he reached the threshold he ordered, "Kennedy, with me."

Only years of training as a soldier enabled Con to tear himself away and to follow the captain, silently, to the bridge.

They arrived to find the command crew abuzz and Lindstrom, Lateef, and Sasaki conferring over the linguist's console. Aqila clasped Con on the arm and asked, "How is she?"

He shook his head. "No change."

Ricci nodded at Lindstrom while asking abruptly of Sasaki, "What can you make of the communiqué, Commander?"

"Quite a bit, sir. As I was just explaining to Commander Lindstrom, their language is quite accessible with algorithm MA913."

"Great. Are they hostile?"

"No, sir, the communication is an offer of...well, détente, I guess you would say."

"That's *something*," Ricci said. "Let's find out if they know anything about those fuc—" He caught himself and more calmly amended, "About those birds that attacked Decker."

"Sir, they *are* those birds who attacked Decker."

***

An hour later, the command staff was gathered in the war room so Sasaki could report on his interactions with those everyone was calling, "The Bird People."

"It seems that the...Burangasisti – that's as close as I can come to a translation of their name for themselves. Anyway, the Burangasisti initially mistook us for Eternals."

Lindstrom asked, "They said that?"

"Well, they wrote it. I'm unable to make sense of their vocalizations due to—"

"We get it, Commander," Ricci interjected. "Please continue."

"They thought we were Eternals until they observed our concern...no, I think that would translate more to our distress and alarm about Lieutenant Decker. I would guess that no Eternal ever showed the slightest concern for a fallen comrade."

"That's true," said Kennedy. "They never broke a sweat when one of their own crumbled away right in front of them."

Sasaki nodded and continued, "So, the Burangasisti concluded that even though we look exactly like Eternals, we weren't them."

Ricci asked, "They think we look *exactly* like Eternals?"

"Yes, sir. To their eyes, there is no difference." Sasaki consulted his notes. "They were attacked by the Eternals some...time ago, I think years. As far as I can gather, they were able to manufacture the toxin to render them harmless." Sasaki added, "They don't believe in killing."

"Just in bestowing a fate worse than death," Con spat out.

113

Clemente said, "What do you mean, 'they manufactured' the toxin? That bird – or whatever – attacked Decker with its beak."

"Well, 'manufactured' is an imprecise translation. Their culture is very...organic in nature. I think what they're telling us is that their scientists can manipulate their own biochemical processes to...well, make this toxin in their systems and then deliver it through their beaks."

"Oh! Could they 'manufacture' something to counteract it?" Clemente exclaimed.

"I can make that request, Doctor. They have expressed sorrow that they attacked Decker in error."

"Wow, they're all heart," said Kennedy.

Aqila patted him on the shoulder. "Still, it's a bit of hope, right?"

Ricci nodded in agreement then asked, "Is there anything else they had to say about the Eternals?"

"Oh, yes, they had a lot to say. The Eternals cut quite the swatch of destruction through this part of the galaxy. Attacked many planets, enslaved...um, something that doesn't translate at all – they might be talking about the Gak there – stole technology...or maybe weapons...from...this translation might be the name of yet another unknown species—"

"The Rock People!" Lateef interjected. "They stole those drones from the Rock People."

"Who also mistook us for Eternals," Ricci concluded. "As did the Gak."

Sasaki concurred, "Very likely. That would explain why they were so fearful. And why the Rock People attacked as soon as I sent them the handshake package. It contains a depiction of humankind."

"Great," Ricci said resentfully. "It's not enough that those gray scaly bastards...." He shook his head, stating, "Okay we're wasting valuable time. Sasaki, contact the...Buranga-whatevers *immediately* and make an urgent request for an antidote."

"Yes, sir."

***

Sasaki, Lateef, and Clement walked along the corridor of one of the strangest buildings they had ever seen. Of course, Aqila had almost been expecting to see huge bird nests everywhere, so an actual building was a plus. The walls appeared to be of some soft, spongy, flocked material and the floors were the same. There were no corners or hard edges anywhere and everything was laid out in an endless spiral. The rounded doorways were covered by retractable panels that opened automatically whenever a Burangan approached.

The Burangasisti were undeniably avian, though their wing tips were prehensile. Their general height ranged anywhere from four to five feet tall with wingspans that were much greater. They were covered in bright deep-blue feathers and had pale yellow legs and beaks.

As Sasaki had indicated, their vocalizations were impenetrable squawks. All communication between the two species was carried out by trading handheld screens back and forth. The Burangasisti didn't need to type on them since their squawks were directly translated as written language, to which Sasaki then applied his algorithm. He entered the human response and reversed the algorithm, handing the screen back to whichever Burangan they were

115

trying to communicate with. It was a slow, laborious process.

Maybe due to this lack of verbal communication, or maybe because it was simply the truth, Aqila had the sense that their welcome was a cool one. The three Terrans were met with unblinking stares everywhere and their guide was continually squawking back at various passersby, what she imagined to be assurances that the humans wouldn't be staying long.

Finally, they made it to what Lateef was privately calling, "the lab" though the Burangan word for it didn't translate. The guide pointed out the Burangan scientists who'd been working on the antidote and called them over.

Screens were traded back and forth to accomplish their halting conversation.

"Was the antidote ready?"

"Yes."

Rita took the screen and entered, "Do you have any idea what side effects this might have on human physiology?"

"No."

"How should it be administered?"

"As was the original toxin – inject into major artery."

"All of it?"

Clemente and Lateef shared a look of concern when this question prompted a five-minute conversation between the two Burangan scientists, yet the final response was simply, "Yes."

"How fast will it work?"

"If it's working, you'll know...." The next word was untranslatable.

"Quickly?"

"Yes."

"Thank you. We'll take the antidote now."

Aqila watched in what she hoped was well-concealed shock, as the one scientist picked up a vial and regurgitated a viscous green liquid into it. He or she, Lateef wasn't sure since she hadn't yet identified any gender differences in the Burangasisti, capped it, and handed the vial to Clemente.

Now, the moment Aqila had been steeling herself for. She took the screen and entered, "Could we get a sample of the original toxin, too?"

Much squawking ensued before the answer finally came back. "What use would you make of it?"

"We would hope to use it in our own fight against the oppression of the Eternals."

"How would you do this? You cannot manufacture it."

Aqila smiled to herself as she responded, "We do not have your gift but we can manufacture substances using tools outside our bodies."

The scientist had a conversation with their guide and the guide finally answered, "This request must go to our leaders."

"Of course."

For the first time, their guide gave a response that wasn't an answer to a direct question. "It is likely to be approved." This was followed by a long declaration but hardly any of it translated.

When the small landing party was back on the shuttle with the precious antidote in hand, Aqila thought to ask Sasaki, "What do you think that last statement was, after they said we'd probably get approval for the toxin sample?"

Jeff smiled faintly and said, "Hard to say but if I was forced to venture a guess, it would be something along the lines of, 'The enemy of my enemy is my friend.'"

***

117

Though she had announced major injuries and even deaths to him, Dr. Clemente had never before chimed at the captain's door with this much trepidation. When she heard his voice call, "Enter," she felt her mouth go dry.

He was at his desk, working, as always. He rose to meet her. "Doctor, what can I do for you?"

"It's about Lieutenant Decker, Captain."

He looked concerned, as was to be expected. "Yes? I thought you said the antidote seemed to be working?"

"It did. It worked fine; the problem is now with her liver. The original toxin and the antidote were too much for it. I'm afraid Decker suffered extensive liver damage."

"But you can regenerate it, can't you?"

"Yes, I've started that procedure but it's going very slowly. I thought if I could get some healthy cells to inject, it could boost the process." The captain nodded, encouraging her to go on. "I performed a tissue match against everyone onboard."

"And you found a match." It wasn't a question.

"Yes, sir." She looked him in the eye as much as their height difference would allow. "It's you." The expected start of surprise was not in evidence. Rita would hate to play poker against this man. She looked down nervously at the tablet in her hands. "In fact, Captain, the genetic analysis indicates that you're—"

"Her father," he finished calmly.

The surprise came but it was Rita's in the end. She stared at the captain before exclaiming, "You know?!" The only answer she got was an affronted glare. "Her medical records indicate, 'father unidentified.'"

"Yes, you see...." Ricci paused, obviously uncomfortable making this explanation. He cleared his throat and started again. "When we were dating, I was a cadet and Naomi was a teaching assistant. Not exactly forbidden but frowned upon enough that we kept the relationship secret. Then we both got the Ionian flu."

The realization dawned for Clemente. Back then, they hadn't yet discovered that the Ionian flu could inactivate the birth control shots. "Oh, I see."

"Yes...when she discovered she was pregnant, Naomi wanted to own up to our relationship, take our lumps, and have the baby while I...." Matt swallowed and paused again for a long moment. "While I did not. This was our solution." He straightened his uniform and asked briskly, "How long will it take for you to harvest the tissue? Do I need to turn over command to Lindstrom?"

"No, sir. It won't take more than twenty minutes and I can do it under a local."

"Good, let's go."

They had just reached the door of his office when Ricci turned back to her and said firmly, "This is all to remain *strictly confidential*, Doctor."

"Of course, Captain." She thought a second before asking, "Does that include Lieutenant Decker, sir?"

"Don't worry – *she knows.*"

***

Ricci entered Med-Bay late that night but none of the beta shift crew paid him any mind. His insomnia was well-known, and he often checked up on injured crew late at night. He slowly made his way to Naiche's room. She was still under, but the monitors all indicated she was doing well; her body had lost that dreadful rigidity and the color had returned to her skin.

Ricci noted the presence of Kay, stretched out under the hospital bed, and he bent down to scratch the dog's head. The entire time Decker had been in Med-Bay, they kept kicking the dog out, but he always made his way back. Finally, Matt had given the order to leave him be. "Keeping watch, huh, fella?" When Ricci straightened up, he saw Naomi's locket hanging on the bedpost; he swore that it was an involuntary motion that brought it to his hand.

Matt hadn't held that necklace in eighteen years – not since Naomi's memorial service. His mind flashed back to that terrible day. In a cruel twist of fate, Ricci had been assigned to head up the recovery mission for Lt. Commander Decker's ship. They didn't recover much besides the moonstone locket Naomi had prized. Only he and three other officers knew how few remains were actually contained in that urn they were interring in The Rock's commemorative courtyard. During the entire service, his hand was in his pocket, clutching the necklace. He missed every speech, staring at Naiche standing with Naomi's father, wondering how he was going to give her the locket.

Finally, the service ended, and he saw the Deckers walking towards the exit gate. He ran after them calling, "Mr. Decker? A moment, please, sir?" The old man had turned and looked at him with dull, pain-filled eyes; his granddaughter was gripping his hand, welded to his side. "I'm Lieutenant Commander Ricci," he said, as if by way of an explanation. There was no response other than a nod. He couldn't tell if the name had any particular meaning to either Decker. "I have something here for Naiche." She didn't look up, so Matt reached over and gently placed the locket around her neck. She grasped the pendant with both small hands and, for the first time all day, the child started crying. Tears welled in Ricci's eyes as he said, "I'm so sorry about your mother, Naiche. She was a wonderful woman. We were...good friends—"

At last, the little girl looked up, interrupting him to say softly, "I know who you are."

Before that moment, Matt would have sworn that five toneless one-syllable words could never cause such searing pain. Now he knew better.

With no acknowledgment of what Naiche had just said, Gus Decker thanked Ricci for the necklace. He looked down at his granddaughter and said a few phrases to her in Chiricahua. Matt didn't know precisely what he said but it was clear that he was telling her that they had to be on their way.

Once again, Matt watched the Deckers leave the courtyard. This time he let them go. He had no reason, no right, and no claim to do otherwise.

***

From her windowed office, Clemente had seen the captain enter Med-Bay, where she was working late to monitor Decker's condition herself. She debated whether to approach him. Maybe he needed to talk – she was the only one onboard who knew his secret. Rita briefly wondered if Decker had confided in Kennedy; she decided in the negative. Con's attitude towards Ricci betrayed absolutely no resentment; in fact, the two men were quite friendly. Apparently, father *and* daughter had kept their relationship to themselves.

When she quietly entered Decker's room, she found Ricci staring, lost in thought, and holding the moonstone locket. He looked up at her approach and nodded towards the patient. "She seems to be doing well."

"Yes. Very well. Thanks to you." Ricci inclined his head at that comment but remained silent. "I might be able to release her as soon as the day after tomorrow."

"Good. That's all I needed to know. Thank you, Clemente." Matt abruptly turned to leave. He must have realized he was still holding the necklace since he stopped and looked down at his hand. Then he reached over and carefully placed it on the bedside table. Without looking at Rita, he explained, "It was her mother's."

"Yes, I know."

Ricci faced her, nodding. It didn't seem as if he had any more to say, but finally he spoke, in a faraway tone. "I was the one who passed it on to Naiche." He gestured towards the bed, while elaborating, "It was at the memorial service." He stared in silence at the sleeping patient before adding softly, "That was the first time we ever met."

"First...and last until the *Lovelace*?" Rita asked.

"No." His reply had a bitter twinge. "When they kicked her out of Medical at The Rock I tried to intervene."

"They kicked her out! What happened?"

"Chuck Delay happened."

"Oh no." Rita shuddered at the name of that notorious womanizer, who had been a first-year medical instructor at The Rock. He'd finally been booted out four years ago but much too late in her opinion.

"Oh yes. Apparently, Naiche fell for him, hard. Found out in the worst possible way that she wasn't the only cadet he was romancing."

"What did she do?"

"She laid him out cold. They were still regenerating his teeth a week later." Rita wondered if Matt realized how much like a proud papa he sounded about that. She wisely remained silent. "So, I got involved, and made things worse."

"How?"

"Every piece of advice I gave her – she'd do the opposite, I guess just out of spite. Wouldn't defend herself, wouldn't contest the suspension." Ricci sighed heavily. "After a while I stepped back, and her advisor eventually got her reinstated on a probationary basis. The next thing I heard was that she had entered the Tactical course."

The captain looked so defeated that Clemente almost let it go but she eventually said, "Maybe if you had tried later—"

"Rita, I did!" Ricci insisted. "When she graduated, I offered to get her a good position – nope, she refused my help and went to the front instead." His mouth was set in a hard line before he recalled, "I think I learned quite a few Chiricahua curse words that day. And then again," he added in a deliberate tone, "I contacted her after her fourth comrade kill. I was worried about her."

"And?"

Ricci looked Clemente in the eye. "Let's just say, thank God that conversation was by holo-message – so I could cut it short." Through gritted teeth he stated, "If *anyone* else had *ever* spoken to me like that...." There was a long drawn out breath before he dispassionately offered, "Since then, we've just tried to stay out of each other's way."

Every doctor's instinct she possessed told her to leave this scar alone, but Clemente couldn't resist venturing, "And yet...here you are."

His lips twisted in a mirthless smile before asking, "And you tell me, Doctor – where would that be?"

Rita had no answer for him. She was still pondering the question days later at Decker's release. She found her dressed, sitting on the bed swinging her legs, reading over her recovery instructions.

Decker looked up at her approach, and asked, "No alcohol for a month? Really?"

"Yes, that's right." Clemente wagged her finger, explaining, "We want to break in the new liver slowly, understand?"

"Got it."

"Any other questions?"

Decker slid off the bed and handed her the tablet. "So...the health record said that you had to get some donor tissue, is that right?"

"That's right." The medical record had indicated that and no more. The donor wasn't named.

"And you found a match right here on the *Lovelace*! That's *amazing*," Decker scoffed, her voice dripping with sarcasm. Rita said nothing as Decker went on to add, with a bitter chuckle, "Damn, that must have been painful for him."

"Actually, the harvesting procedure is relatively painless—"
"I wasn't talking about the procedure, Doc." Naiche waved behind her back as she walked out the door, calling, "You're the best! I'll recommend you to all my friends."

Chapter 8

The Consequences of Anger

"How much more grievous are the consequences of anger than the causes of it." Marcus Aurelius

The *Lovelace* was still in orbit around the planet Balkquwala, home of the Burangasisti, a week later. With Sasaki's help, Lateef was consulting with Burangan scientists, trying to learn as much as possible about the toxin the birds had developed to render Eternals inert. As predicted, the avian species had agreed to supply samples of it to the Terrans, and the hope was that the UDC could learn to synthesize large amounts of it and use in the fight against the Eternals.

The rest of the crew was taking advantage of the time to take rare shore leave. The insular Burangasisti didn't open up their city to the Terrans but allowed them access to the grassy plains outside. Twenty crewmembers at a time were given free rein in the space, in rotating four-hour shifts. Commander Lindstrom, who had been in the city checking on Lateef's progress was due to head back with the latest group and was irritated when he found that Decker didn't have them ready to go on time.

He found them playing a boisterous, disorganized game of football; Decker grabbed a fumble and was promptly tackled by the opposing team. Lindstrom made a mental note to check with Rita as to whether Decker was even cleared for such activity. She promptly jumped up, proving unscathed. But when he heard her screaming, "Time out!" Lindstrom stopped, wondering if she had gotten hurt after all.

It didn't seem to be the case as Decker went on screaming, "I got it! I got it! Here's the perfect plan. We stack 'em up like cord wood on that sterile moon near Antiliac, what's it called?"

One of the other players yelled back, "Longoris?"

"That's it! Yeah okay, so we stack 'em up on Longoris and set them all on fire with an incendiary device from orbit!"

There was a chorus of, "Decker wins! Decker wins! Best idea yet!"

Decker held her hands aloft in an apparent claim to whatever obscure victory was in discussion. "Decker always wins!"

Loudly enough to get their attention, Lindstrom said, "She wins at everything except timeliness it would seem."

"Oops!" She turned and started jogging over towards him. "I'm sorry, sir. Lost track of the time." Decker looked over at the group and yelled, "Okay, back to the shuttle. On the double! We've already kept the Commander waiting." She said to Lindstrom, "I'll ready the shuttle, sir," and then sprinted off, Kay at her heels, apparently unwearied from the recent activity.

Impressed by both her stamina and ebullience, Lindstrom was muttering, "Ah, youth," to himself when one of the tactical corpsmen, Modi, came up to him.

"Commander?"

"Yes?"

"The guys and I were wondering if we'll be getting home any faster than we got here?"

"Back to the ship?"

"No, sir. Back to Uniterrae. You know, now that we're turning around and going back."

"Wherever did you get that idea?"

"Lieutenant Decker told us, sir."

"Yeah!" said his companion. Then they high-fived as they said, "Mission accomplished!"

***

Ricci was working in his office a short while later, when the door chimed. "Enter," he said, thinking this had better not be about another squabble over shore leave times and schedules or he would be tempted to cancel the whole thing.

He was bracing himself for a report like that when Lindstrom slid into the seat in front of him and said, "Do you remember what the penalty is for 'inciting crew riot with risk of mutiny?'"

"If I remember correctly, it's general court-martial with ten years minimum." He raised an eyebrow at Lindstrom, asking, "Keeping your options open, Commander?"

"I just thought we might need that information handy for a conversation we're going to have to have with Lieutenant Decker."

Matt propped an elbow on his desk and put his head in his hand. "What has she done now?" he groaned.

"She's been telling her crew that the mission is accomplished and we're ready to declare victory and go home."

"She what!? Why the hell would she do that?"

"I suppose because she believes it."

"How could Kennedy let this happen?" When Lindstrom just cocked his head in reply, Ricci said, "If you say, 'youth and inexperience,' by God, Nils, I'll be arranging two court-martials."

"*I* don't have to say it, Matt. You just did."

Ricci refused to answer; instead he turned to the AI unit on his desk and snapped, "VICI, locate Lieutenants Kennedy and Decker. They are to report to my office immediately. Priority situation."

Minutes later the two very concerned lieutenants were sitting in front of the captain's desk, with Lindstrom observing, propped up against the wall. Both were in full uniform but Decker, for once without Kay in tow, was obviously fresh from a shower – her hair was still damp, and rather than her usual crown of braids, it was twisted into a bun at the nape of her neck.

"I'm not going to beat around the bush," Ricci growled. "Lieutenant Decker, have you been telling your crew that our mission is over and we're going home?"

Decker threw a nervous glance at Con before answering, "Yes, sir, I suppose I have been."

Kennedy broke in, admonishing her, "Deck! How could you? That's the captain's place to announce that!"

"Well, I didn't think...it's not classified, is it? I was just so happy...I mean, everyone *knows* about the toxin and the stacks of Eternals, right?"

"That's not the point. Information like that has to go out all at once. From the top!" Kennedy turned to the captain.

"I'm very sorry, Captain. Unfortunately, Decker's lack of shipboard experience—"

Matt had been staring at Kennedy, momentarily aghast. "Kennedy! The point isn't that Decker made that announcement before I could, the point is that an announcement like that isn't going to be made at all!"

Con was clearly puzzled. "It's not?"

"No. Our mission is not finished. We haven't yet discovered the host species for the eprion."

Decker broke in. "But what do we need that for? When you have a rabid coyote, you don't worry about what bit it in the first place, you just put it down!"

"And what does that colorful metaphor mean, Lieutenant?" asked Lindstrom.

"It means screw the host species. We have the toxin. We need to get it back to Uniterrae and use it against the Eternals. You know, so we can end the war. Now."

Ricci fought hard to keep his voice patient. "We don't even know if we can synthesize this toxin in large amounts. Lateef is finding it very difficult to—"

"All the more reason to get it back home and put every scientist in the UDC on it! Now. Every minute we waste, means the war goes on, more lives lost, more wounded and—"

"Decker, don't you dare presume to lecture me about a war I've been fighting since you were seven years old. I decide what our mission is and when it needs to change. In case you haven't noticed, we're obviously the command ship that is on the correct trajectory. We're the ones who can find the source of this—" Without permission Decker sprang out of her chair and headed for the door. "You haven't been dismissed, Lieutenant. I'm not finished."

She turned back with a bitter laugh. "Yeah, well I am. I must have been crazy to think I could ever live in this *N'daa* world." Naiche waved her hand around the room as if to illustrate her point and headed towards the door, saying, "You people don't even know how to fight a war. You don't know what's important. The dead cry out for justice!"

Lindstrom blocked her progress towards the door. "Not *everything* is about *your mother*, Decker."

Ricci and Kennedy both jumped up, knowing that Lindstrom had just thrown fuel on a raging fire. Kennedy stepped in between the combatants but Decker leaned around him shouting, "Well, it is for me! None of you were even worth her sacrifice!"

Ricci's order, "That's enough! Stand down," was roundly ignored by both furious parties.

Lindstrom fired back, "You're a disgrace to the name Decker!"

"You don't even understand the name Decker, *daadatlijende*! Chiricahua know how to fight a war. When your people met mine, you pissed yourselves in fear at the sound of our war cries!"

Ricci turned Decker around to face him, biting off each word, his own fury barely contained. "I said, 'enough', Lieutenant! One more word out of you and you'll be in the brig. As it is, you are relieved of duty and confined to quarters." He stared at her for a long second, daring her to disobey his direct order. She drew a shaky breath then wordlessly left the room.

The captain turned to Con and barked, "Kennedy, dismissed! You go clean up this mess she created!"

When they were alone, Ricci snapped at his first officer, "You should never have brought up her mother."

"Why not? It's the elephant in every room she's in! Decker needs to understand that the UDC is not a vehicle for her personal campaign of revenge." He turned to go. "Am I dismissed, sir?"

"For now," answered Matt, realizing he was going to have to give everyone time to cool off, including himself, before he could address this debacle.

***

At the end of that long, miserable day, Kennedy entered his quarters and threw himself on his bunk. His distasteful duty had been delivering the truth to every crewmember whom Decker had unwittingly misled: their mission continued unchanged. As he might have predicted, every soldier who had fought at the front took it particularly hard. For the first time since he'd accepted the position of chief tactical officer, Con doubted the wisdom of that move. He thought both Ricci and Lindstrom were dead wrong but realized he had no choice but to appear to support their decision fully. He'd chosen this path; he had to walk it.

He sighed, feeling alone and miserable. He couldn't even IM Deck without breaking protocol. Maybe it was for the best. Con reflected for a second, reluctantly admitting he wished that Decker could learn to control herself just a little bit. But then, she was what she was and had ever been. He remembered when he had first known her, as a raw recruit. He thought her both the most beautiful, and angriest woman, he'd ever met. She had a lot to be angry about though – continually compared to her mother and found wanting, her entire family gone: never had a father, mother murdered, grandfather dead after a long, painful illness. And she had channeled that anger into becoming a fierce,

131

effective soldier, quickly becoming Con's right hand. *And I am the one who talked her into coming aboard the Lovelace. If I have anyone to blame...it's myself.*

His hand-held buzzed and he pulled it from his pocket reluctantly; he dreaded the possibility of it being from Ricci or Lindstrom, or even one of his crew. When Con saw it was an IM from Aqila letting him know she'd be back aboard *Lovelace* for a late dinner, it seemed like the first break he'd gotten all day. He smiled at the message, especially when she said she'd arranged for them to eat in her quarters. As a Lieutenant Commander, her quarters were pretty spacious and the ability to have meals served there was one of the additional perks of her rank. Con pushed himself off his bunk and went to shower; at least the day would end on a bright note.

Hours later, Con was seated at the small table in her quarters, smiling at her enthusiasm, as Aqila minutely described her work with the Burangan scientists. "It would be so much easier if we could just *talk*. The organic nature of the toxin makes it so difficult to define chemically. It's not as if I will be able to test out my attempts. I wonder if I can get another look at the bloodwork Medical did on Decker...I'll have to talk to Doctor Clemente." Aqila took a bite of her salad then asked, "I haven't seen Deck since she was released. How's she doing? Back to her old self?"

"Yeah, she sure is," Con answered with a slight grimace.

"What? Is something wrong?"

"Unfortunately, yeah. Deck had a run-in with the captain and Lindstrom today. Ended up confined to her quarters."

"Oh no! What happened?"

"Well, she tried to spread a little cheer amongst the crew by telling people her very natural assumption that we

132

would be going home immediately, with the toxin. Ricci and Lindstrom dressed her down because apparently we're *not.*" Con threw up his hand in disgust to punctuate that bewildering thought. "It kind of spiraled out of control from there."

"Why would she think that in the first place? We haven't yet ID'd the host species."

"*Because*, as she rightly pointed out, we have the toxin – you know the thing that can render the Eternals inert? The thing we would have killed for before we set out on this wild goose chase?"

"It's not a wild goose chase! The hypothesis is based on sound scientific principles."

Con tried to dial things back before they ended up having the same fight Deck had had with Ricci. "I understand that, Aqila, but we could end the war – right now – if we can get that toxin to the soldiers at the front."

"Even if we could, which isn't a sure thing, this misery could all play out in the future. Those dormant Eternals? They still had the eprion locked within them. It's not as if it truly eliminates the threat. The eprion could spring up again and again. We owe it to future generations to—"

"Future generations? What about the generation who is bleeding and dying right *now?*"

"I wish I could do more for them, but I can't promise *anything* about this toxin." Aqila learned forward and said earnestly, "But finding the host species will help them, *too.* I'm not sure you're seeing the big picture here, Con."

"Really?" After his wretched day, Con found his usually slow-burn temper quickly heating up. "Well, I think I have a picture you don't – what it looks like to see the soldier next to you vaporized by a projectile, or watching a friend rapidly

133

turning to the enemy or—" He stopped and took a deep breath before saying, "You know what? Forget it."

His rising anger was being matched by an equally tired and frustrated Aqila. "No, please continue – tell me what else *I don't know*."

"All I'm saying is, war looks very different at the front that it does from the safety of a nice clean lab."

"A nice clean lab? I never knew before how poorly you judged the value of my work. How little I actually contributed to the war effort. *Please* tell me more – or are you finished?"

Con tossed his napkin on the table, rising to leave. "Yeah, I think I am finished."

Chapter 9

Light Despite the Darkness

"Hope is being able to see that there is light despite all of the darkness." Desmond Tutu

Late the next afternoon, Ricci found himself standing in front of the door to Decker's quarters, wondering how to deal with this unmanageable young woman. He'd just spent an hour with Lindstrom, hearing him out about Decker but also pointing out all of the ways Matt felt Nils was mishandling the situation. In the end, crew discipline was the first officer's job, but Ricci hoped he'd convinced him to take a slightly different approach.

Suddenly a voice from inside called out, "Did you want to see me, Captain?"

The door slid open. Naiche stood in the opening, wearing regulation gym pants and an over-sized tee shirt. Her hair was down. *God, she looks like Naomi when her hair is down.* It was almost painful for Matt to see.

There was no way she could have been expecting him, so he had to ask, "How did you know it was me?"

135

She moved back and nodded to the dog sitting on the bunk. "Kay knows your footfall."

He stepped inside the cramped quarters saying, as the door closed behind him, "You mean he knows you hate me."

Decker hung her head for a moment then looked up at him, asking, "Why are you trying to goad me into saying something I shouldn't? I'm already in big trouble, aren't I?"

Matt thought to himself, *Okay, let's have this out.* "You want permission to speak freely, Decker? You've got it."

"Truth is, I don't care enough about you to hate you."

Ricci snorted in bitter amusement. "So...you lie even to yourself, huh?"

"What do you want?" Decker looked surprisingly defeated. "Why are you even here?"

"After some discussion, Commander Lindstrom has decided he will allow you to resume your duties, *if* that is, you can offer a full *and sincere* apology." Matt looked her in the eye, asking very deliberately, "Can you do that?"

Naiche swallowed and her gaze shifted to the side. She looked back at him and answered resolutely, "Yes, sir, I can do that."

"You will still be receiving an official reprimand from him for insubordination."

"Understood."

"Be in his office at 0600 hours. He'll be expecting you."

"Yes, sir." After a couple of seconds, she looked at him expectantly, obviously wondering why he hadn't left.

"There's more. What *I* need from you, is your word that you'll control yourself and abide by our mission from here on out."

"Which one, the bullshit one, or the one to win the war?" When Ricci glared at her she said, "Hey, you haven't revoked that permission yet."

"Look, I'm cutting you some *major* slack here because I understand why you're so obsessed with ending the Eternals, but...." Matt paused and put a verbal stop in between each word that followed. "You have got to stop. You're not doing yourself any favors; you're hurting Kennedy's career chances...." Ricci could see that one got to her. "And most important of all, I can promise you that your mother wouldn't want you to feel this way."

"When did you start caring about what my mother wanted?"

Boy, that one stung but he refused to let it show. This youngster didn't seem to realize that he'd been verbally sparring with better than her since she was a toddler. "Do I have your word or not?"

She sighed and said, "Yes. You have my word - as a Chiricahua and an officer."

"Good. Just remember on this ship, you're *a UDC officer first*." Decker made no reply, looking annoyed but nodding in agreement at least. He turned to leave, but hesitated at the door, looking back at her. "Whether you believe it or not...." He paused, as this didn't come easily for him. "I did love your mother."

Naiche's head tilted, her gaze unfocused, as she admitted, "Maybe." She looked him in the eye to add coldly, "Not enough."

As Matt made his way back to his own quarters, his chief thought was that the service file on Decker had been right. Her aim was true – and deadly.

***

Lindstrom heard his office door chime at precisely 0600. "Come in."

Evidently, Decker knew to be prompt and to leave the dog behind. She entered and assumed perfect parade rest. He would be impressed if it weren't for the fact that he suspected her very correct demeanor resulted from having issued similar apologies to other superior officers. "Commander, with your permission, I'd like to offer an apology for my behavior the other day."

"Proceed."

"My behavior was inexcusable, insubordinate, and unbecoming an officer."

"Correct on all counts, Lieutenant. Your service record will be noted to reflect this reprimand."

"I accept your reprimand, sir."

She was obviously waiting to be dismissed but showed no impatience when he hesitated. "How many times have you done this?"

"Request clarification of inquiry, sir."

Nils looked at the set of her jaw and realized he wasn't going to get through to her this way. He had promised the captain that he'd try. "At ease, Decker. And have a seat." She sat down without a word and studied him dispassionately. He gave it a few moments of silence and she waited with no change of expression. "Do you play chess?"

"No, sir."

"Too bad. I think you'd be magnificent at it." She just looked at him. "No response?"

"I didn't realize you were looking for one."

"I am, though. I'm looking for some response that shows you really know what you did wrong."

"Sir, if my apology was insuffici—"

"Stop it. You know as well as I do, it was stultifying in its correctness. I actually believe you're sorry that you said those things. What I don't believe is that you're sorry you thought them."

"You want an apology for my *thoughts*, Commander? That I cannot offer."

"I know." He steepled his hands in front of him. "Did you know that I never wanted you onboard the *Lovelace*?"

"Yes, sir."

"I suppose Kennedy told you?"

"Commander, with all due respect, no one had to tell me that."

Lindstrom felt a sharp stab of shame. Decker was right; he hadn't exactly hidden his opinion of her, had he? Suddenly he wondered how much of her behavior was nothing more than a self-fulfilling prophecy.

"Well, I might have been wrong about you." *Ah, some small note of surprise at last.* "I have on occasion seen signs of the officer you could be, the one Kennedy raved about, the one who...who we need on the *Lovelace*." Now she was watching him closely, waiting for the other shoe to drop. Nils let it drop. "But that officer is so buried under undisciplined anger and bitterness that I fear she may suffocate." Decker shifted her gaze to the side but remained silent. "Get your head out of your ass, Lieutenant. You're not the only one who's lost someone; you're not the only one who's suffered. I've been fighting this war for over twenty years. Do you *really* think that I haven't lost friends...family?"

Decker asked in a faltering voice, "You've lost family, sir?"

"Yes, my younger sister. At the Battle of Yanzu."

"I'm very sorry, Commander. That must have been...unbelievably difficult."

"Yes, it was...and still is. And while I know how rough it must have been to lose your mother—"

"I'm afraid you don't."

Nils checked his irritation. "Okay then, tell me."

A long pause left Lindstrom wondering if she was going to speak, but finally she did. "Like the captain said the other day, I was seven when the war started. My mother didn't get home much after that; it was mainly rushed visits and even more rushed and grainy holo-chats...." Before he could ask, she explained, "The only emitter in our village was at the library."

"I see."

"You said you didn't know her well...yet, I'm sure you knew her better than I did." She pursed her lips tightly and then continued, "Most of my memories come from holos and recordings that the UDC has of her."

"Oh...that is most—" Nils paused his stilted response and simply said, "I'm sorry." When she nodded, he acknowledged, "That's a devastating way to have to remember your mother."

"Yes, and that's what they took from me – a chance to know my mother. That's what can never be made right."

"That's true, you can't get that chance back, but, Decker, you're not fighting that battle alone. We're in this together. At least we're supposed to be. This war would be a lot easier for you if you'd stop fighting it on two fronts at the same time."

"Yes, sir." She squared her shoulders and promised, "I will do better."

"Lieutenant...I think *we both can*." He smiled at her genuine surprise and said, "Dismissed."

She got up and moved quickly to the door. Lindstrom caught her just as she was leaving. "One last thing, Decker...."

"Sir?"

"What does dadat...."

"*Daadatlijende*, sir?"

"Yes, that. What does it mean?"

"Uh, it just means 'blue-eyed people'."

"Oh. Okay, I have to admit I was expecting much worse. But for the just record? My people were Vikings – they never pissed themselves in fear at *anything*."

"Yes, sir."

***

Decker found Con in the mess hall eating breakfast alone. She thumped her tray down across from him and sat down. "Hey, you look like you lost your best friend." She grinned. "Well, she's back."

"I figured; your name reappeared on my duty roster this morning. How'd you get out of solitary?"

"I had to give my word to Ricci that I'd *abide by our mission* and I had to apologize to Lindstrom. And I got another insubordination reprimand on my record."

"How many is that?"

"Counting while I was at The Rock? Four. Two more stamps and I think I get a free dessert in the mess hall." She sighed and smiled sadly. "I'm sorry, Con. I screwed up big time."

"Why're you apologizing to me? It's your record."

"Come on, it doesn't reflect well on you; I know that. Ricci even said my behavior is hurting your career—"

"Does he think I care?" Kennedy spat out.

"I don't know, but he's smart enough to know that *I do*. You've been looking out for me for six years. It's high time I returned the favor."

"It wasn't 'a favor' and you've looked out for me *plenty*. And I'm the one who got us both into this mess...."

"Sounds as if you're having your own trouble 'abiding by our mission'."

"Yeah, I am." Kennedy gave a sudden and particularly bitter laugh.

"What?"

"Oh, it's something Waiguru said to me. 'Only the dead have seen the end of war'." Con sighed. "I didn't know he meant *this* one."

"I know. I thought that toxin was gonna be the answer. Well, at least I got a new liver out of it." Deck took a bite of her eggs then asked, "Is your girlfriend almost done with those bird scientists?"

"I believe Lieutenant Commander Lateef is still engaged with them."

"Uh oh. What happened?"

"We had a fight. She doesn't understand either. Spending the war tucked away in a safe laboratory—"

"Whoa, tell me you didn't say that to her."

"Of course, I did – it's true isn't it? How else would she worry less about soldiers dying right now and more about the eprion and future generations—"

"She said that? Geez."

"Well...she said finding the host could help them both...and that she wished she could do more for them...." Con groaned.

"Sounds like maybe you've got an apology of your own to make."

142

Kennedy shook his head. "You know what? I'm not in the mood for apologies just yet."

"Hey, if I can apologize to a man who hates my guts—"

"He doesn't hate your guts."

"Well, he doesn't love my guts. I think we both know he'd prefer if my guts were elsewhere. Anyway, if I can apologize to Lindstrom, you can apologize to the woman you love."

"I'm not in love with her."

"Con. It's me. I *always* know when you're in love."

He gave a rueful chuckle and said, "Is that true?" When she nodded, he asked, "Did you know I was halfway in love with you when you first joined Force-1?"

"I did. That's why I let you know I wasn't looking for love."

"Ah."

"Turns out I was wrong, though, and I found it anyway."

He leaned forward. "Yeah?"

"Yeah." Decker cleared her throat before saying, "It was just a different kind."

A smile gleaming with pleased amazement slowly spread across Con's face. "Wow, an admission of genuine emotion from the woman who doesn't even let anyone call her by her first name."

"What does that mean?" she asked, puzzled at the apparent change of subject. "That's only because it's almost impossible for *N'daa* to pronounce it correctly."

Con shook his head knowingly at her. "NYE-chey. Yeah, that's a hopeless tongue-twister. Admit it – it's a way of keeping people at arm's length."

"Maybe," she conceded finally, unable to hold out too long against his keen insight. "Maybe it was. But like I just admitted, with you it didn't work."

"Yes, and I'm sincerely impressed that you managed to admit it – to me *and* to yourself."

"You should be." She leaned back in her chair and crossed her arms. "So, if I could do *that*...then maybe you could talk to Aqila?"

He sighed resignedly. "Yeah...okay...later though." Con nodded at her plate. "Eat your breakfast. You're gonna need your strength. We've still got a lot of disgruntled corpsmen to deal with and it's your turn to...." His voice deepened. "Defend our mission."

"Thanks, boss."

"Don't mention it."

Decker shoveled in eggs in silence for a few moments and then suddenly looked up. "Oh...maybe you know...."

"What?"

"What's a Vie-King?"

Chapter 10

Only Suffering in Return

"War demands sacrifice of the people. It gives only suffering in return." Frederic Clemson Howe

As promised, Con apologized to Aqila. In fact, they proceeded to exchange heartfelt mutual apologies and mark their reunion with some enthusiastic make-up sex. A few days later, they ended a romantic evening together in the hydroponics gardens. They had scheduled their date to celebrate Aqila finishing up with the Burangasisti and the *Lovelace* once again being on its way, following the trajectory UDC scientists had mapped out for them months before.

The bench that they were snuggling on was near the bank of lettuce boxes and there was a faint green glow all around them.

"You know, the first time you suggested coming here...." said Con, looking up at Aqila, his head nestled in her lap.

Aqila laughed. "You thought I was out of my mind, didn't you?"

"Well, I thought you were reaching." He closed his eyes and enjoyed the feel of Aqila stroking his hair. "Maybe I should ask, though, how you knew one of the secret make-out spots on this ship."

"You think you're the only man in my life?" she teased.

He opened his eyes and gave her an affronted look. "I did."

"Oh, relax. You are. Bly told me about it; she brings Evelyn here."

"Wow, I didn't realize Scientific had conquered so much of Tactical with their irresistibly romantic ways."

"Yes, you tough guys really have to watch out for us lab rats." She leaned down and kissed him.

Just then, the nearest VICI unit buzzed and Con cringed knowing what was coming next. Or so he thought. "Commander Lateef, report to the bridge. Priority situation."

As Lateef acknowledged the message, Con raised his eyebrows in surprise. "I was sure that was gonna be for—"

"Lieutenant Kennedy, report to the bridge. Priority situation."

"I knew it."

Minutes later they were both on the bridge while Lateef looked over the long-range sensor data that had prompted beta shift to send out an alarm. They had detected signs of Eternal technology on a verdant moon that circled a nearby planet. Aqila was saying, "Yes, those are the metals found in their troop and command ships, for sure. No life signs though."

Ricci asked, "What about eprion?"

"No, none of those either. Not much energy activity of any kind, really."

"Well, we need to check it out thoroughly. It may hold clues to where we should head next." He turned to Lindstrom.

"Commander, please assemble a team. I want as much information as possible. When the Eternals were last there, what they were up to, and most importantly – how long ago it was that they left."

"Aye, sir." The first officer quickly assembled a team of both tactical leads, Lateef, and one of her most experienced science specialists, Lieutenant Mars Kaplita, as well as tactical corpsman José Abello.

***

The shuttle landed near the highest concentration of Eternal technology. Their scans of the abandoned equipment showed that there hadn't been an Eternal presence there in some forty to sixty years but before that they had definitely been using it as a base of operations for a long time.

The deserted complex consisted of dozens of admittedly beautiful buildings and over-grown gardens. All of the low-slung buildings, which were still intact, were made out of a substance that looked like marble but scanned as being a thousand times more durable. Decker swung a hand lightly at the structure saying, "Wow, they sure built 'em to last, didn't they? It seems like the Eternals were planning on staying...and then they just...didn't."

"Only one problem with that," said Kaplita.

"What's that?"

"According to my scans, these buildings are approximately five to seven-hundred years old."

Kennedy mused, "That would mean the Eternals are way older than we thought. Or—"

147

Lindstrom broke in, "Or they didn't build them. So, who did?" He looked around at the team. "Okay, spread out. Scan for other life signs or indications of an older civilization."

For the first hour, the team diligently searched the central buildings. However, they found no trace of anything that looked like, or scanned as, non-Eternal technology or remnants. Kaplita and Abello went to check out the maze of smaller rooms while Con and Aqila started scouting what had scanned as the oldest building in the complex center. Deck and Kay went to inspect the gardens and scan the grounds. Lindstrom split his time between the three groups.

In their building, Con bent down to view some of the carvings in a doorframe while Aqila looked over the items in the cabinets. "It makes sense that the Eats didn't build these," he said. "They never seemed to go in much for aesthetics."

Without looking up from her work, Aqila asked, "What're you basing that on?"

"Those old holo-vids we have of the inside of their Lead Ship."

"How did we get those?"

"From when Deck's mom went over there. Apparently, there was a live feed right up until...the end."

"Oh, God." Aqila stopped suddenly and her hand flew to her face. "You don't suppose Deck has ever watched that?"

"She has."

"Found anything in here?" Con and Aqila both turned to find that Commander Lindstrom had joined them.

"Not yet, sir."

They went back to work while Lindstrom checked something on his hand-held. After a few minutes, Lateef said, "Look at these!" She had what looked to be an actual book in her hand. "I think these are records of some sort."

Lindstrom and Kennedy joined her. There were dozens of the items. "Are they made out of paper?" Con asked.

"No, more like thin sheaves of leather...or something like it." She was paging through one of them. "There's no making anything out of this...writing, I guess it is." She stopped on a page with a full-sized image. "Oh, do you think this was them? The people who built these buildings?"

"What? Those bundles of sticks?" Lindstrom asked.

"Yes, look, there are protrusions from the bottom which could be like feet – or short legs, I don't know. And if you look closely at this one figure, you can see that the bundles can separate into what could be like limbs."

Just then, Lindstrom's comm link crackled, and Decker's voice could be heard saying, "Commander, Kay and I might have found something...uh, significant in that pit we were checking out."

"Ok, on my way." He turned to Lateef and Kennedy. "You two get recordings of a good sampling of those books. Who knows? Maybe Sasaki can make something of that gibberish. I'll go see what Decker thinks she found."

"Yes, sir."

While they worked, Con said to Aqila, "This is kind of cool, isn't it?"

With a smile she answered, "Yes, I'll make a scientist of you yet."

"Scientist? Probably not. Explorer? Hell yes."

"Is that what you want to do?"

"That's why I signed up," Con admitted. "I thought the war would be long over by now and we'd be out exploring the galaxy. Every time I talk to my mom, she asks me what I'm still doing in the UDC – and I'm starting not to have a good answer for her." He put his scanner down and turned to Aqila. "I never intended to be a permanent soldier. If I'd known that was my fate, I think I'd have stayed home and helped my parents run their restaurant."

"Your parents own a restaurant? I didn't know that."

"Well, my mom sold it after my dad died but yeah, they did once." His voice warmed as he said, "Next leave, you should come home to Uniterrae with me." Aqila murmured a pleased agreement while he continued, "I have to warn you though, my mom will feed you until you cry for mercy." He chuckled. "Mom tried that with Deck, but she never complained."

Lateef and Kennedy's comm links came to life at the same time; it was Lindstrom sending out a team-wide message. "Team, Decker has discovered the fate of the indigenous population here, about three hundred meters outside of the complex. I'm sending the coordinates to your handhelds. Please report here immediately."

***

Lindstrom hoisted himself out of the pit using the rappelling line Decker had set up and stood next to Kay who was watching Decker's every move; she stayed behind and continued recording scans of the area. Kaplita held his scanner out over the pit, asking, "What exactly are we looking at here? It's definitely organic material but—"

"It's a mass grave," Decker responded, without looking up from her work. "The remains all date out to the same time period. They were killed within weeks of each other." She stopped her scans and faced them. "There's a dozen of these graves." The pit was filled with remnants of those "sticks"

Lindstrom had seen in the image Lateef found, the sticks undoubtedly being the skeletal structure of those aliens.

"This is obviously what happened to the indigenous population," Lindstrom explained to the group.

With varying degrees of horror and shock at the find, the team watched as Decker nimbly rappelled up and out of the hole. She reached the top, and dusted her hands off, expounding on the discovery, "It looks like the Eternals exterminated these people and pushed their corpses into open pits; they didn't even bother covering them up." As she pulled the rappelling line's anchor out of the ground and allowed the line to telescope back inside, Deck said, "I don't even know if Kay found them all. There might be more, further out."

"We have enough evidence to answer the captain's question about this site. It was obviously their base of operations for the attacks against the Burangasisti and others but has been abandoned for decades. It's also clear that the Eternals gained this settlement by...force." Lindstrom nodded at the group. "Wrap it up. Let's get back to the *Lovelace* with our report."

On the way back to the ship, Lindstrom listened to Kennedy checking in on Decker who was piloting the shuttle. "You okay?"

"Yeah, sure," she said. "We knew they were murderous bastards, right? That sort of thing shouldn't even come as a surprise."

"Still, finding and viewing a dozen mass graves is different than just knowing."

Decker leaned back in her seat. "Yeah, it ain't gonna be the highlight of my week, that's for sure." She turned towards Lindstrom. "We'll need decon after that trip, right, Commander?"

151

"Yes, put it in shuttle bay-1." The exit to shuttle bay-1 led directly into the decontamination air showers. As each person entered the showers, they were met with a blast of high-purity air, which scrubbed them of all particulate matter and foreign microbes, washing the undesirables into the capture area under the perforated floor. The individual then proceeded into the airlocks where a scan confirmed that the decon had accomplished its goal. Only then was the returnee free to rejoin the general population of the ship.

Everyone exited the decon area without trouble until it came to Decker; in the airlock, a warning buzzer sounded, the over-head light flashing red. VICI's voice said, "Decon insufficient. Long-term decon necessary." Long-term meant an extra twenty minutes under the air shower.

"Ah, shit. Probably from being in all those graves." She existed the airlock back into the decon area and used the intercom to say to the group, "You guys go on ahead. Kay will keep me company."

However, when Lindstrom, the last to leave, took his turn in the airlock, the same warning sounded. "Looks like I'll be keeping you company, too, Lieutenant."

They sat on the benches in silence for a while; Lindstrom looked over at Decker who was leaning back against the wall, eyes closed, looking drained of energy. She was idly stroking Kay who sat next to her on the perforated bench. "Sobering day," he offered.

"Yes." Decker sat up and faced him. "But then we've both had a lot of those – fighting the Eats, haven't we, sir?"

"Indeed," he answered, thinking of the twenty-one years of war that had aged him in body and spirit.

"What was her name?"

"Who?"

"Your sister. The one who—"

152

"Ilse." He hesitated, wondering if he wanted to talk about this but then found himself continuing, "She was on the command ship *Taranto*, lost right at the start of the Yanzu encounter." Nils smiled sadly. "She was five years my junior. She followed me first into the UDC and then into Command Operations."

"That doesn't mean you're to blame."

"Of course not," he said briskly, getting up to pace around.

"But you do – blame yourself."

The spike of annoyance he felt at her insistence was tempered by her obvious compassion and the fact that she was right. He nodded at her, conceding her point. "You see much at times, Lieutenant."

"I can...." She cocked her head at him. "Once I got my head out of my ass."

He bestowed the tiniest of smiles on her and said, "Good job. With that – and finding those graves *and* recognizing them for what they were."

"I didn't want to believe it at first but then I remembered who we were dealing with."

Recalling what he'd heard from Kennedy about the video of Decker's mother, Nils said, "I suppose you would know better than most what perfidy they're capable of."

"You mean killing someone who was under a flag of truce?" When Lindstrom nodded, she said, "Yeah, but it's not like that never happened with humans."

"No, I suppose not."

"My grandfather even said, afterwards, that my mother should have remembered Mangas Coloradas."

"Who was that?"

"He was a Chiricahua chief who went to the *N'daaɫigánde*...uh, white soldiers that is, under a flag of truce."

"They killed him?"

"After they tortured him. Then they cut off his head, boiled it clean, and sent the skull to one of their museums." She must have taken his look of dismay for disbelief because Decker added, "It's all true. You can ask VICI about it, if you want."

"No, I believe you. Man's inhumanity to man has a long history."

"Maybe we shouldn't have found it so hard to believe that they came from us."

Once again, Lindstrom couldn't deny her perceptivity. "Maybe not."

Just then, the timing buzzer sounded letting them know that they were free to try the airlock again. Both came out clean this time, or rather, clean of what an air shower could wash away.

Chapter 11

Strange Secrets

"Strange secrets are let out by death, who blabs so oft the follies of this world." Robert Browning

The abandoned Eternals settlement hadn't given the *Lovelace* any indication of where they should head next, but Lateef found something on her long range scans a few days later that looked promising.

"Yes, it's definitely a ship." She looked up at Ricci and Lindstrom who had also been called onto the bridge. "A massive one."

"How massive?"

"Hard to say precisely but at least...five times the size of the *Lovelace*."

"Let's check it out," Ricci said. He looked at his first officer. "Considering our recent run of questionable luck and near encounters with the Eternals, we're going right to DEFCON-beta."

"A prudent move, Captain."

Kennedy saw the side-eye Ricci gave Lindstrom and smiled to himself, wondering how Lindstrom had given such a respectful answer while still making it clear that he hadn't known Ricci had it in him to exercise prudence. He moved to his console to contact his own second in command who also invariably made her feelings clear to him but in a much more direct manner.

And she did just that when they dropped out of L-speed to find the colossal ship in front of them. "What the hell is *that*?" For once Decker had simply voiced what everyone else on the bridge was thinking.

Lateef's estimate proved conservative, as the structure before them was at least seven times the size of the *Lovelace*. The size was so disorienting it took a moment to register that the ship was dead, floating free in space, and apparently powerless. Another moment's observation revealed the fact that the ship was damaged. Something had blown a hole in the starboard side and had perhaps blown away a chunk of what had originally been an even larger structure.

Con and Deck looked at each other with the same thought: *If whatever had attacked that ship was still in the area...not good.*

"Lateef," Ricci barked. "See if you can figure out what attacked that ship." He turned to Tactical, saying, "Kennedy, anything in the vicinity? Anything at all?"

"No, sir. Nothing," Con was busily tuning his scanner for every frequency. "It's as quiet out there as—"

"A ghost ship," Decker supplied.

"Captain," Lateef said. "I'm reading the hull as obduriium." Every head swiveled around at the mention of that ancient precursor to vanadinlum. "I think that ship is...." She paused, evidently rechecking some findings. She looked up, convinced at last. "Captain, that's the *Valiant*."

As both captain and first officer asked in unison if Aqila was sure, Con saw Deck mouth at him, "What's the *Valiant*?"

He leaned over to whisper to her, "It was the sister ship to the *Intrepid.*"

***

Ricci looked at his command staff, gathered in the war room. "The evidence is undeniable. That ship out there is the *Valiant*. I want to figure out what attacked it and if it had anything to do with the conversion of the crew of the *Intrepid* into Eternals."

"Even if it didn't," Chief Engineer Ramsey said. "The *Valiant* was the main ship. It had more of the people, equipment, supplies." Carla shook her head sadly. "The *Intrepid* was primarily the scouting ship; it would have been in big trouble once they lost the *Valiant.*"

"Maybe they got all of that stuff off of it?" Kennedy suggested.

"No," Lateef said. "Our scans indicate that everything that wasn't blown away – personnel and equipment – is still on that ship."

"So, we need to solve a two hundred-year old mystery," Lindstrom said.

Ricci sat down at the head of the table. "Yes. And obviously, the best way to do that is to get a look at the logs. Logs from a four hundred-year old computer. Suggestions?"

Ramsey said, "Just extract the entire units and get them over here. Then we'll try and...well...."

"Get some power to them?" Lateef suggested.

"That's the place to start," Carla agreed. "I wish I had a compuhistorian onboard."

"I do!" Aqila said. "Lieutenant Grieveson."

"Your *astrobiologist*?" Lindstrom asked.

"Yes, it's her hobby."

"Great," Carla said. "We'll be glad to have her help. Once we get them over here, that is."

Ricci nodded. "Yes, that's the first order of business. Okay, let's get to it. I need a team to go over, do some close-range scans, examine that hull damage, and extract those computer units."

Matt was about to tell Kennedy to assemble a team when Lindstrom suggested, "Why don't we let Lieutenant Decker lead this mission, Captain?"

"Good idea," Ricci agreed, pleasantly surprised. In the weeks since their blow-up in his office, it was obvious to him that both combatants were trying to turn over a new leaf. It was equally obvious at times, how much effort it took for both of them but, hey, progress was progress. "Decker, assemble a team."

"Yes, sir." Decker appeared to accept the responsibility with neither obvious pleasure nor dismay. She was all business. "Commander Ramsey, who's the best engineer for the extraction job?"

"Lieutenant Jeong. She works quickly and cleanly and has a lot of experience in low-O suits."

"Good. I'll bring Ensign Muztagh along. We can examine and record the ship's damage and supply the muscle if Jeong needs help – I have a feeling she will. Commander Lateef, who from Scientific?"

"That would be me. And could we bring Ensign Brodie along?"

"To fulfill what role?"

"Oh, practice for her mainly. She's been wanting to get more experience in the low-O suits."

158

"I'm sorry, Commander, but I don't feel that would be appropriate. Next time."

"Why not?"

"That ship is a graveyard. It would be disrespectful to treat it as a mere training ground."

Everyone around the table, except for Kennedy and Ricci, showed some surprise at her firm pronouncement. Lindstrom, clearly perplexed, asked, "Are you suggesting we might *disturb the dead*, Lieutenant Decker?"

Ricci had feared there might be a slightly insubordinate response forthcoming, and was therefore relieved when Decker respectfully insisted, "Yes, sir. That's *exactly* what I'm saying." She seemed mystified at their confusion.

"That's a good, focused team, Lieutenant," Ricci said, cutting off any possible further discussion. "Make it happen."

Ricci and Lindstrom were the only ones left in the room a few minutes later. Matt had recognized that his first officer wanted a private discussion. "Is Decker a believer?" Nils asked.

Knowing that both Naomi and her father had been, Matt considered it likely that Naiche had been reared in the Chiricahua religion. There was no way to give that information without raising too many questions. He just said, "I would imagine so. That's her culture." Ricci knew that believers in the UDC were rare but wondered if there was something else bothering his first. "Why?"

"It simply...never occurred to me." Lindstrom scratched his head. "So, when she said that the dead cry out for justice, to her that's not just some platitude – is it?"

It took Ricci a second to reply and still all he could get out was, "No. It's not."

"Huh." He shook his head as if to clear it and then looked at Ricci. "I guess you've noticed I'm trying to help her develop as an officer."

"I have noticed." Ricci grinned. "Needed a challenge, huh?"

"Well, it is a long voyage, Captain." They got up to leave the room. "It definitely seems that there's more to her than I initially thought. I'm wondering what other layers there are still to unpack."

Matt could think of nothing to say which was neither a lie nor too blatant a truth, so he remained silent.

***

Aqila hadn't thought much about Deck's description of the *Valiant* as a graveyard, until she got over there. She tried to concentrate on her scans but there were frozen, mummified bodies floating everywhere. A few minutes observation had led the team to the inescapable conclusion that, whatever happened to the *Valiant*, it had been sudden and unexpected.

On the comms, Decker and Jeong were discussing the damage. Jeong said, "Looks to me like their fusion reactor lost containment. There's no way to determine what caused it, though."

"There's no evidence of an attack, not that I can find," said Decker. "No signs of enemy fire, no scarring, no beam streaks, nothing. Would the breach alone account for this massive damage we're seeing?"

"Yeah, if they lost containment, it would have been incredibly violent. Like this."

Lateef broke in to ask, "How much warning would they have had?"

"Hard to say, Commander. Depends on how fast the leak was. My guess? It was pretty fast."

"Okay," Decker said. "I think we've recorded enough of this. Let's get to the bridge and see what we're up against with those computer banks."

"You go ahead," Aqila said. "I'm going to scan as much as I can of the rest of the ship. Ensure we're not missing anything important."

"Be careful," Decker warned. "The debris is...overwhelming. Keep your comm line open."

"Copy that." Lateef used her power pack to move inexpertly down towards the lower decks. As she progressed through the ship, she was dimly aware of Decker, Muztagh, and Jeong discussing removal of the computer banks over the line.

The concentration of bodies got denser on the lower decks and Aqila had a hard time avoiding them all. She started feeling a rising panic and told herself, *They were just people...that's all they are...just ex-people....* Then she came across a room filled with children. *Oh God, children...must have been a classroom or playroom. Of course, there were children; this was a generational ship.*

She left that room as quickly as she could but, in the eerie dark lit only by the lights on her suit and her wrist, there were still bodies everywhere she looked. Aqila began to hyperventilate and was starting to feel faint when suddenly Decker appeared in her line of sight. She grasped Lateef lightly by the shoulders and in a calm, soothing voice said, "Hey. Look at me...look at me. Concentrate on my voice. You're okay. Listen to me breathe...breathe with me...nice and slow...don't look anywhere but at my face...you're okay."

It worked; Aqila felt her panic subsiding and her breathing returning to normal. "Thanks."

"No problem. I think you've had enough. Can you make it to the shuttle by yourself?"

"Yeah." She took another deep shaky breath. "I can do that."

"Okay, we won't be long. Turns out those computer units were modular."

An hour later they were all in the decon air shower together. Jeong and Muztagh were excitedly discussing possibilities for bringing the old banks to life after they went through the equipment decontamination process; Aqila and Deck were silent.

When the engineer and ensign were ready to proceed through the airlock, Decker said, "Go on ahead without us. We'll catch up. I need a few minutes; my legs are cramping. Tell the captain he'll have my report by 0100 hours. About the time those banks are through decon."

"You mean you want us to go find him?" Jeong asked.

"No, he's waiting outside decon."

"How do you know that?" Muztagh asked.

Decker rolled her eyes. "I'm psychic." When Muztagh looked skeptical, she added, "Look, if you want to put a month's pay on it, I'm in." He waived the proposition off with a grin and they left.

When they were alone, Decker asked, "You okay?"

Aqila looked at the floor answering, "Just embarrassed."

"Why? That could happen to anybody."

Lateef looked up. "Not to someone who's been at the front, though. Right?"

"Hey, I don't know of a galaxy-wide ranking of horror shows, but if there were? That ship would be *way* up there."

"And yet, you were not only fine but had the presence of mind to recognize that I wasn't – from half a ship away."

"I was leading the mission; that was *my job*. What're you getting at?"

"Con once said that spending the war in a nice clean lab is very different from spending it at the front and I think I'm starting to get a taste of how right he was. Between those mass graves you found and the bodies on the *Valiant*...." She rested her head in her hands momentarily, and then looked up at Deck. "How did you possibly deal with all of that constant death at the front?"

Decker came over and sat down right next to Aqila. "Sometimes not that well. That's how I can recognize a panic attack." She smiled sadly and said, "Soldiers aren't born, they're made."

Aqila ran her hands through her hair and thought of her discussion with Con about his place in the UDC. "I don't know, Deck...what the hell am I even doing here?"

"On the *Lovelace*?"

"In the UDC. I'm not the military-type. I never was. I was seventeen when the war started and already in a special scientific program at school. The UDC came and recruited and I joined up with stars in my eyes because they said they needed scientists for the war effort."

"And we do! We need people like you...the war isn't gonna be won just by grunts like me—"

"You're not a grunt, you're an officer—"

"I'm a grunt at heart. You know...mainly. And that's okay. But, as for you – it's good to have people in this who are still...."

She watched Decker struggle to put her thoughts into words. "Who are still what?"

"Still able to be horrified by death on a massive scale, I guess."

"I think you're selling yourself short there. You were horrified at those mass graves—"

"Bothered? Yes. Horrified?" She shook her head. "No." Deck gave her an encouraging smile. "So absolutely, we need eyes like yours here on the *Lovelace* – and in the UDC."

Aqila stood up and stretched out, feeling somewhat better, not only about her panic attack but also about her place in the war effort. "You give a good pep talk."

"I learned from the best." She winked and said, "I think you know him real well."

"Well, thanks."

"Don't mention it." Deck stood up and they walked to the airlock together. "Seriously, don't mention it. You'll ruin my reputation as a stone-cold bitch."

"You don't *have* that reputation."

"I don't? Man, I've been slacking off!"

***

Three days later, Ricci and Lindstrom were being briefed on the results of the *Valiant* logs' analysis by Ramsey and Lateef. Aqila was saying, "There was a lot of data corruption. That was to be expected. I think we lost everything that might explain the loss of integrity of the fusion reactor."

"Unfortunate," Ricci murmured.

"However, we *can* make out that one of the very last things noted in the logs was a clear distress signal."

"Well, that's to be expected, isn't it?" said Lindstrom. "I'm sure they sent one out as soon as—"

"No, sir, this wasn't sent out," Ramsey explained. "It was received."

"Received from who? And from where?"

Aqila said, "The data are so corrupt on the 'who' question that it's…impossible to be sure. But we can make out the location. It's a planet not more than six astronomical units away."

Ricci said, "Lateef, it looks like you have a guess as to who sent it. Don't you?" When Ramsey and Lateef exchanged a doubtful look, he said with impatience, "I know, I know…scientists don't guess. Just tell us anyway."

"It looks like it might have gone out from the *Intrepid*, Captain."

Chapter 12

To Survive the Day

"To survive the day is triumph enough for the walking wounded among the great many of us." Studs Terkel

Captain Ricci made the decision to move to the location of the *Intrepid*'s distress signal at 0.025 L-speed in order to do a thorough sweep of the area for either Eternals or eprions. The slower speed gave the crew a little over a day to prepare for whatever challenges awaited them at their destination. Based on their recent experiences, Decker felt that there was no preparing, so she just tried to put it out of her mind and enjoyed a lively dinner with Con, Aqila, and Bly.

Con was teasing her about her latest self-induced burden. "How're those chess lessons coming?"

"Would you just shut up about that, *wise guy*." She turned to Aqila in an effort to derail the subject. "You know that's actually what his name means, don't you?"

"It means 'wise'," Con protested. "And you know it." He added in a playful voice, "I *could* tell people what *your name* means."

Bly leaned forward. "Why? What does it mean?"

Feeling as if she'd have been better off staying with the discussion of her chess lessons, Deck announced firmly, "It was originally the name of a great Chiricahua chief and warrior."

"True," Con admitted, ignoring her warning glare. "But it also means trouble-maker...or mischievous one."

"Does it *really*?" Aqila asked, trying and failing to smother a laugh.

"Big mouth."

"Me?" Con shook his head at Deck. "I'm not the one whose big mouth got me roped into chess lessons."

"Let's hear *that story*," Bly said.

"There's no *story*." Deck sighed and then explained, "Lindstrom just asked me if I wanted to learn how to play chess."

"And you said, '*yes*'?" Aqila's surprise was clear.

"No," Deck intoned. "I said I'd rather remove my own appendix with an oyster fork...." She continued, in an imitation of Lindstrom's dry speaking style, "When a simple no would have sufficed."

Bly asked, "Deck, what were you thinking?"

"I wasn't – as usual," she admitted. "But Lindstrom didn't have to be so *cruel*. He could have just sent me to the brig or something easier like that."

Aqila said, "You know, I don't think he's trying to be mean. I think maybe he sees himself as kind of...a father figure for you."

"Right," Deck retorted. "That's all I need."

***

Lovelace had arrived at the planet that was definitely the origin of the desperate plea, sent to the *Valiant* not long before it met its own horrible fate. It was, at first scan, an unremarkable place: barely big enough to sustain an atmosphere and was composed mainly of arid grasslands and sand mountains. Ricci waited for Lateef to report her findings, bracing himself for the word that Eternals or eprions waited below.

"Captain," she said at last. "I'm detecting nothing but human life signs. And not many of those."

"How many?"

"More than ten thousand but less than twenty. They are clustered near the only city on the planet's surface."

"Makes sense," Ricci said. "Evans, hail them. All frequencies." They waited; ten minutes passed. "Well, Lieutenant?"

"Sorry, Captain. No response."

Matt looked at Lindstrom with a raised eyebrow. "Well, I guess we're going to have to go knock at the front door."

"Who gets to lead the team – me or Kennedy?" Lindstrom asked.

"Neither," Matt said brightly. "I'm going to do it. Lateef, Kennedy, you're with me."

An hour later, Ricci was really wishing he'd sent Lindstrom. The team had made their way to all of the obvious entrances to the tiny walled city, but all were locked tight. There was no response to their knocks or shouted greetings. Ricci turned to Bayer, who was piloting the shuttle. "I didn't see any apparent landing places inside the walls – did you?"

"No, sir. Not unless you want to take a chance at landing on a roof top."

Ricci was about to answer that no one was crazy enough to try a stunt like that when he remembered that one exception to that rule was operating the tactical console up on his bridge at that moment.

"Lateef, how many life signs are in that city anyway?" Aqila was checking and re-checking her scanner and didn't seem to hear him at first. "Lateef?"

"None, sir." She looked up. "The readings indicate that the city is deserted."

"Where are those ten thousand people, then?" he asked with mounting irritation.

"That way it seems, Captain." She pointed off in the distance. "About a thirty-minute walk or a short ride in the shuttle." However, no matter how much they searched in the appropriate spot, they found nothing apart from what looked like muddy-pink beetles the size of watermelons. Those interested no one except Lateef. She and Kennedy were now conferring over their scanners.

Matt walked over to them. "Okay, are these people invisible or are your scanners malfunctioning?"

Lateef faced him. "Captain, I don't know what to tell you. According to our scanners they should definitely be within sight."

Matt looked around at the empty grassy plain. To have come this far and wind up empty-handed galled him. Then he got an idea. "Kennedy, contact *Lovelace* and tell Decker to get down here."

"Yes, sir."

"Make sure she brings that dog— that is, Corpsman Third Class Kayatennae with her."

Ricci congratulated himself on having had a great idea when the well-trained dog immediately got the idea and took off following a scent. Decker, just as fast as Kay, shadowed him, leaving the rest of the group trailing slightly behind. When they caught up with her, she was on her knees listening intently and examining the ground.

"What is it?" Ricci asked, impatiently.

She sat up and put a finger to her lips, pointing at the ground. Kennedy crouched down and examined the spot with her; he looked up with a grin. Matt could see nothing at first, but then he noticed a faint circle in the dirt. He was about to ask what was so remarkable about a circle in the dirt when Decker pounded on the ground. It made a hollow knocking sound. They all stood back and waited. Seconds later, the circle lifted up and they were looking at an undeniably human face. The woman put an ancient clunky black radio receiver to her ear and, without greeting them, said, "It's okay. They're not Eternals."

***

They called this place Chelmang and themselves Chelmanians. None of them remembered life before the retreat to underground lairs. But they knew the stories.

In a low-ceilinged, dimly lit chamber, Ricci was speaking with the woman they called Doyen Eva Sampson, leader of the local clade. She was an impressive figure, six-feet tall, with thick blond hair that hung past her shoulders.

"Why don't your people live in the city?"

"It's a dangerous place. There is much about its workings we don't understand; the Eternals kept that knowledge to themselves."

"Was the city only for Eternals, then?" Lateef asked.

"No," Eva said. "All lived there. Eternals ruled and Chelmanians served. Until the rebellion."

"You rebelled?" Ricci asked.

"Some did. The ancestors of those you see here. Many died, though. The ones who lived were the ones who retreated here to the underground."

"Where are the Eternals now?"

"They left in search of worlds to conquer, condemning the rebels to die of starvation. But we have the gubang and waichux."

Ricci cocked his head and said, "I'm sorry, the what?"

"Meat from the gubang," she stopped and pointed to a table where, for the first time, Matt noticed a half-butchered beetle creature. "And waichux." Eva handed around what looked to be disks of flaky cardboard.

Aqila took the waichux and examined it closely. "I think it's a fungus." She looked up at Eva. "Where does it grow?"

"During the rainy season, it grows on the grass. We gather and dry it, so it will last until the next season." Eva gave Matt a wily smile and said, "Now it is your turn to answer a question."

"Yes?"

"You said you come from our ancient home, but you didn't say why."

"We are at war with the Eternals, as were your ancestors. Our people are also dying at their hands. We have reason to believe the Eternals were once human like you and me."

Eva agreed, "So it has always been said."

"We want to understand how that happened. We come in search of answers."

For the first time, Eva's hulking son, David, spoke in a sullen tone. "You won't find them *here*."

Ricci asked, "No one knows *anything* about how the Eternals came to be?"

David exchanged a look with Eva that clearly contained an unspoken question – about what, though, Ricci wasn't sure. Eva turned to the *Lovelace* crew and said, "The story-teller, Sartesh, he knows the most about that tale. We'll send for him."

"Thank you."

"Perhaps you would join us in a meal while he answers your questions?"

Every UDC Captain had diplomatic training, which allowed Ricci to appear to carefully consider the matter and then smoothly suggest, "I have a better idea."

***

Captain Ricci had gone to the planet's surface to escort the Chelmanian delegation to the *Lovelace*. Lindstrom had informed the entire command staff that they were to be available to greet them as a sort of honor guard. With a minute until the shuttle was due to arrive from Chelmang, Decker was running to towards the shuttle bay, hoping to make it in time.

As she came skidding to a stop, Decker saw by Lindstrom's stiff posture that he was on the very edge of annoyance and immediately explained, "Sorry, I'm late, Commander; I had to get the wrinkles out of my dress uniform." She got in line complaining to Con, "I can't *believe* the captain made us wear them to share a meal with people who've been living on bug meat and grass smut."

The dress uniforms were a universally despised shade of robin's-egg blue, consisting of a close fitting, stand-collar, and button-up tunic combined with either slim pants or a knee-length skirt. That choice was entirely up to the individual officer, though most opted for the pants.

Decker had chosen the skirt and Aqila said, "Oh, I've never seen the skirt version before. Is it more comfortable?"

"Not particularly, but I have great legs so...." Deck stuck out a leg as if in demonstration of her boast.

"My, such modesty," Lindstrom interjected.

"Commander, that word has never been applied to me in any definition whatsoever."

"I'm sure." The arrival of the shuttle stopped any further observations he had to make on that point.

The first order of business was a tour for the Chelmanians but the *Lovelace* delegation for that consisted of Ricci, Lindstrom, Ramsey, and Clemente. Meanwhile the rest of the command staff assembled in the war room, which had been transformed by the kitchen staff into a space for elegant dining. After milling about for a while, they started to take their seats. Decker asked, "So, what's on the menu?"

"Bug meat and grass smut étouffée, I believe," teased Con, as he ran a finger under the collar of his tunic.

Decker put a hand to her heart. "Please do not besmirch my memory of your mom's wonderful étouffée that way!"

Lt. Commander Sasaki asked, "What is étouffée?"

"You've never heard of shrimp étouffée?" Kennedy was dismayed to find that Sasaki had never heard of, let alone tasted, so classic a dish from his culture and extolled its virtue at length.

Sasaki had begun to tell Con that as good as his favorite shrimp dish sounded, prawn tempura was even better, when the senior staff and their guests entered the room. Eva was saying, "Your ship is most impressive but so small, Captain Ricci. Or the tales of the *Intrepid*'s size are exaggerated, perhaps."

"No," Matt explained. "Those generational ships were much larger than our command ships. But we can travel much faster now and don't have families as part of the crew, you see."

Another Chelmanian leader, Joseph Danx said, "Ah, so that is why we saw no children."

"Yes."

"But you said your journey could be still quite long. You don't mind leaving them behind?"

"We don't have children," Lindstrom explained.

Danx's daughter, Maria, exclaimed in surprise, "Humans on Earth no longer have children?"

"No, no, no, not at all. I mean, of course they do," Nils protested. "What I meant was that no officer in this room...." He gestured around the space while continuing, "...has any children."

Naiche covertly glanced at Ricci to see how he reacted to that statement. Seeing him display nary a flicker of discomfort, she enjoyed a moment of pleased contempt that she told herself contained no edge of pain. But then, as Ricci had said, she lied even to herself.

During the meal, Maria started asking Con and Jeff Sasaki about their personal lives, *very* personal lives. When Jeff firmly informed her that he had no interest in mating with women, she turned her rather aggressive questioning on Con. "And you, do you mate with women?"

Aqila leaned in and said decisively, "He's spoken for."

David Sampson picked up the thread, inquiring of Decker, "Do you have a mate already?"

"I have many."

"Why do you need more than one?"

"Because there's not one man alive who could—"

"Deck," Con said, warningly.

"I'm still playing the field," she amended brightly.

175

David nodded and then asked, "Would you like to mate with me?"

Decker exhaled as she weighed an appropriate response. "Do you know what an oyster fork is?"

***

After the meal, the storyteller related what he knew of the rise of the Eternals. "The ship, *Intrepid*, was stricken with disease. One that spread quickly throughout the crew. The call went out to the ship *Valiant*, for help, but no help ever came."

"That ship met with an accident," Lateef explained. "All were lost."

"Ah, we always wondered. Our ancestors stopped here to allow the sick to rest and left some healthy crewmembers to care for them. The others took the ship, going out in search of help. They came back transformed, telling of the Pakarahova."

"What is that?" Ricci asked.

"Those are the beings of transformation. The Eternals said that the beings travel this part of the galaxy, looking for people to help. The Eternals were fortunate that they met them nearby, since their home is many years journey away."

"It wasn't really fortunate, though was it?" Decker asked.

"They weren't cruel and arrogant at first," Sartesh said. "They had acquired great knowledge from the transformation. They cured the illness, and then built the city you saw. They converted the ship *Intrepid* to be fast like yours. They went out frequently and brought back wonders. But they kept promising that they would soon ascend and then others could enjoy the transformation."

"Ascend to where?" Lindstrom asked.

"Nowhere. That was a lie to ensure the cooperation of those without the gift."

Ricci clarified, "By gift you mean....?"

"The Eternals don't age, sicken, or die. Is that not a gift?"

"They don't age?"

"No. My great-grandfather told me how they stayed unchanged while he grew from boy to man to elder. The transformation holds the secret to eternal life. That's why they took that name, you see."

Ricci and Lindstrom shared a look of skepticism; both wondering if that was an accurate statement or an artifact of legend. Matt decided, in the end, it wasn't important. "These Pakarahova, they've never visited here?"

"No."

"And you don't know any more about them?"

"Only that their home can be reached with a fast ship like yours," answered Sartesh.

Before the captain could question the story-teller further, Eva spoke. "You will go out in search of the gift givers now?"

Ricci explained, "We search for the source of this...we consider it to be a disease, but yes, we will. We wish to ensure it stops infecting humans."

"That would be a grave mistake. It is too dangerous," Eva insisted. "You would be transformed yourselves and then be a risk to my people!"

"I appreciate your concern," Ricci said. "But we've been fighting the Eternals for over two decades now. We know how to prevent progression of the infect— that is, the transformation. I assure you, the only risk we're taking, is for ourselves."

"You're asking me to believe that you would reject the gift?"

"We've seen enough of the Eternals to understand that the transformation is *no gift*," Ricci avowed. He looked at the Chelmanians beseechingly. "Is there nothing you can tell us that will help us find the Pakarahova?"

"And if there is no help to be found here – what will you do?"

"Either way, we'll continue our search. We have no choice; it is our mission."

Eva was silent for a long time and then said, "Since I cannot persuade against this madness, there is something we can offer...."

"What?"

"I don't know if it can really assist you, but there are records with details of the Pakarahova in the city. There are those who can escort you safely therein. We call them scrappers. They pry away what useful items can still be found." She gestured at her son. "David is one of the best."

David said, "It's a dangerous and sacred place. Your equipment, radios, and such won't work within the walls of the city."

Lateef said, "We already took scans from outside—"

"And you found nothing, correct?"

"That's right."

"Yet the scrappers were there – within the walls."

Ricci said, "Well, I guess we'll see. Tomorrow."

Eva said, "Captain, I will be pleased to be your personal escort." She smiled, explaining, "I was once a scrapper, like my son."

Gallantly, Ricci agreed, "And I am very pleased to accept."

178

Chapter 13

A Gauntlet with a Gift

"God answers sharp and sudden on some prayers, and thrusts the thing we have prayed for in our face. A gauntlet with a gift in't." Elizabeth Barrett Browning

Early the next morning, the Chelmanians escorted a small landing party into the walled city. They were met by decay, rust, and ruin. Kennedy immediately saw that David had not exaggerated about this being a dangerous place. Many buildings were unsound; no building was without unsafe areas, floors that couldn't be trusted, walls that could collapse at any moment. Additionally, David had been correct that once within the city walls, scanners proved useless and comms didn't work.

Adding to Con's dismay was the discovery that these "records" of the Pakarahova were artworks that the Eternals had produced; paintings, drawings, tapestries, all located in what must have been the sprawling city hall or administration complex. All the works were very detailed and evidently accurate but still: *artwork.*

Every UDC officer was assigned a scrapper to guide them, but Con felt uneasy about the presence of the watchful Chelmanians. Towards the late afternoon, he found a moment to confer with Decker out of their escorts' earshot. Decker immediately started complaining, "I can't believe we're spending the day in Hell-Hole City, gathering up wall rugs."

"Something about the Chelmanians strike you as odd, Deck?"

"They are definitely seven kinds of creepy," she said. "I can tell Kay even thinks so. He watches them like he would bears on the prowl." She sighed before admitting, "But then, what do you expect from people who've been living on scraps for generations?"

"No, it's more than that. I'd swear they're up to something."

"What?"

"I don't know...but the needle on my 'something's wrong here meter' is buried in the red."

"Yeah, I get that." She looked around. "Maybe the captain is ready to call it quits soon? Where is he?"

"He and Eva went over to the east wing."

"I thought Ramsey was covering the east wing?"

"No, she and Aqila and their escorts are covering the entire outer ring of rooms."

Just then, David and, Alsop, Con's silent escort, appeared at their elbows. "We must keep busy; we'll be losing the light soon."

"How many more...records are there?" Con asked.

David said, "Let's ask my mother. She'll know better than me. She's right outside in the main chamber."

Kennedy went willingly, thinking that whatever Eva thought, Ricci must be close to calling it a day. However, when they found Sampson, she was alone. David asked her, "Mother, how many more records are there?"

"Not many, we should have most of—"

"Where is the captain?" Con interrupted.

"He hasn't returned? I sent him on ahead an hour ago when I went to check on the outer ring party."

"What? I thought you said it was unsafe for us to be alone!"

"It was not more than a few hundred meters. He should have been able to travel that distance safely."

Kennedy immediately got to work. "David, take me to Commander Ramsey, now. She needs to be informed that the captain is missing." He turned to Naiche. "Deck, you and Eva retrace their path. See what Kay can turn up."

***

In the growing dark, Deck traveled with Eva all the way back to the east wing with no sign of Ricci but she saw many more Chelmanians than she had realized were present. Decker could tell that Kay was finding traces of the captain's scent; he started pawing at a huge set of rusty, locked doors. "What's behind those doors?"

"Not much, there's no floor behind them. They haven't been opened since I was a girl."

"Can you open it so I can see?"

"No, the key was lost long ago."

"Well, we gotta find a way in. Kay senses that there's definitely something behind them."

"He's mistaken. His scanner can't work in the city any more than anyone else's."

"His scan...? No, that's not how...." She sighed and turned back to examine the doors muttering, "I guess they've forgotten what a dog is." She looked up and noticed that the top of the wall had crumbled away near the doors. "I'm going to get up there and have a look." She went to climb the crumbling walls.

Eva pulled her away. "I can't allow this. It is not safe. You're wasting valuable time when your captain is certainly elsewhere."

"You've got a point." Deck gestured with her hand. "Please lead the way back." When Eva turned, Deck used the butt of her pulse pistol to knock her out. She turned to Kay and said, "I hope you're right about this, buddy. Otherwise I just bought myself one shiny new court-martial."

When Decker made it to the top of the walls, and was able to see down into the space, she found that Eva had told the truth. Behind the doors was an empty elevator shaft. Looking down, Deck could just about make out the inert form of Captain Ricci at the bottom of the two-story structure. She jumped quickly back down to the floor, trying to figure out how to get down there safely. She ran to the nearest stairwell, yanked the door open, and inspected the stairs; they seemed sturdy enough. Deck and Kay raced down.

Once in basement, Decker faced the same kind of rusted metal doors as upstairs. She used her pulse pistol to burn the lock off and with great effort, pulled the protesting doors open. She swiftly assessed Ricci's injuries. Luckily, the floor was mainly dirt, so he wasn't as badly off as he could have been. He was out cold, his leg was bleeding from having landed on shards of broken glass, and his shoulder looked to be dislocated. She gingerly picked the glass out of his leg and tied her jacket tightly around it to staunch the bleeding.

Decker weighed her options; none of them were good. Going for help meant leaving the captain unguarded;

sending Kay meant his facing the Chelmanians on the way, some of whom were armed. Their weapons were old but deadly enough. Taking the captain with her meant facing those same Chelmanians while she was hampered. No, she needed to get Ricci to a safe location and then she could come back for help. Searching for an exit, Deck shone her light around the darkened basement and suddenly noticed one of those ring structures in the wall that she'd found in the ground outside the city.

***

The first thing Matt perceived when he came to was pain, pain in his head, pain in his shoulder, and an even worse pain in his leg. He saw nothing but darkness. "What the fuck?'"

"Oh, you're up." He turned to see Decker crouching beside him, shining her wrist-light on him, Kay next to her. "That's good, I guess."

He groaned as he tried to sit up. "What do you mean, you guess? And where the hell are we?"

"No, don't sit up," she said, pushing him down gently. "We're in an abandoned warehouse, as far as I can make out anyway. About a kilometer and a half from where Eva shoved you down that elevator shaft. That is what happened, isn't it?"

"What? No...." Ricci tried desperately to remember. "I was with her...she was taking me to the main art gallery and...."

"And?"

"And that's the last thing I remember. Why don't you ask her what happened?"

"Because I knocked her out cold."

"You what!? Goddamn it, Decker! Have you *lost your fucking mind*?"

Her voice burned with indignation as she snapped, "Eva lied about where you were and probably tried to kill you. Don't shed any tears for her." She lifted her daypack onto her lap. "Now, if you don't mind, I'm going to stitch up your leg before you bleed out."

"Stitch up my leg? What the hell does that mean?"

"You know what you think it means?"

"Yeah?"

"That's what it means. That's why I said I wasn't sure it was good you came to. Then after the stitches, I gotta pop your shoulder back into place. Brace yourself; this is all gonna hurt like hell."

Suddenly Ricci realized all Decker had probably already done for him at that point, and how ungrateful he had been. "Well, don't enjoy it too much," he said with grim humor.

***

It was nearing afternoon when Decker heard the captain coming around for the second time. He sat up with a groan. "How're you feeling?" she asked.

"My head's a lot clearer. The rest of me is...well, better than last night at least. How long did I sleep?"

"About nine hours. It's good; you needed it."

Decker could have laughed at how quickly the wounded man morphed into "the captain." "What's our situation? Report."

"Well, like I told you before, we're in an abandoned warehouse—"

"How did you get me here?"

"I carried you. I did a year of S&R, remember?"

184

"Through the streets?"

"No, this city is riddled with tunnels. My guess is that they lead out to the settlements we were in before. The Chelmanians are looking for us; they're crawling all over that building I got you out of and all of the ones next to it."

"How do you know?"

"I've been up on the roof several times, doing recon."

"Any sign of *Lovelace* crew?"

"No, but from the roof, I saw flashes of light inside the admin complex all night. They're probably still in that maze, looking for us there. The Chelmanians, on the other hand, know to look elsewhere." He gave no argument, seeming to remember or recognize that the Chelmanians were not their friends and were responsible for their present predicament. "I've been canvasing the near-by tunnels and I almost ran into some Chelmanians, but thankfully Kay alerted me in time. I was trying to sneak back over to where our crew is but had to turn around."

"Didn't you get any sleep?"

"No. I don't sleep well when...." She sighed and just said, "I don't sleep well." Decker looked him over speculatively; his color wasn't too bad. "Do you think you could eat something?"

He laughed. "Like what?"

"Elk jerky."

"Really?"

"Yeah, I always have it in my pack." She left Kay guarding the door and retrieved the jerky, along with a silicon tube of water, and handed it over. Deck watched him cautiously start to chew.

"Does someone send you this from home?" he asked.

"No, it's synthetic." She sat down on a sack across from him. "No one at home talks to me that much. They sure as hell aren't sending me presents."

"Oh...I'm sorry to hear that."

Decker shrugged, ignoring the distant ache talking about home always brought. "It's not their fault. I was supposed to stay and be a doctor. They needed me to do that." She forced a smile. "They don't understand why I had to...why I had to come to the UDC. Only *shitsúyé* - my grandfather," she clarified. "Only he would've understood." To change the subject Deck nodded at him, asking, "How're you doing with that?"

"Not bad," he said. "I'd kill for a cup of coffee though."

With a snort of amusement, she answered, "You and me both." She reached around for her daypack. "I do have caffeine tabs, if you want one."

"What's the insomniac doing with caffeine tabs?"

Deck smiled, admitting the incongruity. "Because, if I don't get coffee – or one of these...." She held it up. "I get a terrible migraine."

"Yeah? Me, too," Ricci said, in a curiously amused tone.

"Have one." As she was handing it over, the penny dropped. Decker nodded her head slowly while digesting this new information. "Oh...I see."

"Afraid so," he answered, pausing to down the caffeine tablet before adding nonchalantly, "The insomnia, too, by the way."

"Great," she drawled out. "Did I get anything good from you? You know, genetically speaking?"

"Well...your mother wasn't the pilot, was she?"

Her head snapped up and Deck stared at him in silence for a second before confirming, "You were a pilot?"

"Not of Micro-craft but yeah, I was a pilot. I flew fighters the first two years of the war."

"I never knew that."

Ricci took another sip of water before shrugging and saying, "There's a lot of things you don't know about me."

"Yeah?" she snapped. "I don't think that's my fault."

Deck was surprised at the sadness in his tone when Ricci answered, "Nope. It's not."

***

"No," Ricci was explaining to Decker, later that night. "Whatever is blocking all of our signals would have to be *huge*. The Eternals' technology was good, but it was of its time."

"Why would they even bother making something that would do that?"

"Good way to shut down a rebellion, isn't it? Shut down all communications between the rebels. Probably why they responded by building all of those tunnels."

"And it's still running?"

"Apparently." He squinted up at her; by the dim light filtering into the building, he could see her pacing the space between them. Decker certainly was a restless soul. "When you were doing recon, did you see anything high up – something that was covered in spike aerials?"

"Maybe." She stopped and nodded thoughtfully. "There *was* something like that...I assumed it was a water tank. Let me have another look. There's a moon out tonight – I should be able to see."

Matt watched with shock as she suddenly took a run at one of the many pallets of synth-fiber sacks, bounded off them onto another stack and then up onto the crumbing walls, which she proceeded to clamber up. "Decker! What in the hell do you think you're do—" It was too late; she was already nearing the high bank of broken windows and crawling out onto the roof.

Ricci was still shaking his head with exasperation when she jumped back down beside him. "Yes, I can see it. It's on a high rooftop not far from that admin complex." He just glared at her. "What? How did you think I got up there before?"

Rather than deigning to answer, Matt said, "I really don't understand how you've survived for twenty-eight years."

Decker laughed and said something in Chiricahua.

"What was that?"

"I said, 'I can't die because heaven won't have me, and hell is afraid I'll take over.'" Her smile radiated affection as she explained, "That's what they used to say about my great-grandfather."

"The one you were named for?"

"How do you know about that?"

Ricci didn't know whether he wanted to laugh or cry at her apparent shock. Without even noticing, for the first time in many years, he addressed her using the given name that they had just been discussing. "Naiche, don't you think your mother and I talked after you were born? After she came back to the UDC?"

"I didn't know...I didn't think you talked about *me*."

"Of course, we did." He hesitated before adding, "I know she talked about me to you...right?"

"Yep, she did." Suddenly all business, she asked, "So...how do we take out that signal dampener?"

"Give me your pulse pistol."

"I don't think that's gonna do it."

"They can be rigged to over-load."

"No, Artillery Engineering fixed that."

"You still can do it, if you understand the original design flaw." At her questioning look, he explained, "Captain's privilege." Deck rolled her eyes and handed over her pistol. While he worked on it, Ricci couldn't resist returning to their former subject. "What exactly did she say about me to you? Your mother, I mean."

"She said that...." Decker paused, sighed, started again. "She told me about what happened between you two, and she said that you had every right to make the decision that you did and...." There was another long pause while Matt studied her from underneath his lashes. "And that I should never think it meant you weren't a good man."

When he trusted himself to speak again, Ricci said, "She was...a remarkable woman." He looked up at Decker and she just nodded, with tears glittering in her eyes. He held up the pistol. "You can activate it by pulling back on the trigger. It will lock up. Then you'll have anywhere from fifteen to twenty minutes to get out of the way. How're you gonna deliver it?"

"I'll go over the rooftops."

"What?! No."

"Those rooftops are no more than three to four meters apart; those are easy jumps. I can get within six meters of that dampener. Then it's just a long free throw."

In spite of the danger they were discussing, Matt couldn't help but smile. "You play basketball?"

"Yeah, Con taught me." She held out her hand. "Okay, let's do this." She looked at the pistol he'd handed her and stuck it back in its holster. Suddenly she pulled her necklace out from under her shirt and placed it gently onto one of the sacks. "Glows in the dark," she said. She quickly patted Kay, saluted Ricci, and then she was gone.

While he waited for Decker to return, Matt couldn't resist picking up that locket again. He examined it closely and activated it for the first time in years. The first image he saw was of the little family that could have been his – had he made a different choice.

By watching Kay, Ricci knew immediately when Decker had made it back onto the roof; he breathed a sigh of relief. She was beside them both in moments saying, "Piece of cake. Now we wait."

"Any sign of Chelmanians?"

She didn't seem to hear him as she was looking all around her. "Did you see what happened to my locket?"

Belatedly, Ricci realized he was still had it. He handed it to her, explaining, "I wondered if it still worked."

"Why wouldn't it?"

"It was already an antique when I gave it to your mother."

"Oh," she breathed. Looking down at the locket in her hand she said, almost to herself, "You *were* the one...."

"You didn't know?"

"No, she never said." Naiche stood still for a second, biting her lip, but then she put the necklace back on, admitting, "I always wondered...even way back when you gave it to me...if that's where she got it."

"Why didn't you ask?"

Decker shot him a piercing look. "Honestly?"

"If we can't have the truth between us now...." He waved his hand to indicate their precarious situation.

"I didn't want to know. I wouldn't have wanted to wear it if I knew for sure...it was from you."

"I see." He tried to ignore the sudden stab of pain – after all, he'd asked for it. Matt swallowed hard before offering, "That *is* honest."

Her voice was laced with annoyance as Naiche explained, "Look, I was just a kid, all right? And no matter what *shimáá* had said about you – in my eyes you were just the man...." She gave him a hard stare and continued, very deliberately, "The man who'd never wanted me."

Matt stopped trying to fight the pain; he let it goad him into challenging, "And later, at The Rock? Where you *just a kid* then?"

"No, by then I didn't see what right you had to come busting into my life, issuing orders, and directi—"

"I was trying to help!"

"I didn't ask for your help."

"Your advisor did."

"Right," Naiche snapped. "I *never* believed that. Out of all the people in the UDC, Gordon just happened to ask you—"

"He asked me because he knew."

"He knew your dirty little secret?"

Vehemently, he asserted, "You were *never* a dirty—"

"I've been with the UDC for ten years, Ricci. Nobody knows – nobody even *suspects*."

That was too true for contradiction, so Matt just insisted, "Gordon knew. He'd been my CO."

"So?"

Ricci couldn't go there. They were edging into dangerous territory. "Never mind. Forget it."

"Why?" She crouched down to study him. "What aren't you telling me? I thought we were finally trading some truths here?"

Naiche refused to turn away, so reluctantly, Matt haltingly explained, "Gordon knew...because I kept having to take leave to go back to Uniterrae. That spring after your mother died. To go to court...tribal court." She was staring intently at him as he talked, her body stiff and tense. "I was trying to get my parental rights reinstated."

"What?!" Decker rocked back on her heels in surprise. "You were trying to get *custody*?"

"No! I just wanted a chance...." Matt shook his head and his tone softened as he elaborated, "I thought we should get to know one another. I just wanted to spend some time with you."

"You didn't have to go to court for that! My grandfath—"

"Would not let me near you."

"I don't believe you!"

"Believe what you want," Ricci shot back. "You always have."

Decker jumped up, started pacing again, ranting to herself. "*Shitsúyé* would have told me. He never kept *anything* from me. We were...." Suddenly she stopped in her tracks, stricken silent and immobile.

"What?" There was no immediate answer, so Matt asked again, "Naiche, what's wrong?"

Gradually, she turned around and admitted, "He *was* in court back then – three times that spring. He said it was a land dispute." She was shaking her head slowly, explaining, "But we had no land...other than the house." After a moment of silence, Naiche whispered, "*Ádíídíí díík'eh dáándí,*" before hunching over, as if in physical pain. "I can't believe he didn't tell me...he *never* told me...not even when he knew he was *dying*."

192

Matt was close to tears, longing to comfort her, stuck where he was due to his injuries. This was the very reaction he had dreaded. "He did it *for you*," Ricci explained. "Gus told me as much after the verdict came down in his favor." She hadn't seemed to hear him. "Naiche, your grandfather thought he was protecting you," he insisted.

At last, Decker straightened up and stared at him. "Protecting me from *what*? From you?"

"From me, from the UDC—"

Her bitter laugh stopped him mid-sentence. "Well, that *worked*. He must be so proud of me. Lieutenant Decker – of the UDC." Ricci started to protest her self-reproach, but she simply held up her hand. "No, please...let me appreciate the beauty of this. As different as the three of you all are, I still managed to become a disappointment to *every one of you*."

Just then a roaring boom sounded, rattling the ancient warehouse. The pistol bomb had worked. Without hesitation, Decker put her hand to the comm link in her ear and said, "Decker to Kennedy, come in. Kennedy, do you copy?"

Con's voice could be heard in the room. "Deck, I copy. Where the hell are you?"

Chapter 14

To Speak the Truth

"It takes two to speak the truth - one to speak, and another to hear." Henry David Thoreau

Ricci suborned Dr. Clemente into releasing him from Med-Bay after forty-eight hours. He had managed that feat by promising to stay away from work and to rest in his quarters until the next day. The promise he'd extracted in return was for Rita to tell Decker that the medical skills she'd learned from her grandfather had proved invaluable during their recent ordeal. Clemente had readily agreed.

Within the first couple of hours of prescribed rest, he was thinking that his promise was going to be a difficult one to keep. When the door chimed, Matt was glad for the distraction even if it was just Clemente checking up on him.

"Enter," he said. The door slid open to reveal Decker, standing on the threshold. They hadn't seen each other since their rescue because Ricci's visitors in Med-Bay had been limited to Lindstrom. Everything Matt had wanted to say to her suddenly flew out of his head. The answer to the question he'd asked Clemente weeks ago – what were they to each other? – he still didn't know. All he could do was tell her to come in.

Decker walked in, followed by Kay, and surveyed the space. "Hey, *nice*."

"What? Oh, my quarters."

"Yeah, very spacious." She seemed unusually nervous, shifting her weight from foot to foot. "Um, I just heard they let you out today. How're you doing?"

"Pretty good. Thanks to you."

She waved his thanks off, and pointed at the dog, now sitting at her feet. "Thank Kay. He found you."

"As grateful as I am to him...." He paused and gave Kay a two-finger salute. "I don't think he could have done it alone." In a more earnest tone he said, "Really, you did *good*. Your mother would be *very proud*." He knew the next statement was a risk, but he took it anyway. "I think your grandfather would be, too."

Decker gave no sign as to whether she agreed or not. "Yeah, about that. I wanted to...I'd like to say something personal, if that's okay?"

"Of course."

She seemed to have a hard time starting, wasn't meeting his eye, and then suddenly blurted out, "I'm not good at this – apologies, I mean. Not personal ones, anyway, so if you'd just let me get through this without comment, it would really help." She finally looked him in the face. "And then I just need a yes, no, or maybe answer. Okay?"

He nodded, saying, "Okay."

Decker exhaled and said, "It seems that I misjudged you—" She stopped and shook her head. "No – let me try that again. I *willfully* misjudged you because doing so suited my...personal narrative about you. And every time you

196

reached out to me...I was unfair and unkind...in the *extreme*. And I'm sorry. I hope you'll forgive me." She let out another deep breath and looked at Ricci expectantly.

"There's nothing to forgi—" He stopped at her reproving look and said, "Yes, of course I forgive you."

She finally relaxed and said with a smile, "Okay! Great. Good stuff." She rubbed her hands together and then pointed at the door. "I'm gonna go now because I think that's all the touchy-feely-ness you and I can stand all at once." She turned to leave, trailed by Kay.

"Naiche, wait—"

She didn't stop. "No, no, I think it's better—"

In his very best captain's voice, Ricci said, "Lieutenant, halt! That's an order." She stopped and turned, Matt guessed mainly by force of habit and he suddenly realized there were some advantages to being your child's CO.

"I really don't think—"

"Quiet. That's also an order." She again obeyed. "Now, I'm no good at apologies, so if you'd just let me get through this without comment...." Naiche started smiling broadly but let him continue. "...it would really help. And then I want a yes, no, or maybe answer. Okay?"

She laughed but said only, "Okay."

Ricci swallowed past a lump in his throat and his tone turned serious. "I never thought about what it was like for you, growing up thinking—" *No, Matt*, he said to himself, *be as honest as your daughter was.* "—knowing that your father didn't want you, and I regret that you *ever* thought I was ashamed of you or disappointed in you. I'm not. I never was. But I can see why you thought that and I'm deeply sorry. I hope you'll eventually find a way to forgive me. For everything."

197

Her eyes were wet but her smile bright as she offered quietly, "Yeah, I can do that." They nodded at each other for a few seconds and then she said, "Phew. I really think that's enough for one day."

She turned to leave again and had almost reached the door when Matt called out, "Decker!"

Naiche turned, her expression wary. "Sir?"

"What do you do when you can't sleep?"

"Oh." She was visibly relieved at the question. "Um, I read, sometimes. Mainly I go down to the gym and shoot baskets – until I'm tired enough to sleep."

"Ah, good plan."

Naiche was smiling faintly as she asked, "What do you do, Captain, when you can't sleep?"

"I work usually...occasionally I wander the halls...." He cocked his head and offered, "Maybe I'll wander by the gym sometime, see if there's someone to play basketball with."

"You should definitely do that," she agreed and once again, she and Kay headed out the door. "I'll even spot you a few points."

"You don't have to do that, I'm actually pretty good."

Just as she was making her exit, Decker called out, "I probably do, I'm actually *really good*."

***

The *Lovelace* was still orbiting Chelmang when the command staff gathered the next day. Scientific staff had been pouring over the artwork they'd retrieved from the Eternals' abandoned city to see if it actually had value or had merely been used as a lure. Lateef was giving her assessment. "The depictions are all of a single star system, of that I'm certain. The artists were obsessive about it."

"But can we glean anything useful from any of them? Anything that would help us determine the location of the Pakarahova home world?" asked Ricci.

"Not just yet, but I had an idea. I'm having Ensign Brodie convert each image to a digital representation. Then I plan to create an average composite and match that composite against local star maps."

Commander Ramsey asked, "Won't averaging a muddle of hundreds of artworks together just create a worse muddle?"

"Not necessarily," Lateef explained. "There's a theory about the aggregation of information in groups often yielding excellent results."

"Meaning, what?" Lindstrom asked.

"Meaning, if you ask a hundred people to estimate the distance to the nearest planet, you'll get a wide variety of responses but when you average them, you get a surprisingly accurate result."

Lindstrom said, "But that will only work if they weren't just copying from each other."

"I don't think they were. The works were all produced within a very short time period. Our scans indicate, within the first ten to twenty years after the initial transformation."

"And then what?" inquired Clemente.

"And then they all just stopped. Or those works weren't preserved. I don't know."

Kennedy asked, "Why were they even painting, or drawing, or whatever, a system they had never visited?"

"I don't know that either. My guess is that the eprion may confer some kind of...race memory for lack of a better term."

"Just when you thought they couldn't get any *creepier*," Decker said.

"There's something else. We noticed that in many of the artworks with words in them, they state things such as, 'we are many, we are multitudes, we are legion—'"

Ricci broke in, "We get the picture, Commander. What's significant about that?"

"They're often followed by lists of alien words...." Aqila stopped and glanced at Jeff Sasaki. "Commander Sasaki and I spent some time attempting to translate them and we agree – they seem to be the names of many different alien species." She saw the dawning realization on the faces around the table but clarified anyway. "I'm afraid that if and when we do get to the right star system, we need to be prepared to possibly find...more than one host species or more correctly, more than one infected species." Lateef saw by the troubled faces of her colleagues, that she had conceivably just delivered the worst news of the trip.

"Thank you, Commander," Ricci said. "It may turn out that many species have faced infection. That shouldn't surprise us, when we think of it. There's no reason to assume they're *all* in that star system but we should be prepared to find...much more than we originally bargained for. As far as I'm concerned, that changes nothing about our mission; we need to proceed to this star system if we can find it." He looked at his team, "Any objections?"

"I think we all stand with you on this point, Captain. We're not turning back now," said Lindstrom. He looked around the table. "Though I suppose it's presumptuous of me to speak for everyone. Does anyone think differently?"

There were general murmurs of support from everyone, ranging from Sasaki's "Certainly not, Commander," to Kennedy's, "Not a chance!" to Decker's "No, hell no."

"You have your answer, Captain. 'Into the jaws of Death, into the mouth of hell, rode the six hundred'," said Lindstrom.

"Thank you for that literary interlude, Commander." Ricci said wryly. "Though I would have appreciated a comparison to a less disastrous battle." Lindstrom had no response other than a sardonic shrug. "Any other business before we adjourn?"

"Yes, sir," Aqila said. "I was wondering what we're going to do about the Chelmanians?"

Ricci shook his head as he replied, "There's not much we can do, Commander. We have no jurisdiction here and it seems like the people stand with Doyen Sampson and her group of conspirators. It looks like her only punishment will be the severe concussion she received from Lieutenant Decker."

"If I'd known that, I'd've—" Decker stopped upon receiving a suppressing glare from Lindstrom.

Lateef objected, "That's not what I meant, Captain. I meant what are we going to do to help them?"

"Help them?"

Ricci seemed stunned by the suggestion, as did Lindstrom who said, "I'd like to help them into the brig but I don't want to be stuck with them for the rest of the trip."

Aqila gathered her courage and persisted. "Sir, I know what they did was wrong but—"

"Wrong?!" Decker interjected. "They tried to kill my...*our captain*. Did you miss that part?"

Con patted her arm and gave her a smile. "No one missed that, Deck. Just hear her out, okay?"

Aqila was heartened by the encouraging look Con gave her. In the same strong voice she'd used to defend her research at symposiums she said, "The Chelmanians were afraid; they still are. Eva saw history repeating itself – us going off in search of the 'gift-givers', coming back as Eternals, and once again enslaving and oppressing them." Lateef looked around the table. "Desperate people do desperate things."

Ricci put up a hand. "Okay, Lateef, let's say for the sake of argument, we did decide to *help* the people whose leader conspired to push me into a goddamn—" he paused, and in a calmer tone, continued, "...who thought that step one in fouling up our mission was getting rid of the captain of the *Lovelace*. What would you have us do?"

"Because of the...odd circumstances of their ancestor's dependence on the Eternals, they lack some basic skills and tools. We could give them seeds from the hydroponic gardens, with some instructions on how to plant and harvest. I could even get some eggs out of the stasis chamber and engineer them to be fertile. With accelerated growth enzymes—"

"Who's going to sit on the eggs?" Lindstrom asked.

"They have incubators in the lab, Nils." Rita said.

Passionately, Aqila pressed her point. "This is the furthest humans have made it out into the galaxy. We sent them out here; remember? And they survived against incredible odds. Yes, they made an awful mistake, and Captain?" She turned to Ricci. "I know you almost paid a terrible price for it, but I think we can rise above that."

Ramsey said, "Couldn't we just promise to send out ships to bring them back to Uniterrae, when we get home?"

"We've already made that offer and we *will* do that but a lot of the Chelmanians insist that they don't *want* to leave. They feel that this planet *is* their home," Kennedy explained. "They'd die to defend it. Just like we're willing to do for Uniterrae."

202

Lateef said, "We've all been fighting a war to ensure that humankind stays...human. Maybe in a small way, helping these people *now* is part of our mission, too?"

Ricci was nodding his head while saying, "Okay...okay, maybe you're right. I can't believe I'm saying this but okay. We give them the seeds and...chickens, if I'm hearing you right. Anything else?"

Aqila looked at Decker. "They could probably use some better medical skills."

Clemente said, "Okay, I'm in."

"I'm glad of what help you can give, Doctor, but they don't really have modern technology available to them." She turned to Naiche. "I was hoping Lieutenant Decker would teach them some of her basic medical skills."

Decker put her hand to her forehead. "You want *me* to teach medicine to the people who *three days ago* were hunting me down like I was a hare they wanted for the stew pot? Just so we're clear on this, that's what you want?"

With a softened tone, Lateef said, "Deck, do you know how the Burangasisti knew we weren't Eternals?"

"No, I kinda' missed some stuff there. You know, being in a vegetative state and all."

"They knew because we cared about each other – for each other. Unlike the Eternals." Aqila saw Naiche mulling it over and pressed, "I guess I could have Con ask you...."

"No, you don't have to play the trump card," Decker said, winking at Kennedy. "I'll do it."

"Thank you, Deck. I know this isn't easy for you...."

"No, I can see that you're right. I guess it's like if someone hurts you and you hit back at them even harder without trying to figure out what happened in the first place, then you just set up this endless cycle of hurt." Decker had seemed to be talking to the table but at this point she gave a quick glance at the captain. "And nobody wins that."

Lindstrom said approvingly, "Why, Lieutenant, that was a speech worthy of your mother."

Decker laughed and said, "Commander, are you certain you ever *heard* any of my mother's speeches?"

"A sentiment worthy of her, then."

The group adjourned leaving behind only Lateef, Ricci, Clemente, and Lindstrom who wanted to hear more details about her ideas to educate the Chelmanians. They ended up agreeing that the time it took to complete Brodie's work on the aggregate star map, could be used to enact her plan.

As they broke up, Clemente insisted on herding Ricci into Med-Bay to check on his healing injuries and Lateef was left alone with Lindstrom. Flush with victory, Aqila decided to go for broke and broach a subject that she knew was near and dear to Con's heart. He hadn't yet found the opportunity to do anything about it, but maybe she could. "Commander, I was wondering if I could have a word with you about Lieutenant Decker."

"Of course. Is there a problem with her?"

"No, sir. It's with you."

"Me? In what way?"

"Well, not just you...I wish *everyone* could stop comparing Deck to her mom. Con tells me it started the day she showed up at The Rock. That wasn't fair. She's not her mother. As far as I can see, she was never meant to be."

"Well...point taken." He seemed accepting of her opinion but also slightly astonished. "This certainly is your day to hand out home truths, isn't it, Commander?

"I hope so, sir. I think everybody should get at least one." Against all odds, they both left the room smiling.

Chapter 15

Into that Darkness Peering

"Deep into that darkness peering, long I stood there, wondering, fearing, doubting, dreaming dreams no mortal ever dared to dream before." Edgar Allan Poe

After two weeks of concentrated effort by Brodie, Lateef, and the rest of the scientific department, Aqila's plan to create an aggregate map appeared to have worked. There was a definite match to be found, the Mu Cassiopeiae system, and the *Lovelace* headed for it. They seemed to be nearing their journey's end, an end that was viewed with differing levels of fear and hope. With how much fear versus how much hope, well, that varied by crewmember and every crewmember had their own internal swings between highs and lows.

A week into that journey to the MC System, Clemente was in her office dictating her orders for beta shift when she heard Kennedy come crashing into Med-Bay, yelling, "Coming through. Injured captain here!" She ran out to find Ricci, limping, supported in-between Decker and Kennedy.

"What happened here?" Since they were all dressed for basketball, Clemente already had a good idea of what had happened.

Kennedy and Decker started talking at the same time.

"Deck slammed the captain into the support—"

"We both went after a loose ball and—"

Ricci held up a hand, indicating 'stop', and said, "Merely a hazard of the game, Doctor."

"I see," Clemente answered. "Kennedy, please help the captain into exam room-1."

Twenty minutes later, she was putting a healing boot on Ricci's ankle, when Nils entered the room. "Hello, Captain. I understand I'll be taking over command tomorrow, is that right?"

Matt looked thoroughly annoyed. "It's just a sprain; I can manage."

Rita said, "It's a bad sprain, I'd like you to rest for twenty-four hours and give the boot a chance to do its job." She turned to Lindstrom, "So, yes, plan to take command tomorrow." Ricci rolled his eyes and sighed but didn't object. The doctor offered this reassurance, "Don't worry – if we go to DEFCON-alpha, you're back on the bridge."

Just then, Kennedy and Decker popped their heads around the doorjamb. "Is the captain going to be all right?" Decker asked.

"I shall live to fight another day."

"If we're talking basketball, not for another week you won't," Clemente objected.

Decker said, "Sorry to hear that. We'll keep the court warm for you, sir."

"You need help getting back to your quarters, Captain?" Kennedy asked.

"No, you two go ahead," he answered. "Once Clemente gets this boot on, I'll be fine."

Over his loud protestations, Clemente did end up sending an aide to ensure Ricci got back to his quarters without problem. When they were gone, Lindstrom observed archly, "So...he and Decker seem much *friendlier* these days, don't they?"

Rita smiled, saying, "Yes, I think they...bonded during that ordeal on Chelmang. It's good."

"Really? *Good*? That's an odd way to pronounce, 'ill-advised'."

"What is *ill-advised* about the captain and Decker having a...a better rapport?"

"Is that code for an affair?"

"That is *not* the nature of their relationship." She stood up on tiptoe to get as close as possible to looking him in the eye and enunciated clearly, "Trust me on this."

He looked at her fondly, but his tone was ever so slightly patronizing. "Dear Rita. You can be so naïve."

"Get the hell out of my Med-Bay or you'll be needing a healing boot of your own."

He laughed but did leave, calling out, "I love you, too, Doctor."

Rita was left wondering why she had chosen such a completely impossible man.

***

Weeks later, after checking six likely planets in the MC System and coming up empty-handed, the *Lovelace* had zeroed in on the small rocky world furthest in. The ship had been circling it for the past hour; the planet was entirely black desert, burnt continually by the near-by star.

Everyone on the bridge was wondering if this barren place could be the home of the Pakarahova.

Lateef was at her station, reporting her findings to the captain and first officer. "The planet's surface is extremely absorbent. Scans just don't get back to us with much information but there are definite life signs down there. One species has the strangest life signs I've ever encountered."

Ricci asked, "Do you think this could be the Pakarahovan home world and that the host species?"

"I don't think it's the intelligent host species, sir, but they might be infected with the eprion in some form. These creatures give off the weirdest energy signatures...not an eprion signature exactly but maybe a residual sign of it...I don't know." Lateef shook her head. "But either way, this is the closest we've come to finding anything that might even be related to the Pakarahova. I really think we really need to investigate."

The captain considered his options. "Ok, I want a strong team; Lindstrom, you're going to lead it. Take the large shuttle, a robust tactical force, and how many from Scientific, Lateef?"

"Me, plus Lieutenant Grieveson should be plenty, Captain."

"Okay." He said to the first officer, "Commander, assemble your team."

Without hesitation, Lindstrom turned to the tactical consoles and said, "Kennedy, Decker, you're with me. Get Modi, Perham, and...."

"Abello, sir?" Kennedy suggested.

"Good choice. Okay, let's move."

***

Thirty minutes later Decker was piloting the shuttle towards the surface, which was split evenly into day and night. "Anywhere in particular you want me to land, Commander?" she asked of Lateef.

Aqila said, "Well, daylight would be nice."

"Of course. No other stipulations?"

"No, those life signs aren't concentrated in any particular area."

"Got it." She skimmed the surface, but it was black sand and black rock and not much else. "Guess one place is as good as another," Decker mused, before settling down in a wide-open spot.

"Before we go out," Lateef said to Lindstrom, "I want to take some wide range scans for eprion signatures."

"Excellent idea," replied the first officer.

Lateef and Grieveson got to work; in the meantime, Lindstrom, Kennedy, and Decker were looking out at the burnt surface. "You ever see anything like that before, Commander?" Con asked.

"Thankfully, no."

"This look anything like that desert you told me about back home, Deck?"

"The Chihuahuan? No. That has life, this is...endless dead sand and rock. Looks more like Longoris, that empty moon near Antiliac, than anything on Earth."

Just then, the two scientists reported their findings. "No trace of eprion at all, but there are definitely life signs in the area, might be the very ones we were looking for."

"All right," said Lindstrom. "Let's move out. We'll split into two teams, each lead by a science officer. I'll go with Grieveson and I want one of the tactical leads with me." He turned to them and asked, "Do I have a volunteer?"

"Yes, that would be me," Decker said. "And as a bonus, you get Kay."

Lindstrom responded, "Wonderful. Day made."

As they assembled their gear, issuing particle rifles and daypacks to each tactical officer, Con whispered to Deck, "Have you gained a sudden fondness for Lindstrom?"

"Ah, he's not so bad," she answered. "Besides, do you really think I'm gonna get in the way of true love?"

Kennedy shook his head and said with a laugh, "I knew it." Decker just waved a hand to indicate that it wasn't any real sacrifice on her part.

**

Lindstrom's group quickly found the source of some of the near-by life signs; first to be spotted were what looked to be a type of armor-skinned wild boar. They had tusks and evidently rooted in the ground for whatever lived below the surface. Lindstrom turned to Grieveson. "Is that what we've been looking for?"

"Negative. The ones we're looking for give off a faint energy signature. We need to keep looking."

The group moved on, constantly checking Grieveson's readings. The boar-like animals were definitely much more common than whatever it was they were searching for. Finally, they found one of the probable creatures in question, basking in the brutal heat.

"Looks like a big-ass lizard," Decker mused, viewing it through her oculiscope.

"What's a lizard look like again?" asked Lindstrom. His family had immigrated to the Centauri settlements when he was young, so he remembered very little of Earth's native wildlife. He knew the name from coursework at The Rock but couldn't place it.

"Like that, except you know, not 500 kilos," Decker answered. "And not pitch black. And not half jaw." Lindstrom gave her a glance that was an even mixture of amusement and annoyance. "Okay, maybe not *that much* like a lizard," she conceded. She looked down at Kay, "You're not going to be chasing *these* lizards, buddy. Quite the reverse."

"I don't think they're up to chasing him, either." Lindstrom said. "It sure doesn't do much, does it?" he inquired of the astrobiologist.

She didn't disagree. "No, sir, it seems completely dormant. I'm going to get closer to get better readings."

Decker said, "Okay, Abello, and I will accompany you." She turned to Nils, asking, "Do you wish to stay here, sir?" while gesturing at the shade they'd found in a rock outcropping.

"Yes, I think I will do just that," he answered, never being one who appreciated heat.

Twenty minutes later the group returned, looking none too happy. Well?" Lindstrom asked.

"Not, much to report, sir," answered Grieveson. "It doesn't add up. If their energy signals were this low all of the time, we shouldn't have even been able to detect them from orbit. Not the way this planet absorbs scans."

Lindstrom put a hand to the comm link in his ear and contacted the other group to see if they had any better luck. Lateef's results replicated Grieveson's precisely. They rendezvoused at the shuttle. Lindstrom asked the chief science officer, "Shall we abort, Commander, or do you want to try something else?"

"I do have an idea...." ventured Grieveson.

"What's that?

"These creatures may be entirely nocturnal. The energy they absorb during the daylight may be emitted during the night. That would explain why some of the readings could be detected from the *Lovelace*."

"Yes, of course!" said Lateef. "They absorb energy all day, that's why they're so sluggish. I'd really like to get readings from them when they're emitting that stronger energy. We might have to wait—"

"We don't have to wait," Decker interjected. "I can fly us over to the dark side of this rock right now."

The party boarded the shuttle and Decker put it in a low orbit over the planet's surface. They hadn't been airborne for more than two minutes when an alarm sounded on the panel. Kennedy, who'd been in the back talking with Lindstrom and Lateef, looked towards the pilot's seat. "What's up, Deck?"

"Shit! Uh, there's a sudden burst of activity from that star." She nodded at the nearby light in the sky. "Ionic front on its way to us."

Kennedy ran up and took the seat next to her. "Everybody strap in!" he ordered. "It's gonna get rough." Seconds later his words proved to be an understatement as the shuttle was buffeted by the ion storm and tossed about. "Hold her steady, Deck." She only nodded in response, obviously concentrating all her efforts on piloting the wayward shuttle.

Just then another strong wave hit. A klaxon sounded, accompanied by a flashing red light. All shuttle lights, other than the few emergency lights and the control panel, went out. "It took out the power rod," Decker announced tightly. She frantically moved her hands over the panel. "Gonna switch to auxiliary...." They were still losing altitude. She shook her head, muttering, "Fuck! The whole system's fried." Without looking up, she gave the grim warning, "We're going down."

"Prepare for crash landing!" Kennedy announced, as Decker fought the rebellious shuttle, desperately attempting to guide it to the best possible landing. A minute later they landed, in the dark, with a thundering jolt.

***

Kennedy was taking stock of the situation: not great but it could have been a lot worse. No one was injured other than a few bumps and bruises. They were below the storm, which had moved entirely into the upper atmosphere, and they could wait it out here. Either *Lovelace* could send another shuttle for them when it was over or maybe Decker's efforts to repair this shuttle would pay off.

The floor compartment near the pilot's seat was open and she was poking around with gloved hands, surveying the damage by the dim emergency lights. "There's no fixing this damaged power rod but if I could just get it free without...yeah, that'll work." Decker glanced over at the open tool kit. "The spare is intact, so I might figure out how to replace it." She looked up at Con, while gently pushing Kay out of the way; he'd been looking into the compartment with her, as if hoping to offer some advice. "That would get the power back on in here but I'm not sure about the hull integrity or the navigation system; it's not like I'm an engineer. I wouldn't risk taking it back up to *Lovelace*."

"Well, then don't knock yourself out; *Lovelace* will send help when the storm abates."

"Might as well get the power back on if I can. I got nothin' better to do, right?"

"Well, I do," announced Aqila.

"What's that?" Lindstrom asked

"I'd like to take a party out and see if we can get better readings off of those energy-creatures at night."

Kennedy looked at Lindstrom. "Any objections, Commander?"

"No, we may as well get something out of this God-forsaken—" He caught himself. "Out of this trip."

Decker sat up, saying, "You guys go ahead. Kay and I will stay here and work on the shuttle."

"He's going to assist?" Lindstrom asked.

"Yeah, he's going to help by staying out of my way." She wagged a finger at the Blue-Heeler. "Right?"

Lindstrom looked at Con. "You lead the party, Lieutenant. I'll stay and assist Decker in replacing the power rod and determining if this thing can fly again or not. Or rather *she* will assist *me*." Both tactical officers looked at him in mild surprise. "Yes, I'm an engineer. I wasn't commissioned out of The Rock as a first officer, you know," he caustically reminded them.

Con's first instinct was to ask Deck if she was okay with that but it's not like they could countermand Lindstrom's plan anyway, so he just said, "Very well, sir." Once again, he handed out particle rifles to Perham, Modi, and Abello and grabbed one for himself, saying, "Okay, wrist-lights on everybody. Let's move out." He grinned at Aqila. "We're doin' science!"

The group traveled several hundred yards in the pitch black without encountering much. The planet had no moon and the black sands seemed to absorb the beams from their wrist-lights. The effect was eerie; you couldn't see more than fifteen feet in any direction. Con watched as Aqila consulted with Grieveson over their scanners. "Wow, those readings did jump up."

"You were right, Angie," Lateef said. "Those creatures are definitely nocturnal."

"I want to approach them with caution. They seem very timid."

Lateef agreed and added, "Before we head out, we should set an alarm on our scanners for eprion signatures."

Kennedy wasn't bothering looking for the energy alligators, as he had mentally dubbed them, but he did ensure his and everyone else's scanners were also set to alarm at the slightest sign of eprion signatures.

Grieveson pointed off to the right. "Seems to be a small concentration of the creatures over there." She led the way and the rest of them trooped after her. Con brought up the rear; the only one he could actually see was Aqila directly in front of him, though he could hear the quiet padding sound of boots against sand.

Suddenly the quiet was broken by a scream of agony. Con rush up to see Grieveson, under attack from one of the creatures, which looked anything but timid as it lunged at the biologist and slashed her with its powerful jaws. All four tactical officers opened fire; to their horror, it had no effect. In less than three minutes, the terrible screaming had stopped but only because it was clear that Grieveson was dead. Con ordered, "Go! Everyone, back to the shuttle NOW!"

The group hadn't progressed thirty feet, before two more of the creatures appeared out of the darkness, the first one advancing steadily on Modi. He fired desperately at the creature but that didn't give it the slightest pause, in fact, it seemed to move faster the more they fired. Kennedy yelled, "Stop firing at it! It's absorbing the particle energy!"

By then Modi was screaming as the creature tore into him. Con rushed up and started battering at the animal with the butt of his rifle. He had almost freed Modi when Con was assaulted from the left by the other creature. He felt a searing pain in his side but ignored it as he desperately bashed the attacking animal over and over, screaming orders to the group to go on without him. He saw Aqila hesitate and shouted more urgently, "Go!" That time they listened.

Left alone, Con valiantly fought the creature with everything he had. He knew that if it got its jaws around him, he'd suffer Modi and Grieveson's fate. Finally, Con managed to free himself by gouging the creature repeatedly in its huge eyes. With a mad shriek, it ran off into the darkness; its companion was still finishing off Modi.

Ignoring his pain and disorientation, Kennedy desperately headed for the shuttle; his heart started beating even faster when he heard another agonized scream up ahead. He caught up with the others to find Perham, blood running down her face, desperately bashing at one of the animals while Abello, in Aqila's arms, held his bleeding stump of a hand under his armpit. Con joined the fight, shouting, "Aqila, don't wait for us. You two, get back to the shuttle – now!" They stumbled off, and he ordered, "Perham, go for the eyes!" Together they drove the last creature away.

Bleeding and panting with exhaustion, they caught up with Aqila who was almost carrying Abello now; they all headed back to the shuttle together. The group hadn't gotten far when they heard the unmistakable scuffling sound of something coming towards them in the dark. Con's heart sank; they wouldn't survive another attack. He held up his light to see how many there were this time. The circle of light was finally breached by none other than Decker and Kay.

***

Not for the first time in his life, Lindstrom doubted the wisdom of humankind's foray into space, as he surveyed the state of his shuttle crew. He and Decker had finished replacing the power rod and discovering that the shuttle still couldn't fly when they'd been alerted by Kay that something was wrong in the distance. Decker had grabbed a particle rifle, saying she would check on it and headed out with the dog. When Nils heard the faint sound of screams, he took a rifle for himself and went to follow but was met by the bloodied group on their way back to safety. The relative safety, that was, of the disabled shuttle.

Decker had the first-aid kit out and was seeing to the wounded as best she could; Aqila was helping. "I'm going to have to cauterize this," Deck said to Abello, looking at the left arm, now minus a hand. "I don't have much for the pain. I'm sorry." The most horrifying thing was that Abello hardly reacted at all.

Finally, Decker came over to report to Lindstrom, leaving the wounded behind, stretched out on makeshift beds. Aqila remained beside Con, holding his limp hand. "Con's lost a lot of blood and is in shock; same with Abello. Perham is unconscious; she has a massive head wound that could be really serious. I don't know; I'm just a medic." Lindstrom was grateful that Rita had insisted, after Chelmang, that if Decker was going to 'play medic' she should come into the 31st century and had taught her basic modern medicine. "The sooner *Lovelace* can send down a rescue party, the better off we'll be." The ion storm was still raging overhead; they hadn't been in contact with *Lovelace* for over an hour. Lindstrom knew they had no recourse other than to wait it out.

Just then, loud scraping, screeching, scratching noises sounded from outside the main hatch. Lindstrom looked at Decker. "What the hell is that?"

"I'll take a look from up top." She quickly hoisted herself up to the top escape hatch, opened it slightly, and shone her wrist-light out. She dropped back down. Her eyes were wide but her voice dispassionate as she reported, "There's two of those creatures out there. They're trying to fight their way in."

Chapter 16

For Others and the World

"What we do for others and the world remains and is immortal." Albert Pine

Thirty minutes later, the energy creatures were still trying to breach the shuttle, and rather than lessening, the terrifying sound of their gnawing and scratching had grown louder. Aqila, who was slumped with exhaustion in one of the passenger seats, asked Lindstrom, "Do you think they can get in?"

"This shuttle is made of vanadinlum; if anything can withstand them, it can." He had answered Lateef with a lot more faith than he possessed and then he turned his attention to Decker who was jumping down from her perch on one of the seats. She'd been taking another look out of the top hatch.

"Any change?" he asked.

"Nothing good," was her only answer.

Lindstrom didn't even bother asking what she meant but watched her move to the rear to check on the patients.

All were out cold except for Kennedy, who had been sleeping fitfully. Her whispered conversation with the groggy man alarmed Nils.

"How're you feeling?"

"Been better."

She crouched down so they were face-to-face. "I want you to know something." Con just looked at her and she continued, "You're the best man and best friend I've ever known. I'm grateful for every day we had together."

Kennedy took a moment then asked weakly, "Am I dying?"

"No way. I would never let that happen to you. You know that." She clasped him on the arm and held his hand briefly, watching him fall back to sleep before moving to the front of shuttle.

Lindstrom observed her activity in puzzlement. She took one of the extra-long, heavy wrenches and stuck it in the straps that crisscrossed her back, used for holding a daypack. He wondered if the stress had gotten to her when she started stretching her legs as if preparing to go for a run. He went to talk to her. In an undertone, so as not to alarm Aqila, he asked, "What are you doing?"

When she looked at him, he noticed her jaw was firmly set. "I'm going out there."

"Out there? Are you *crazy*?"

"No. There's three of them now. They're gonna make it through that hull before dawn – it looks to me like they're gonna get through it within the hour. You know how badly it was damaged by the crash and their jaws are...formidable. We won't stand a chance in this confined space. Especially the wounded."

"If the storm stops, *Lovelace* can—"

"Commander, we both know that's a very long shot."

220

"So, what's your plan? Fight three of them single-handedly with a wrench?"

"No, the wrench is insurance. I'm gonna run."

"Run? That's your plan?"

"If they act like most hunting animals, their instinct will be to give chase. From what Aqila told us, they're not that fast. I just have to stay ahead of them."

"For how long? All night? You can't do that."

"Our species, ours and his...." She nodded towards Kay. "...invented persistence hunting. One thing we're both good at is running long distances for long times. We'll run towards where dawn will be breaking. It's our best chance for survival."

"You don't even know how many more might join the chase."

"You're right, I don't, but we're all out of options." Decker shook her head at him. "Commander, you know it; this is the only way."

"Then I'm going with you. We'll stand a better chance togeth—"

"I appreciate that, sir, but I think you need to stay here in case more of them come. It seems to me that they're following the blood trails here, so they might. Then—"

"I'll get my chance," he finished.

"Yes, sir." He watched her gather herself for a second, and then she quickly unzipped her jacket. Decker removed the ever-present necklace and handed it to Lindstrom. "Do me a favor, give this to the captain. He'll understand." She smiled sadly and said, "Tell him I'm glad that we...." She paused and blinked, as her eyes were growing wet. "Tell him I'm glad we made up." Lindstrom was too choked up to say anything. She turned to Kay and said, "Come on, Kayatennae, we're going for a run."

221

Suddenly Decker's path was blocked by Aqila; she'd obviously been listening. "I'm not going to let you do this."

"Aqila, please—"

Lateef nodded towards Kennedy. "He'll never get over it if you—"

"Yes, he will. He'll remember that he's the one who trained me to be a soldier." Aqila started crying. Decker put both hands on her shoulders, saying, "It's all right. It really is...." With a shaky breath, she finished, "I always knew I was gonna die young. All the women in my family do." She gave Aqila a quick hug and whispered, "Good-bye."

Without further comment, she quietly opened the emergency hatch and hoisted Kay through it. The agile dog silently climbed out onto the shuttle roof. Decker followed him, pausing only to salute Lindstrom, saying, "Commander, it's been a genuine honor."

He could offer nothing more in return than, "The honor was mine."

Decker disappeared through the hatch. They heard two muffled thumps that must have been the woman and dog jumping down on the opposite side of the shuttle. The last sound they heard from Decker was a whooping call off in the distance. The gnawing outside stopped. The creatures had given chase.

***

One hour and forty-nine minutes later, Lindstrom knew exactly because he'd done nothing but watch the chrono and listen intently for the sound of more creatures, the radio crackled to life. It was Leticia Evans, calling from *Lovelace*. "Shuttle L3, come in, this is the *Lovelace*. Shuttle L3, do you copy?"

Lindstrom leapt to answer. "*Lovelace*, this is shuttle L3. We copy. Is the ion storm over?"

It was Ricci who replied. "Negative. According to Scientific, it's only a break in it, but we wanted to take the opportunity check in on you. How are you holding up?"

"Very badly. We've been attacked by an indigenous species. Grieveson and Modi are dead. Kennedy, Perham, and Abello are badly injured. We've sustained heavy damage to the shuttle – it's inoperable. I need you to get medical personnel down here immediately if it's at all feasible."

"Hang on," was all Matt said.

The next thing he heard was Rita asking, "What are the injuries? Let me talk to Decker."

"She's not here."

"Where the hell is she?" Ricci barked.

"She's out—" Lindstrom paused. "Captain, I'd really rather explain that part in person. Can we risk getting a shuttle down here?"

"Consider it done."

"Ensure that the tactical personnel have non-energy weapons. We might need them."

In a puzzled voice, Ricci said, "Copy that. *Lovelace* out."

When the shuttle landed, even though it was strictly against protocol for the captain to join a mission where the first officer was already present, Lindstrom felt he shouldn't have been surprised to see Ricci emerge. He was more relieved to see Rita, one of her nurses, and the three tactical specialists armed with some of the rare projectile weapons available onboard.

They all crowded into the crippled shuttle as the ion storm resumed outside, worse than ever. Rita and the nurse saw to the patients while Lindstrom filled the others in on the grim story; he could barely look at Ricci as he relayed the last part, about Decker. Nils handed him the necklace; as Matt's hand closed around it, he thought he'd never before seen a more heartbroken man.

"You should have stopped her!"

"I tried."

Aqila stepped in. "We both did. She just wouldn't listen. She said—" Lateef couldn't finish through her tears.

"What? She said what?"

"She said that she knew she would die young...." In a near whisper, she finished, "All the women in her family do."

"Like hell they do." Matt turned towards the closed hatch. "I'm going after her."

Lindstrom blocked his path. "Captain, have you lost your mind? We have no idea where she is, which direction—"

"I've got to try!"

"I am not going to allow this." He grabbed Ricci by the arm. "Stop and think about what you're doing. I know what she means to you—"

"No, you don't."

"Of course, I do." He looked him in the eye and said very deliberately, "I really do, Matt."

Ricci's head whipped around. He glared at Clemente. "I thought better of you, Doctor." She was too busy to pay him any mind.

"What does Rita have to do with it? I figured it out myself."

The two men were shouting by now and all aboard the shuttle clearly heard the next exchange.

"You figured it out?"

"Yes!"

"You figured out *all on your own* that Naiche is my daughter?"

224

"Yes! I figured out...." Suddenly Lindstrom comprehended what Ricci had just said. Aghast, he demanded, "What? She's your...daughter!?"

Lateef was staring open-mouthed at the captain while Clemente left the nurse in charge of the patients and made her way over to them. She shook her head and said quietly, "Right now, I really don't know which of you is the bigger idiot."

***

Dawn was nearing by the time captain and first officer were able to sit calmly in the rear passenger seats of the L2 shuttle and talk quietly.

Lindstrom was still pondering the recent revelation. "She's really your daughter?"

"Yes."

"She doesn't look anything like you."

"No, she doesn't."

"But the necklace...she wanted you to have her mother's...oh, you knew her mother...."

With mounting irritation, Matt demanded, "Do you need a refresher course in human reproduction, Lindstrom?" When Nils just slumped back against his seat in response, Ricci asked, "If you didn't know Naiche was my daughter, what did you mean when you said—"

"I'd really rather not discuss that, Captain." His eyes were on the necklace Matt was still clutching. "You know, I do think she might have made it."

"She didn't think so."

"Well, in the months I've known her, I've learned two things about that young woman."

"What's that?"

"The first is, they don't come any tougher and the second is...." He paused and then finished with the trace of an encouraging smile, "She's been wrong about a lot of things."

Just then Ensign Bayer, who had been monitoring the scanner, abruptly announced, "The storm's over!"

Ricci sprang into action. "Bayer, get this thing in the air. Scan for life signs – human."

Lindstrom stayed behind with the L3 shuttle, awaiting rescue from the L1 shuttle, while Ricci, Bayer, and Clemente went out in search of Decker. For an hour, Matt's eyes hadn't strayed from the scanner, desperately willing it to chirp. Finally, as if in answer to his whispered, "Come on, come on, come on, Naiche," it did.

"We've got it, Captain!" Bayer said. "It's weak but it's somewhere over there."

They scanned the black rocky area, but Decker was nowhere to be seen. Upon exiting the shuttle, they heard it – from up above, the thin wail of a howling dog.

After climbing the rocky hill, they found Decker, passed out, and wedged into a narrow opening in the rock. Clemente went to work with her medical scanner. "She's received some major lacerations and lost some blood but she's not in critical condition." She looked up at Ricci. "It looks like she's suffering more from exhaustion and dehydration than anything else."

Decker's hand was still curled around the wrench; it was covered in sticky yellow fluid, obviously from one of the creatures she'd fought off. Kay had gashes on his face and torso and was limping badly.

"Okay, Bayer," the captain said. "Let's get these two back to *Lovelace* ASAP."

226

***

Decker slowly edged into consciousness; she immediately recognized the pinging sounds of the monitors in Med-Bay. It wasn't the first time she'd awoken in this condition, but it was as disorienting as ever. She heard Clemente say, "She's coming around!"

By the time Deck felt up to opening her eyes, she found Clemente, Ricci, and Lindstrom all looking down at her. "What the hell happened?"

Clemente asked, "You don't remember?"

"No."

Lindstrom said, "Well, you're a hero. Does that help?"

"Umm...." she searched her memory and the previous twelve hours came flooding back. She sprang up saying, "Oh God, Con, is he okay?"

"Yes, he's in the next room. Now lay your ass back down," Ricci growled.

She didn't immediately obey, instead asking, "Kay! Is he—"

"Yes!" Clemente said. "Con's going to be fine, Kay is fine—"

Ricci pushed her back down while interjecting, "And by some absolute fucking miracle you're alive, too."

Lindstrom looked over at the doctor. "You know, Rita, I think we should give Decker some private time with her father."

Decker faced him, forcing out a weak laugh. "With my *what*?"

"Your father."

"Where did you get a crazy idea like that?"

"From me," Matt answered.

"Oh."

"And by the way, your grandmother is still alive."

"What?"

"And both of my sisters, too. Not that they're *that* old...."

She thought for a second before asking, "I missed something didn't I?"

"Yes," Rita laughed. "Your dad will fill you in. Come on, Nils, let's go."

When they left, Decker looked up at Ricci and asked, "Am I in trouble?"

He nodded, answering, "Yes." Matt leaned his forearms on the bed rail and smiled wearily at her. "Situation normal, in other words."

***

Aqila beamed at Con, while scraping the bottom of the bowl of soup she'd been feeding him. "Looks like you ate it all, champ."

"Yes, I can eat a bowl of soup. Yay, me."

"Don't make fun of your progress; you're doing great, Doctor Clemente said."

"Yes, maybe tomorrow I can eat it all by myself." She offered him some water from the cup on the bedside table. As he sipped it, he said, "You know, there are nurses, if there's something else you have to be doing—"

"There's nothing I'd rather be doing. Why? Are you trying to get rid of me?"

"Well...no man likes to appear weak in front of the woman he loves."

"Weak! I watched you fight off those—" She stopped mid-sentence and said, "Wait a minute, did you just say...that you love me?"

He shot her a cocky grin. "Yes, I think I did."

"Conroy Kennedy! What a way to tell me."

He laid back down as he answered, "Thank you, I thought it was rather inspired."

"You know if you weren't already hurt...."

"Yes?"

"Never mind." She leaned down and kissed him on the forehead, whispering, "I love you, too." With one hand, Aqila gently stroked the side of his face. "I hope it didn't take a near-death experience for you to figure this out."

"No. Deck told me a while ago; I was just trying to figure out how to tell—"

"Wait – how does that work?! Deck told *you*, that you were in love with *me*?"

"Yeah, she knows me just that well."

Lateef felt her exasperation fade easily away when she couldn't help but laugh at Con's response. She sat back down but slipped her hand through the bed rails so she could hold onto his arm. After musing for a few seconds, she asked, "You know Deck equally well, right?"

"Of course."

"Meaning you know about her father?"

"The sperm donor?"

A few minutes later Decker, who was in Con's room at least ten times a day, appeared in the doorway holding up a small cup. "Hey, you want my tapioca? I hate this glop."

Aqila really wished she'd been able to take a holo of Deck's face when, rather than answering the question, Con bellowed, "Ricci is YOUR FATHER?!"

Lateef got up and pointed at her chair. "Have a seat, Lieutenant. You've got some explaining to do."

***

Naiche slid into the proffered seat and smiled guiltily at Con. "So...." she drawled. "How're you feeling? You look a lot better."

Kennedy pulled himself into a more upright position and shook his head at her. "I probably look about the same as I did when you were in here this morning – telling me everything but the one thing that mattered."

"I've never told *anyone* the truth about me and him. And for the record, Ricci and I *did* have a run-in my first year at The Rock so that wasn't exactly a lie."

"It wasn't exactly the truth, either."

"No, it wasn't," Deck admitted softly.

"Were you ever planning to tell me? I mean, now that everyone on this ship knows."

"Of course, I was!"

"Then why the hell did I have to hear it from Aqila?"

Seeing that she'd hurt Con with her reticence was an arrow to the heart for Naiche, and she struggled to explain herself. "I wanted to tell you this morning, that was my plan, but...." She reached over and briefly grasped his hand. "But I didn't know how to start. I didn't know how to explain why I'd never told you before." Deck shrugged. "How can I explain something I don't really understand myself?"

"With anyone else, I might take that for bullshit but with you...." Con's sigh was laced with mild exasperation.

"Yeah, I guess I've never been big on self-reflection."

"Well, how 'bout giving it a try? It's gotta be less painful than fighting off three energy alligators by yourself."

"I wasn't alone; I had Kay. And it was only one of them. The other two dropped off about—"

"Stop trying to change the subject."

230

"All right...." Decker nodded in recognition of Con's perceptivity. She quieted her mind and made space for some long-buried truths to surface. "I guess I never told you – or anyone else – because...because I didn't want to claim him."

"You didn't want to claim Ricci as your father?"

"Yeah. If he didn't wanta' be my father, well then, I didn't wanta' be his daughter. When I was little, he didn't want anything to do with me but when I got to the UDC he started acting like he had some goddamn right to—" Deck paused to check the primal anger that still automatically arose in her regarding this subject. "Anyway...I guess I never wanted to talk about...how fucked up things were between me and the man who...between me and him. Especially since everyone else in the UDC thought he was such a great guy. Even you."

"Oh, Deck," Con breathed. "That must've felt awful, knowing that. I'm sorry—"

"No," she said, waving her hand in a gesture of negation. "Save your sympathy. Turns out, I was wrong about him. And I was wrong about...my grandfather. Ricci's not some demon, *shitsúyé* wasn't some saint—" She stopped abruptly, closing her eyes briefly and taking a deep breath. "I mean...he made a mistake. A well-intentioned one but...still, a mistake." Deck exhaled in bitter amusement as she declared, "So, I was wrong. Once again, Naiche Decker is wrong about *everything!*"

"You're not wrong about *everything*. You just have to stop trying to put people into little boxes marked: 'demon, saint, good, bad'. *No one* is all bad or all good—"

"Like hell! You are. All good."

"No, I'm not." Con shook his head and said forcefully, "How can you even say that? After Cat. What I did to you – or didn't do...."

231

"That wasn't your fault." Deck wiped the side of her hand across her forehead and swallowed thickly. "I should *never* have asked you to help her out. That was my job—"

"Goddamn it! No, it wasn't," he insisted angrily.

"Look, I'm not going to fight with you about this." She stopped and tilted her head back and to the side in an effort to keep the tears from falling. "You need to understand – the main thing that helped me get through...it, was knowing that I spared you from...." Naiche just shook her head, unable to do more than repeat, "Knowing that I spared *you*."

Con's eyes were wet now, too, and he seemed too choked up to speak. Finally, he said, "I really don't know what I did to deserve a friend like you."

Decker smiled through her tears and said, "I don't know either – but it must've been pretty awful. Maybe you *aren't* all good." Glad to see Con manage a shaky laugh, Deck asked, "How the hell did we get on this subject anyway? We were supposed to be talking about me and Ricci."

Kennedy offered up a fond smile and said, "Okay then, why don't we do that? Tell me all about...you and him."

"It's kind of a long, convoluted story."

"That's fine. I got nothing to do but sit here and eat your tapioca pudding – and listen."

Deck said, "Okay. I guess I should start at the beginning." She let Con pick up the cup of pudding and start eating before she launched into her tale. "I was five years old when *shimáá* first told me about my father...."

Chapter 17

On the Road to the Stars

"The Moon is the first milestone on the road to the stars."
Arthur C. Clarke

Two days later at 0700, Ricci and Lindstrom where having their usual morning debrief. Lindstrom was explaining, "Perham won't be back on duty for at least two weeks; Abello can be on desk duty about that same time but a permanent replacement hand will have to wait until we're back home. Kennedy should be fit for duty a little sooner – probably ten more days, and *as I'm sure you already know*, Decker was released for full duty today."

Ricci must have noticed Lindstrom's emphasis and said, "If there's something you want to say to me about her, then just come right out and say it."

"Okay." Lindstrom sat back, crossed his arms, and unloaded. "You should have told me, Matt. I'm your first officer; that was information I deserved to have."

With only a brief glance his way, Ricci answered, "It's not like I'm the father of record and I didn't help raise the girl."

If Ricci had just told him to fuck off, Lindstrom would have been less incensed by his response. "Save that line of bullshit for the admiralty, okay?" he retorted. The captain was still refusing to meet his eye. "After all these years, I would have thought you trusted me enough—"

Matt finally looked up and assured him, "I do. You know that. It wasn't a question of trust."

"Then what?"

He paused briefly before answering, "Shame, I guess."

"You were ashamed of fathering a child?"

His voice tinged with fury, Ricci snapped, "I was ashamed of *not* fathering her – all because I didn't want a wife and child slowing me down. I threw away the woman I loved and my daughter for the sake of my ambition!" Biting off every word, he added, "It's not exactly my proudest moment."

Suddenly Lindstrom realized he had pressed on a still open wound. "Oh, Matt," he murmured. "You were...what? Twenty?" When Ricci nodded, Nils continued, "Show me a man who's not some kind of an idiot at twenty and I'll show you...."

"What?"

"Nothing, 'cause that man doesn't exist." Nils stood up and clasped Matt on the shoulder. "Give yourself a break. Seems to me like you've already paid enough for the decision that a very young man made."

Ricci shook his head. "Naiche paid." He held up his right hand. "I got the pretty gold braid on my wrists."

"I still hold that you both paid – one way or another. And it's time to stop." Nils lounged against the wall.

234

"Decker's here now, part of your life. And all in all, she turned out to be a damned fine human being."

"I don't think I can take any credit for that."

"I don't know," he drawled. "Ever since I found out, I've been thinking it sure explains *a lot*. She seems to have inherited most of her...*personality* from you."

Lindstrom was glad to see Ricci come out of his funk and observe sharply, "Why, thank you, Commander. I'll take that as the compliment you undoubtedly meant it to be."

"Of course, sir," Nils answered with a grin and turned to leave. "I guess you know the ship is abuzz about this."

"Yeah, I figured." Matt leaned back in his chair. "It gives the crew something to talk about besides the fact that we've been in this star system for weeks now and all we've found so far is some murderous night lizards."

***

After the disastrous encounter on the desert planet, the *Lovelace* fruitlessly explored the MC system for two more weeks. The restless crew had long been bracing for the encounter with the Pakarahova but had apparently been unprepared to find...nothing. Nerves were fraying.

Con, Aqila, and Bly were eating dinner in the mess hall and watching Deck wend her way towards them with her tray. As she passed a table of engineers, one called out, "Hey Decker, why don't you ask *your daddy* how much longer we're gonna be wandering around aimlessly?"

She turned on her heel and said, "I don't know why you're complaining, Fisk. Wandering around aimlessly would seem to be all your four brain cells can handle."

Fisk unfolded his massive frame from his chair and started towards Decker. His CO, Avery, grabbed him and

235

said, "Sit down. As entertaining as it would be to watch her lay you out, I don't wanta' deal with filling out all those forms."

When Deck got to the table, she sat down with a sigh, closed her eyes, and moaned, "Why, why, why, did Ricci have to let *everyone* know?"

Aqila said, "It was a very emotionally charged moment. You can hardly blame him for—"

"I know, I know." She shook her head and said glumly, "You'd think by now I'd be used to being considered as nothing more than somebody better's kid."

While Con was exchanging a significant look with Aqila, she said, "It's not that *at all*. The news is just a novelty right now. People will get their fill of the gossip and move onto something else soon enough."

Bly said, "Well...at least now you know who your father is...right? That's something."

"Uh...." Deck answered while rolling her eyes. "I've always known."

Bly tapped her chest and said, "Oh, deep down inside, you've always known?"

"No. My mother told me when I was a little girl, so I've always known."

"But you told us your father was a sperm donor?"

"Yeah...see...it's a very complicated...well, for the longest time...."

Con came to her rescue. "Deck and Ricci had to come to terms with what was a very...dynamic relationship themselves before they could talk about it with anyone else."

"There you go," Deck said, waving her hand at Con. "My emotional translator."

Just then, Con spied Ricci entering the mess hall with his own tray. "Speak of the devil."

Con tried to get his attention while Deck was whispering, "Don't you dare wave him over, Conroy Kennedy, I will kill you where you sit; I swear I will."

Privately, Con thought it was ridiculous the way Deck and Ricci had avoided socializing in public since their relationship had become general knowledge. He was about to put a stop to it. He whispered back, "It's like ripping off a bandage, Deck. Just get it over with."

The captain had seen them and was now headed their way. Once at the table, he stopped and cleared his throat. "Mind if I join you?"

"It would be a pleasure, sir. Please." Con waved his hand at an open seat, aware that every eye in the room was on their table but doggedly ignoring that fact, as was Aqila. Bly, however, was taking full notice and as for Deck, well, he'd literally seen her face death with less apparent anxiety. He looked over at Ricci. *Oh, that's where she gets it.*

Ricci sat down and nodded at everyone. With a stiffness Con wouldn't have believed possible, he said, "Good evening. Hope all are well." Con thought, *What have I gotten myself into? Now I'm responsible for two of them.*

Everyone answered in the affirmative, even Deck managing to mumble, "Just fine, sir."

"So...what were you all just talking about?"

Bly started chocking on a mouthful of potatoes. While glaring at her, Deck suddenly announced, "Bly won't shut up about that ice moon she wants to visit."

That had actually been the topic of conversation the night before, so Bly looked at her blankly. "What?"

"Yes, the ice moon, Bly," Aqila insisted, while Con managed to not break out in hysterical giggles, but just barely. "Now is your chance to make your case."

"Ohh, the ice moon," Brodie said.

237

By now, Ricci was smiling broadly. "Well, I've heard the term 'ice moon' three times now. Want to fill me in?"

"There's a moon orbiting one of the outer planets that has some very unique physical properties, Captain. Not least of which is that it seems to have an internal luminosity."

"Like Dione?" Ricci asked, naming one of Saturn's moons. "That's where we get Dionian moonstone from." He and Decker exchanged the briefest of smiles and Con finally relaxed, knowing for the first time, he'd done the right thing in asking the captain to dine with them.

"That's what I was thinking," Brodie said. "But the light spectrum doesn't match any known element. We might be looking at either a new element or a new source of chemiluminescence."

"And you'd like to check it out?"

"Very much so," Bly said, earnestly. "I know our mission is the most import—"

"Well," Ricci drawled. "Considering how little of interest we've turned up in MC so far, I think we can spare a few hours for you to take some scans and samples."

"Oh, thank you, Captain," Brodie gushed. She nudged Decker. "See, it does help having a father in high places!"

Aqila was visibly cringing; Con was almost afraid to look at Decker but when he did, he was relieved to see her laughing. She looked at Ricci and to the general confusion of the others said, "And you wondered how *I* survived this long?"

***

The *Lovelace* had arrived at the ice moon which so fascinated Ensign Brodie. It was small and cold and devoid of all life, but it definitely had an odd, ghostly gray glow to it, deep in the impenetrable center. It yielded no great secrets to the scans from the ship, but Bly was determined to take close range scans and samples of the ice. Aqila had originally planned to go as well but at the last minute decided to let Kaplita go in her place since he had experience at extracting ice core samples. Decker volunteered to fly the shuttle over and Con was going as much for something to do as any real tactical reason.

Kennedy spent most of the morning giving Bly some last-minute pointers in the low-O suits and the landing party headed over. The surface was slick and smooth as cold marble. The four explorers moved about carefully for the first hour before they become comfortable with navigating the moon.

Con was helping Kaplita extract and label the ice core samples; Deck was assisting where required, while trying to keep an eye on Brodie who was darting everywhere with her scanner. "I don't understand the light source at all," Bly said over the comms. "Nothing is adding up." She skated over to Decker and said, "I want to check out the north side – I saw a crater there, the floor is much closer to the moon's center. Maybe I can determine something from that. And there must have been an impact event that caused it."

"Okay, I'm coming with you." She let Kennedy and Kaplita know where they were going and then followed Bly to the crater.

Once there, they used their power packs to navigate down into what looked like an immense bowl carved into the surface. They were surrounded by walls of semi-translucent ice. When they looked down, it seemed as if the gray light was visible deep in the center of the moon, far below them. Above them was the dark sky. Decker suddenly felt that she had entered another dimension, in this ghostly gray cavern of shimmering ice.

Brodie looked around saying, "Oh my God, this is the coolest thing I've ever seen." She proceeded to scan for signs of the chemiluminescence that she suspected was behind the moon's glow.

"It is beautiful, isn't it?" Decker said as she contacted Kennedy over the comm link. "Hey, you really should come see this. It's...unworldly."

"Well, I guess so, we're not on a world," he answered with a laugh.

"Okay then, wise guy, you can just see the holo-vids." Decker turned her scanner on and started recording.

"Let me help Mars get these samples onto the shuttle, then I'll come and take a quick look. We're supposed to be back soon."

"I know, but you really gotta see this."

A few minutes later Kennedy joined them and asked, "Wow, what the hell caused this? Impact crater?"

"I don't know," Bly said. "None of the scans match up with what I would expect from an impact crater."

Con said, "I think Aqila's going to be sorry she missed this."

Just then Decker asked, "Is the light moving up the walls?"

"It is!" Bly exclaimed. "Awesome!"

All three of them watched transfixed as the walls started to glow stronger and stronger with the gray light until they shimmered and pulsed with it. They stared open-mouthed as the light appeared to coalesce in a ceiling above them and they were completely surrounded by it.

Deck was staring up at it and the hair started to stand up on the back of her neck. It looked familiar; it looked like.... "Con," she said, trying but failing to keep the panic out of her voice. "What does that light look like?"

Kennedy stared silently for a second and then reached over and gripped her arm as if steadying himself. "It can't be...that's *impossible*." He started repeating quietly, "Okay, okay, okay." Deck wasn't sure if he was trying to calm her, himself, or both. Evenly, Kennedy said, "I'll just tune my scanner...and check it out. And then we'll see...it's just our imaginations."

Her mouth had gone so dry that Deck couldn't even form words, so she silently watched Con reach for his scanner and tune it to detect eprion signatures. They stared in hushed horror as the signal immediately jumped off the scale.

At last, Brodie turned and must have noticed the tactical officers' stricken figures. "Is something wrong?"

Decker found it in herself to answer after a second or two. "Yeah, something's really fucking wrong."

***

Ricci was on the bridge getting impatient for the shuttle to return from the ice moon. Brodie had promised a two-hour trip at most and it was edging into three. "Lateef, contact your landing party and see what their ETA is."

"Yes, sir." She tuned the comm on her console to reach Kennedy's channel. "Con, it's Aqila. Are you guys heading back soon?"

Every ear on the bridge perked up at Kennedy's panicked response. "We have a situation here."

"What? What's wrong?"

"Scan this moon for eprion signatures."

"What? We already swept this area, weeks ago. Why would we—"

"Please, Aqila, just do it."

Ricci came over to the Science console. "Did he just ask you to—"

"Yes, he did." Without further comment, Lateef did as Kennedy had requested. By then Lindstrom had joined them at the console and all three watched in shock as her scanner read out more eprion signatures than could be quantified.

Ricci leaned over and barked into the comms, "Kennedy, report! What the hell is going on over there?"

"We're surrounded by a wall of eprions, Captain."

"What?"

"Aqila, pick up the feed from Deck's scanner. Put it on screen there." Lateef did as Kennedy suggested. The bridge crew had suddenly had a picture of what the landing party was seeing.

When Ricci said, "Holy fucking shit!" the entire bridge could only agree.

Chapter 18

By a Foe

"The truth is forced upon us, very quickly, by a foe."
Aristophanes

The tense situation on the moon had stretched to an hour. *Lovelace* was at DEFCON-alpha and the bridge was in both visual and audio contact with the trapped landing party. Aqila was in frequent communication with Kaplita on the shuttle, but there was nothing he could do to rescue the stranded trio without wading into a sea of eprions himself. At this point, the bridge was just listening to the conversation between Kennedy and Decker who had either forgotten that the bridge was listening in or didn't care. Brodie was completely silent.

Deck said, "If they get me first, you'll do it, won't you, Con? You've got your pulse pistol, right?"

"Yeah, I do, and yeah, I will. You know I will."

"I know. And you know I'll—"

"No doubt in my mind."

"And then I'm gonna turn my suit off so they can't get me without someone to…help me out."

"Yeah, that's my plan, too." There was silence for a moment then Con said, "We should ask Bly what she wants us to do in case…."

Decker looked over at Bly who seemed transfixed by the sight of the swirls of gray light. She asked, "Bly, how do want us to handle it if they…if they infect you?"

There was no response and Con said, "Give her a few minutes to think it over."

***

Ricci was steeling himself not to cry on his own bridge; Aqila had no such compunction and was weeping openly. Lindstrom appeared at Matt's elbow. "If you need me to take command briefly so you can—"

Matt blinked the tears back from his eyes and said, "Thanks, Nils, but I'm not going anywhere. If they can stand it, so can I."

They could hear Decker asking, "How the hell can they just keep floating around free like that? I thought they needed…."

"A host, I know," Con answered. "What're they waiting for? Fuck, I can't take this much longer."

For a long time, there was no answer from Decker. Finally, she offered a non sequitur. "This must be what happened with Cat."

"What?" Con said.

"Cat. A free-floating eprion must've got her." Decker's voice brightened a bit as she said, "Maybe I didn't miss it."

"You didn't miss what?"

244

"I gave the all clear that day, don't you remember? I did the recon from the air and I gave the all clear for Eat life signs. Maybe it wasn't my fault after all."

"Deck, have you been blaming yourself all this time?"

Her voice fell to a whisper as she admitted, "Yeah. I guess I was."

Ricci vowed to himself that every admiral who had decided to keep the information about the full capabilities of the eprions from the troops was going to get a copy of this conversation wrapped up with a bow. And if that alone didn't cause the shame to follow them to their graves, well, then Matt planned to help them out with that.

Decker said, "Better see if Bly made up her mind." She called out, "Hey Brodie, what do you want us to do if they get you? Do you wanta' go over the hill or do you want us to...to help you out?" Again, there was no reply. "Bly, you need to tell us. We won't do it for you unless you let us know...that's what you want."

At this point Lateef put her head down on her folded arms and sobbed, and Lindstrom dashed an arm across his eyes.

All of a sudden, Bly spoke for the first time since they had been trapped by the eprions. "Binary."

Everyone on the bridge stared at one another unsure they'd heard correctly. Con said, "What? What does that—"

"They're blinking in binary. Don't you see it? I thought there was a pattern and there is."

In a whisper, Decker said, "Oh God...Bly's lost it. Can't blame the poor kid—"

"I think they're trying to communicate with us," Bly insisted.

Con asked, "Who's trying to communicate with us?"

"The eprions."

Decker's disbelief was palpable as she confirmed, "You think the wall of disease is trying to talk to us?!"

Bly didn't seem to hear her and was mumbling, "I can rig up a binary translator on my hand-held...let me see."

The stunned silence stretched from the frozen moon to the bridge of the *Lovelace*. No one blamed the young ensign for completely going over the edge, but no one knew what to say about it either.

After a few minutes Brodie said, "Oh, they want to know what we're doing here."

On the bridge, Aqila hit the comm to Brodie and said, "Bly, who wants to know what—"

Con's incredulous voice broke in. "Are you trying to say the eprions are *talking to you*? In binary?"

"Yes. Uh, got another message...let me see...huh, they want us to leave."

Deck said, "Okay. This is nuts but go ahead and tell them...wait, how do you say, 'get the fuck outta' my way' in binary?"

Ricci leaned into the comm at Lateef's station and said, "Ensign Brodie, are you quite certain that...you're having an actual dialogue with these...things?"

"Well, so far it's been one way, sir," answered Brodie. "Let me check if I can send something to them. I'm gonna ask if they can understand me." On the screen they could see Bly's hand-held flashing out a message in binary to her surroundings. Then everyone, on moon and bridge, waited breathlessly. Finally, Bly said, "Yep. They do. I'm gonna ask them to move back so we can get to the shuttle."

Brodie flashed out another message followed by another moment of silence then Con said, "Oh my God, it worked." On the moon and on the scanner feed, the gray

246

swirls of light could be seen retreating below the surface once again.

Con and Deck hurried to evacuate from the crater, but Bly was lagging behind. "Brodie," Con yelled. "We're moving out. What are you doing?"

"I'm asking if we can talk some more...once we're back on the *Lovelace*."

Kennedy barked, "Ensign, get your ass—"

Aqila broke in to say, "No, Con, she's right. We need to...well, we need to talk to these things. If we can."

Decker exclaimed, "Okay, have Con and I transformed, and this is actually what happens or has everyone else gone completely insane?"

Bly only responded, "They said yes! Deck, leave your scanner here so we'll be able to see them. We can go now."

***

The next day, Ensign Brodie and Lt. Commander Sasaki were on the bridge, addressing the command staff together. Jeff was saying, "So, with Ensign Brodie's assistance, I was able to rig up this translator. It should enable us to speak with...the eprions."

Ricci asked, "I just talk and it translates my speech to binary code flashes?"

"Yes, and it will translate their flashes into speech that you'll be able to hear."

The captain turned to crew and said, "Okay, here goes nothing." He said to Sasaki, "Turn it on, Commander." Ricci looked at the translator doubtfully for a second then said, "I'm Captain Matteo Ricci of the Uniterrae Defense Corps. Can you understand me?"

A synthetic voice answered, "We can."

"Who are you?"

"We are the Pakarahova."

The reactions to that statement on the bridge ranged all the way from Decker's "What the fuck?" to Brodie's, "I knew it."

The synthetic voice continued, "You are human?"

Ricci answered, "Yes, we are."

"We cannot bond with humans. It is forbidden. There is nothing we can do for you. You need to leave."

"Not so fast," Matt objected. "Some of your...kind have been attacking humans for hundreds of—"

"We do not attack. We bond with permission and help species such as yours escape your prison of meat and become like us."

Ricci mouthed 'prison of meat' at Lindstrom who just shrugged helplessly. Ricci spoke into the translator with a slight edge to his tone, "Yeah, well, that's not what's been happening. Two hundred years ago, some of our people, on a ship called *Intrepid*, met up with some Pakarahova—"

"We know what occurred. When we bonded with humans, at first, all seemed well, but your kind refused to ascend at the proper time. You reject the beauty of pure consciousness and cling to your organic forms since the bond gives vast knowledge and extends your lifespan. You become arrogant and obsessed with power. You thwart our mission."

"What is your mission?"

"Since before there was time, Pakarahova have existed. As organic species have formed and gained consciousness, we have made it our mission to do what we can to preserve that consciousness. We have enabled many species to become like us. That is how we grow our numbers. Humans are our only failure. You are unsuited for—"

"We didn't ask you to force your way into our minds and transform us into monsters!"

"We cannot force. Pakarahova can bond only with permission."

Decker suddenly yelled out, "That's a lie! I've seen it with my own eyes. You infect people against their will. They scream and they fight—"

"Sometimes the bond is painful at first, but permission is always given during the initial meld."

"Liars!" Deck insisted.

Lateef said, "No, wait, they may be telling the truth. That's why some people were resistant! They didn't want the bond."

"That is correct," the Pakarahova answered.

Ricci observed, "Hold on, originally you said that bonding with humans was forbidden. How did you allow the situation with the *Intrepid* crew to happen in the first place?"

"It became forbidden once we observed how you infect us who bond with you."

His tone spiked with outrage, Kennedy asked, "Wait – we infect *you*?"

"Yes. Those who bonded with humans became addicted to the form. They do not listen to us. Even when freed, they keep finding humans to bond with. Pakarahova and human has proved to be a most unsuccessful association."

Decker looked at Sasaki and asked, "Don't they have a term for fucking disaster of cosmos-ending proportions?"

Ricci said, "Is there no recourse available to you to fix this...unsuccessful association, which after all, you had equal responsibility for starting?"

"We have gathered here on our home for just that purpose. There is a solution, but it is an unacceptable one. We have been pondering the situation for this short while."

"Short while!? It's been two-hundred years!" Each word ascended in volume with increasing disbelief on Ricci's part.

"Captain," Lateef said, in a whispered aside. "They are billions of years old. Two-hundred years is the blink of an eye to them."

"Well, isn't that special?" Ricci turned back to the translator. "In *the short while* you've been pondering your solution, infected humans – or infected Pakarahova – however you want to look at it, have inflicted indescribable misery on...on many people, many species."

"We are aware. These organic species have such a short time to begin with; some did not have consciousness yet worth preserving. A little time less...can it make such a difference?"

Decker broke in, "That's it. How do you kill a beam of light?"

Ricci waved a hand at her to tell her to calm down and said, "The unacceptable solution you mentioned, what is it?"

"We could recall our infected members by force. They would not survive the process. This is in direct conflict with our mission to preserve pure consciousness."

"Look, aren't they lost to you either way?"

"You may be correct. Yet, we still hold out hope for them."

"In the meantime, they're causing the destruction of many beings. An entire conscious species looks to have been wiped out. Is that not also in opposition to your mission?"

"Yes, that is why this is a grave decision. It cannot be rushed."

Ricci threw up his hands in a gesture of disgust and frustration. He took a deep breath and tried again. "I know our time seems like *nothing* to you but it's…everything to us. Our friends, our family who are dying, who we are losing every day, are *everything* to us. If you could just feel what we feel…."

There was a long silence but finally the translator spoke. "Are you suggesting a meld?"

"What?"

"A Pakarahova who melds with an organic does experience their…emotions during the meld."

Ricci said, "No, we have no desire for this bond—"

"A meld is not a bond. We will not bond with humans ever again. Only during the meld are the emotions transferred from organic to Pakarahova. Only the Pakarahova who melds experiences this. It is not transferred back to us until that Pakarahova rejoins the whole."

"No, we couldn't risk even—"

"I'll do it!" Decker said, rushing up to Ricci's side.

Ricci said, "Naiche, no. You can't possibly mean—"

"No, let them *feel it*. Let them know what they did to me. What they took from me."

"No." Matt turned her to face him directly. "I will not allow this. No."

"Then I'll do it," Lindstrom announced.

"Nils, why?" Ricci asked.

"Because she's right. Let them feel what I felt, what I suffered when Ilse died."

"Me, too," said Con. "Let one of them feel what ten years of this war did to me, took from me, continues to take from me."

Ricci said, "No, enough of this! If anyone is going to do this – it's me. It's my place. I'm the captain, here."

Decker answered, "No, you can't...I couldn't stand to lose—"

"Yes, you can. Someday you'll have to anyway." He reached a hand out to her shoulder and offered up a sad smile. "And I lost her, too, remember?" Ricci turned back to the translator and said, "Okay, I'll meld with one of you."

"There is no limit to the number. We can send four; if you wish."

Ricci said to Lindstrom, "Commander, a private word?" Lindstrom nodded and they moved off to huddle together at the back of the bridge. "We can't both risk this. One of us has to stay in command. I'll take this one."

"With all due respect, Captain, my loss was much deeper—"

"I know. But if the worst happens and transformation occurs...whoever is in charge will have to give the order to...kill the infected." He glanced at Decker and then back to Lindstrom. "Either way, I will not *survive that*. So, it may as well be me."

Lindstrom said, "I see." He swallowed briefly and then stated, "You're right. I'll take command."

Captain and first officer walked back to the front of the bridge together. Ricci said, "Send three. I'll do it, as will Lieutenant Kennedy, and Lieutenant Decker."

"Let the three stand together."

Almost immediately three swirls of gray light appeared on the bridge.

***

The group of volunteers readied themselves for their ordeal. Ricci turned command over to Lindstrom, officially. Con hugged Aqila as if in a final good-bye; Decker ordered Kay

252

removed to her quarters saying she didn't want him witnessing this. "He won't understand and it will upset him."

Lindstrom was thinking that the dog was no different from any of the humans on the bridge in that respect, but he simply asked Kennedy, "May I have your pulse pistol?" Con kissed Aqila on the cheek and then silently handed the pistol to Lindstrom. Nils said, "And I need each of you to confirm—"

Ricci ordered, "Don't even hesitate."

"Take me out," said Con.

"With extreme prejudice," was Decker's answer. Then she said, "Okay...so you know what you're looking for...the point of no return is when the body starts to grow and the muscles...it looks like snakes moving under the skin."

"Okay," was all Lindstrom could manage.

"That's usually when the screaming starts."

"Got it."

"We're ready," Ricci announced. The three swirls of gray light disappeared, and Ricci, Kennedy, and Decker dropped to the floor, limp and unresponsive. To Lindstrom's horror, their skin immediately turned gray and started to scale.

"Oh God," Lateef moaned. "They're transforming."

"Not yet, not yet," Lindstrom chanted quietly, waiting for the signs Decker had imparted to him, pistol at the ready.

The bridge was deadly silent as everybody waited. The skin on the three individuals melding with the Pakarahova had become completely inhuman. Time had seemed to slow to a crawl.

Chapter 19

Expect the Best and the Worst

"We should expect the best and the worst from mankind, as from the weather." Vauvenargues

Decker came to on the bridge of the *Lovelace* with a pounding in her head that was worse than the most painful migraine she'd ever had. She sat up and looked to her right to see Con who appeared to be in an equally bad state. Aqila was hovering over him. Deck wanted to check on Ricci, who was lying beside Con, and who seemed to be out cold still, but she was in too much pain. She laid back down with a groan. Dr. Clemente appeared in her field of vision and said, "Just stay where you are," while waving a med-scanner over her. "You're going to be okay."

"Is this some new definition of the word, 'okay'?"

"Hey, don't start on me. Apparently, you volunteered for this fool stunt as did your two friends here."

Decker heard Con say, "Did it work?"

It was Aqila who answered. "Well, all of you passed out and your skin changed, so I guess so."

"Did it get all gray and scaly?" Deck asked.

"Yes. It was...awful."

Ricci said, "Glad I missed that."

"How long were we out?" Con asked.

Aqila answered, "In relative time? At least a year. In objective time? About twenty minutes."

Decker said, "That makes sense, twenty minutes used to be about how long the resistant people took to come out of it, too."

A few minutes later, all three of them were feeling well enough to sit up. Con asked Deck, "What do you remember?"

"I remember...sensing that I wasn't alone in my own mind. It was weird and...really repulsive. That's about it. What about you?"

"Pretty much the same."

Decker cautiously pulled herself to her feet and offered Con a hand up. He took it and then she turned to Ricci, but he waved her off saying, "I can get up." He did so very slowly, while Clemente watched closely and Deck thought, *Oh, that's where I get the stupid stubborn pride.*

She asked Ricci, "What did you experience, Captain?"

"Same as you two. But I also remember my skin starting to itch and burn; considering what we could have faced...not that bad." Ricci looked over at Lindstrom and said, "Well, Commander, you didn't get to live out every first officer's fantasy, after all."

"I assure you, sir, not this first officer." Before Ricci could acknowledge the compliment, he added, "My life would be so dull without your...."

"Antics?" Ricci suggested.

"Sure, let's go with that."

Ricci cleared his throat and said, "Before I resume my antics, could I have your report? What have we heard from the Pakarahova?"

"The only thing we've heard from them was that, in their words, 'the melds were successful'."

Ricci addressed the Pakarahova through the translator. "This is Captain Ricci. Did the melds help clarify the situation for you at all?"

The machine voice rang out across the bridge. "They were most enlightening. We see how your pain has been amplified by this war you fight with the bonded ones. So much pain crowded into such short lives. No wonder our fellows were moved to try to help your species ascend. It is a shame it was unsuccessful. They paid a terrible price for their mercy."

"Thank you for the empathy." Deck could only assume that Ricci was trusting that sarcasm couldn't carry through the translator. "Have you changed your minds about putting a stop to the Eternals' rampage— to this unsuccessful association?"

"We are at this time reconsidering enacting the forced recall."

"Thank you. Please remember that our entire lifetimes stretch for only half as long as you've already been considering it."

"We understand. The timing will be extremely brief. We will render our decision in what you consider...if we understand correctly from the meld, to be...a day."

"Until tomorrow then."

Dr. Clemente said, "That leaves plenty of time for the three of you to get a thorough exam in Med-Bay."

***

The next morning the command staff, including Chief Engineer Ramsey and Dr. Clemente, and augmented by Ensign Brodie, was gathered on the bridge awaiting word from the Pakarahova. Ricci and Lindstrom were in whispered conference at the command chair. "It either ends today...or not in our lifetime, I guess," Ricci said. "The Pakarahova could be pondering the fate of their lost brethren for the next millennium."

Lindstrom answered, "I'd hate to go back to HQ and tell them how close we came to ending it and then...didn't."

"It's going to be hard enough explaining why you and I were fighting for the privilege of being infected by an eprion."

Lindstrom glanced over at Decker sitting at her tactical console. "You know, I'm not entirely sure that's the biggest thing you're going to have to explain, Captain."

"Yes, well, let's hope the story of a secret daughter pales in comparison to a successful mission."

"From your mouth to the Pakarahova's...binary ears."

As the time ticked on, everyone on the bridge stopped even the pretense of working and simply waited.

Finally, Decker said, "I hope they didn't get a day confused with a year."

Ricci, fearing a mass bout of hypoglycemia on the bridge, was just about to order his staff to take a late lunch when the translator came to life. "We the Pakarahova have made our decision."

"This is Captain Ricci. What is your decision?"

"It is done. The recall has been made. The ones you call the Eternals are no more."

Matt waited for the feeling of elation that did not come; all he felt was exhausted relief. "Thank you. Humankind will trouble you no more."

"Yours is an interesting species and we may decide to reconsider the matter as you continue to evolve. We will review your fitness for ascension in a reasonable amount of time." Ricci was just about to tell them to keep their reconsideration to themselves, when they continued, "A thousand of your lifetimes might be sufficient."

"We'll make a note of that. See you in a hundred thousand years." He turned to the pilot, saying, "Petrović, set a course for Uniterrae." Ricci looked at the chief engineer. "How soon can you get us home, Ramsey?"

"Well, if I push it, a lot faster than we got out here. Say, three months...maybe two and half, since I noted some short-cuts on the way here."

"Great! Let's get going then." He hit the comm button on his chair and announced to the entire ship, "This is Captain Ricci. I'm happy to announce that our mission has concluded successfully and we're on our way home. Congratulations to one and all. You should be very proud of what you've accomplished. I am. Ricci out."

After Ramsey went down to Engineering and Clemente back to Med-Bay, Kennedy was the first to speak. "So, they're gone. All the Eternals...just crumbled away to dust. I can't believe it."

Decker said, "I thought it would feel better than this. That they finally got what they deserved."

Aqila asked, "It doesn't?"

"No. After what we've learned...it was just...I don't know...it could have been any of us, right?"

"That sums it up pretty well," Lindstrom agreed. "Any student of human nature will hardly be surprised to find that our species can't handle immortality and immense power very well."

Ricci said, "We have met the enemy and he is us."

"Who said that?" Sasaki asked.

"Pogo. Twentieth Century philosopher."

Decker asked, "That Greek guy we learned about at The Rock?"

"No," Ricci said, trying to hide his amusement. "You're thinking of Plato. Pogo's a bit more recent than that." He turned to Naiche and said, "I'll send you some of his work. I think you might like it."

"Wonder what they're thinking back home," Brodie said.

"If Commander Ramsey's optimism is justified, we'll be in communication range of Ptolemia in about six weeks and we can find out." Ricci was silent for a moment before musing, "Whatever the immediate reaction was, I have a feeling there's a...reckoning in store for humanity. Or there should be...."

"A reckoning, Captain?" asked Kennedy.

Before Ricci could respond, Decker interjected, "You mean because we're the only species out of thousands who met up with the Pakarahova and couldn't...or wouldn't...."

"Ascend to a higher plane?" offered Lateef.

"Precisely," Ricci answered. "I'm still not sure what living as pure consciousness really means but the cold hard fact is that we met with a big test of our...our *character* as a species and frankly, we failed." He stood up and continued, more cheerfully, "But, like any failure, it's an opportunity for us to take a good long look at ourselves. And improve."

"Yes, and it's not like humanity has ever had *that* kind of opportunity *before*," Lindstrom acerbically observed.

"Don't give up on us yet, Nils. Even the Pakarahova held out a glimmer of hope for humankind."

"I would love nothing better than to be proved wrong, Captain."

"While we're waiting for that *rare event*," Ricci quipped, "who would like to join me for lunch?"

"I'd be glad to, sir," Lindstrom said. "Anybody know what the entrée is today?"

"I think it's gubang fritters, Commander," Decker teased.

"Excellent. My absolute favorite."

***

Since *Lovelace* had been in contact with the UDC prior to their arrival, they came home to a hero's welcome and to find the reconstruction efforts well under way. The entire crew left the *Lovelace* for its well-deserved renewal at UDC HQ on Ptolemia and traveled to Uniterrae, specifically The Rock, for the many welcome home ceremonies.

Ricci had to spend the bulk of his time in the administration building, attending meetings and de-briefings; his first afternoon was taken up by Captain Kei Chen's report on her efforts to rehabilitate and resettle the surviving Gak. Chen's ship had been the first of the long-range vessels to return to Uniterrae and she had immediately volunteered for the challenging assignment. It was going slowly, at best.

Late in the day, Matt was finally able to leave the noise and backslapping behind and find a seat on a bench in the commemorative courtyard near where Naomi was interred. He faced her plaque and thought of all he wished he could say to her. In a whispered conversation he said, "She's really something, Naomi. You and Gus…you have a lot to be proud of." He was silent for a short time and then said, "It was you, wasn't it? You brought her to me. I'll always believe that." He wished her peace and got up to leave. He turned back briefly and said, "Thanks. It was a lot more than I deserved. But then, so were you."

Ricci had just reached the gate, when he ran into the very object of his recent conversation. She was accompanied by the faithful Kayatennae. "You come here, too, huh?" Naiche said.

"Yes. When I can. Do you need some company?"

"Nah, I'm just gonna tell her all about the trip." Deck smiled warmly. "And you know all of that."

"Right. I'll meet you at my quarters later."

"Yeah, about that…."

"What?"

"I was thinking…it's gonna be really crowded at your place with your family there and all, so I'm just gonna stay in the barracks and catch up with you all—"

Ricci reined in his frustration, reminding himself this was all very new for Naiche. "Okay, in the first place, they're *your family, too*. And in the second place, I am a dead man, *dead*, if my mother shows up and you're not staying with me. Do you understand me? Dead man."

She laughed and shook her head. "Captain, are you telling me you're afraid of your own mother?"

"Yes," he admitted without a trace of shame. "So, take pity on your old man and go get your things out of those barracks and into my quarters, pronto. Got it?"

She saluted and said, "Yes, sir."

As Ricci left the courtyard, he ran into none other than Commodore Grace Stein. "Well, well, if it isn't the conquering hero! No time for your old friend?"

"I was actually going to message you to see if you wanted to be my date to the gala."

"You're going to make me watch them give you the Founder's Medal, eh, Ricci?"

"You're a tough broad, Grace. You can take it. Besides, aren't they naming that metal you discovered on your voyage, 'steinium'?"

"They are." She winked at him and said, "I shall live forever. Speaking of which, congratulations are in order, aren't they? I hear it's a girl?"

Since Matt had been hearing pointed witticisms like that constantly since his return, he was able to shrug it off and say, "Thank you, yes. She's 344 months now. You'll be able to meet her at the gala."

"I don't know whether to be intrigued or frightened. I've always heard she's quite formidable."

"Grace, you wouldn't be frightened if the last Eternal popped up in front of you right now so just try being nice. And don't start anything with her because even you will not win." He kissed her on the cheek and said, "I'll talk to you later. My family's due in tonight. Gotta run."

***

Decker paced the entranceway to Ricci's spacious quarters and studied herself in the mirror for the tenth time. She'd chosen a simple silk shift and had her hair down; in her hands, she was twisting the small bouquet of lilacs she had for her grandmother. *Grandmother. I have a grandmother and two aunts.* She'd never known her maternal grandmother and Naomi had no siblings, so this was a strange concept for her. "Maybe I should have worn

263

something with sleeves, what do you think? I could go change."

"I think you should calm down," Ricci said. "I've seen you face an eprion infection with more fortitude than this."

"I shouldn't have worn heels. I'm pretty tall in heels. Are they tall?"

Matt walked over and put his hands on her shoulders. "Stop worrying. You're just meeting some family – not one of those energy lizards."

"Okay, just remember that, when you're meeting *my family*."

"I'm very much looking forward to meeting your family and seeing where you grew up."

"You say that now but I'm warning you, my Great Aunt Loza is probably scarier than your mom."

"I didn't say my mom was scary, I said that *I* should be scared of her. I kept her granddaughter from her for almost twenty-nine years."

"It wasn't all your fault."

"I don't blame your grandfath—"

"No, I don't mean that." Naiche took a deep breath. "Do you remember that message you sent me on my first day at The Rock? Asking if I wanted to meet up with you sometime?"

"I remember your two-word reply."

"Yeah, what you don't know is that my first reply was one word. 'Okay'."

She could see she had managed to surprise him. "Why did you change it?"

"I don't know." Naiche shook her head. "*Shitsúyé* always said, I was one who'd cut off my nose to spite my face." She looked at him with a sad smile. "I tend to be my own worst enemy."

264

"Well, I think you come by that honestly. For one thing, look how I behaved that first day you showed up on the *Lovelace*."

Deck chuckled. "Yeah, you acted as if I'd taken that posting solely for the purpose of undermining your authority at every turn."

Ricci put his hand under her chin so she'd face him directly. "Okay, new rule – no more letting our base impulses overrule our heads...and our hearts. As soldiers we run into enemies enough – we don't need to add ourselves to that roster."

"Sounds good to me. At last – a UDC rule I fully endorse!"

There was no opportunity for Matt to make a reply because the doorbell rang and seconds later, the room was filled with the Ricci family: Matt's mom, his older sister Damiana, his younger sister Carmella, and her husband Joe. Naiche hung back while the women all hugged and kissed her father and commented about how he'd gotten much too thin and explained that they were late because the hotel had messed up Carmella and Joe's reservation.

Then it was her turn. Her grandfather and his siblings had been loving but, in the Chiricahua tradition, not overly demonstrative people, so this was a brave new world. She was hugged and kissed and fussed over to within an inch of her life and told to start calling them Nonna, Aunt Dami, Aunt Caro, and Uncle Joe immediately. Deck bravely accepted the treatment with grace and was agreeable to all their demands; she even let them call Kayatennae, "her dog," without mention.

Damiana and Carmella were both commenting on how pretty Naiche was but she was wholly unprepared when

Dami said, "Thank God, she didn't take after you, Matty, with that nose."

Ricci took this in stride, apparently quite used to his older sister's bluntness. "Thanks, Dami."

Damiana turned to Naiche and explained, "It's our father's nose and he was a wonderful man, but Caro and I were always grateful we got our looks from the Lorenzo side."

Deck was torn between defending her father, who she'd always thought, even during their estrangement, was fairly handsome and offending her aunt so she just said, "Yeah, I definitely take after my mom." She figured the best way to change the subject was to hand her grandmother the bouquet she had for her and she did so, explaining, "Captain Ricci told me these are your favorites."

When all three Ricci women stared at her open-mouthed in horror, she desperately tried to figure out what she'd said wrong. However, in unison, they'd swung round and glared at Matt. His mother demanded angrily, "You make her call you *Captain*? Your own daughter calls you 'Captain Ricci'!"

Naiche tried to fix her mistake by explaining, "Oh no, it's not his fault. See, on the *Lovelace* it wouldn't be appropriate—"

Her grandmother turned back to her, insisting, "Well, you're not on the *Lovelace* now, *are you*?"

Deck's immediate thought was, *Wow, she is scary,* and she placated her by agreeing, "No, ma'am, I am not."

"So now, you're going to call him...?"

"Matteo?" Naiche guessed, in a faltering tone.

"Papa! You should call him Papa."

"Uh, sure. Papa. You bet." She looked over at Ricci hoping for a reprieve. "That okay by you...Papa?"

266

"Of course, Naiche." Matt picked up his mother's suitcase and said to her, "Grab Dami's stuff and let's get them settled into their room."

She followed his order, muttering along the way, "Sure thing, *Papa*. 'Cause it's not like that's *super-weird* or anything."

Ricci murmured back, "Behave."

Deck could only explain, "I'm trying."

***

The next night at the gala, Ricci got his Founder's Medal of Honor, which, in his acceptance speech, he sincerely explained belonged to every crewmember of the *Lovelace*. As first officer on what was rapidly becoming a legendary mission, Lindstrom received the Exceptional Service Medal, and much to the joint delight of both captain and first officer, Kennedy, Decker, and Brodie all got promotions. Lateef and Sasaki received special recognitions for outstanding contributions to their respective fields. Even Kayatennae, who was present, was awarded a special commendation.

Deck was getting a drink at the bar and had just promised the next dance to the intriguing Lieutenant Diego Romero when Kennedy appeared at her elbow. "What a nice *young* man, emphasis on the young."

"Very funny, wise guy." After a second of reflection, she sheepishly admitted, "Okay, maybe 'daddy-issues Decker' is no more."

"'Bout time. But still, remember to save a dance for me."

"Really? You're going to tear yourself away from your fiancé?"

"Shh. I haven't asked her yet."

"That ring's gonna burn a hole in your pocket if you don't make your move soon."

"I will." Kennedy looked around. "Some night, huh?"

"Did you ever imagine anything like this when you talked me into coming on the *Lovelace*?"

"Sure, I figured I'd meet the woman of my dreams, we'd come home heroes, be promoted, and you'd have a new grandmother commenting on how short your dress is." While Deck broke into laughter he added, "And an Aunt Dami who says it's okay because you have great legs which apparently you inherited from her." He took a sip from his drink and asked, "You?"

"Absolutely. I knew we'd help end the war; I'd mend my ten-year feud with my father, make peace with my mom's death, and need to compose a Best Woman speech. It's all *exactly* what I would have predicted."

Epilogue

A True Friend

"Hold a true friend with both hands." Nigerian Proverb

Decker watched Kennedy pacing the small room adjacent to The Rock's non-denominational chapel. "Don't work up a sweat; that damn robin's-egg blue shows every stain."

"I'm not going to sweat, it's not like I'm nervous."

"Of course not."

"Do you have the ring?"

"Nope, I ate it. It was *delicious.*"

"You are the worst Best Woman in the world."

"On the contrary, I'm the best Best Woman in the world because I have the ring...." Deck held up the item in question. "As well as an extra copy of your vows in case you blank on them, *and* a speech for the reception which will leave not a dry eye in the house."

"Sorry," Con said with a deep sigh. "You *are* the best – best friend ever. I guess maybe I am a little nervous."

"Maybe a little." Decker smiled. "But you're entitled; this is a lot. Getting married right before we ship out for six months."

Con's smile glowed with his happiness. "I can't think of a better way to start married life than spending six months just exploring the galaxy. Besides, we do get a week for our honeymoon."

"Yes, a whole week." Naiche's mind was also on their upcoming space exploration voyage. "It *will* be good to get back on the *Lovelace*."

"So...I did the right thing in recruiting you, huh?"

She grinned and nodded. "Yeah, you know you did. You helped me find something I've been missing for a long time."

"What's that?"

Rather than answering directly she said, "When Ricci and I visited my family, my cousin Motsos reminded me of a conversation we'd had the morning I left for The Rock. He'd warned me if I stayed away too long, I'd be a stranger everywhere. And for the longest time he was right...I didn't really feel at home anywhere."

"And now?"

"And now, I know my home is on the *Lovelace*. With my family."

Con archly corrected, "You mean with your father?"

"Oh, shut up. You know I meant not only him, but also you and Aqila and—" She stopped suddenly and said, "It just occurred to me that between you and Aqila, Lindstrom and Clemente, and Ramsey and – what's her wife's name again? The chef?"

"Maisie Collins."

"Ramsey and Collins, the *Lovelace* is really living up to its name."

"Next we gotta get you coupled up."

"Nah, I think I take after Ricci in that department."

"Well, he has a...relationship, doesn't he?"

"Yeah, I don't know what to call what he has with Commodore Ball-buster but it ain't quite a relationship."

"Is it like what you have with Diego?"

"No, we like each other in and out of bed. We're just not...in love. Definitely in like, though."

Just then, Ricci stuck his head in the door. "Okay, Aqila's here and I'm going to take my place. You two should come out front when you hear the music start."

"Sure thing, Pop." When Deck turned back to Con, she found him grinning and chuckling. "What?"

"You call him 'Pop', now?"

"No! I said, 'Cap'."

"You did not. You absolutely said 'Pop'. Oh my God...you're *never* living this down."

"You tell *anyone* about this, Conroy Kennedy-Lateef...."

"Not yet Kennedy-Lateef."

The music had started playing out in the chapel. "Okay, then," Naiche said with a warm smile. "Let's go fix that." She pulled Con into a quick one-armed hug and then they headed out the door together.

Chiricahua Glossary

Ádíídíí díík'eh dáándí – all of this is true
Bik'ehgo'iindáń - the Creator
Daadatlijende – blue-eyed/green-eyed people
Naaghéé – monsters
N'daa – stranger, enemy, non-Apache people
N'daałigánde – strange, non-Apache people, who are white skinned
Shimáá – my mother
Shitsúyé – my grandfather
Tsiłkizhéne ndé – foolish ones/people
Ya a teh – greetings/hello

Other Exquisite Fiction
from D. X. Varos

The Inquisitor's Niece
Erika Rummel

Immortal Betrayal
Daniel A. Willis

Immortal Duplicity
Daniel A. Willis

Immortal Revelation
Daniel A. Willis
(coming June 2019)

Prophecy of the Awakening
Daniel A. Willis

The Heiress of Egypt
Samuel Ebeid

274